THE HA... ...ND
GRINN... ... PIPER

"You come to speak to He Who Should Not Be Named in the Dark?" he asked. "My master will grant you an audience, spotted horse. If you can gain admittance from Anor, the Executioner. And Anor does not care to let you pass."

The Executioner's clawed hooves clicked against the rocky earth in a deadly rhythm. His one yellow eye gleamed in dull rage.

"You know the penalty if you fight him and lose?" asked the Hound. "You will die—forever."

But Piper had no choice. Unless he could face Anor's dread master, the Dark Horse himself, and call out that one's Name—the Name only Piper knew—the souls of all his breed would perish.

"I accept the challenge," Piper said.

Without warning, Anor charged . . .

MARY STANTON

PIPER AT THE GATE

BAEN
FANTASY

Acknowledgments:

Elizabeth Mitchell: who started it
Donald Maass: who vetted it
Amy Flinn: who typed it
Brian Kress: who asked for another one

PIPER AT THE GATE

This is a work of fiction. All the characters and events portrayed in this book are fictional, and any resemblance to real people or incidents is purely coincidental.

Copyright © 1989 by Mary Stanton

All rights reserved, including the right to reproduce this book or portions thereof in any form.

A Baen Books Original

Baen Publishing Enterprises
260 Fifth Avenue
New York, N.Y. 10001

First printing, May 1989

ISBN: 0-671-69820-6

Cover art by Thomas Kidd

Printed in the United States of America

Distributed by
SIMON & SCHUSTER
1230 Avenue of the Americas
New York, N.Y. 10020

This book is for my father
William Bishop Whitaker

TABLE OF CONTENTS

A Note From The Author:

Those of you who love fiction featuring animal characters will recognize the origins of this novel's title. It comes from a chapter in Kenneth Grahame's *Wind in the Willows*, called "The Piper At The Gates of Dawn." The chapter describes the rescue of a baby otter by the great god Pan. For me, it's one of the most poignant scenes ever written in an animal story. It's here that the reader understands that Ratty and Moley live in a universe which orders responsibility for the helpless: unconditional love for other beings; the reality of a pastoral heaven. I've longed after Grahame's vision ever since I first read of it. Like all of us, I want it to be true.

With the exception of Richard Adams, there has never been an animal fantasy writer with Grahame's clarity, intelligence and compassion. Adapting his chapter title to my novel is an acknowledgement of a debt to his work and its impact on those of us who love it.

Mary Stanton
Puddle Jumper Farm
Walworth, New York
1988

SWEETWATER'S DANCING PIPER

PROLOGUE

Spring came early to Bishop Farm, spreading pale green against the winter snow. Duchess, Lead Mare of the Bishop Farm brood mare herd, stood in the weak sunshine, inhaling the morning air with mild delight. There was an unexpected softness in the chill air, and she tasted the clear-water scent of daffodils.

She'd had no foal this year, and she watched the brood mares with their weanlings in the adjoining paddock with a little regret. They were all getting old; for most of them, these would be the last foals they would bear. Lilly, Fancy, Cissy had all dropped healthy foals the month before, and their babies played cheerfully in the pasture. Fancy, the Quarterhorse who was Duchess' Second-In-Command squealed as her colt nursed and Duchess blew out in amusement. They were getting teeth about now.

A fly buzzed angrily in her ear and she shook her head to chase it away. Spring was really here, if these nuisances had arrived so early. She walked to

1

the end of her paddock and leaned comfortably against the gate.

"I wouldn't do that if I were you," Cissy called out fussily from the pasture. "It's a stupid habit. You'll spring the latch one of these days and then the boards will have to be fixed." The brown Thoroughbred stopped grazing and looked at Duchess in irritation.

"Every year I think your temper's gonna get better, Cissy, and every year you prove me wrong," said Pony, grazing nearby. The little Shetland curled her upper lip. "Don't ever change, it'd send me straight into conniptions." She winked at Duchess, then walked to the fence which separated the paddock from Duchess' own. "Morning."

"Morning, Pony." Duchess blew out contentedly and stretched. The fly buzzed in her ear. She jumped a little and fell into the gate. The latch sprang and the gate swung open.

"Told you," said Cissy.

Lilly, the grey Arabian Dreamspeaker, raised her head and watched the open gate. A furrow appeared between her fine dark eyes. "This is not right," she said.

"What d'ya mean?" Pony stuck out her lower lip belligerently.

"She means Duchess is breaking the Law of Fences, and she shouldn't," said Cissy, crossly. "But Duchess can do no wrong, can she, Pony?"

Lily's eyes clouded. "The day is darker than it should be. There are black flies too early in the year."

"Paah!" said Pony, who had little time for the Dreamspeaker's fey behavior. "The day feels fine to me. And flies are flies." Pony gazed at Duchess in pleased interest; the Shetland had an appetite for mischief. "So what are you going to do about it?"

Duchess, the spring air teasing her mane and hindquarters, cocked her head, considering. "The Bishops left early this morning, didn't they?"

"Mmhm. Went off in the truck. Don't know when they'll be back. Cory the collie went with them."

Duchess rolled her eye at Pony. "Maybe I'll go visit the Dancer."

"Typical," said Cissy. "You aren't supposed to be walking around. Remember what happened the last time you broke the Law of Fences."

"Ya, Cissy, tell us what happened the last time Duchess broke the Law of Fences," Pony jeered.

Cissy flattened her ears and turned her hindquarters to the Shetland in a classic gesture of contempt. The last time, Duchess had left Bishop Farm with Dancer and been gone an entire year, returning with Pony, and in foal for the first time with Piper.

"Nobody pays much attention to the Law anyways," said Pony to Duchess. "You go ahead and do what you want to."

Duchess nosed the open gate. It swung back and forth. She stepped into the yard and walked into the drive. She hadn't been outside alone with no men to lead her for years, and she kicked up her heels a little. She hadn't been to visit the Dancer for quite a while either; she missed him.

The Dancer's paddock lay in back of the Big Barn, and she'd have to go through the arena to get to him. Emmanual had opened the great sliding doors of the Barn to the spring air that morning. She started through them on her way to the arena and to Dancer's paddock beyond.

Suddenly, Lily called out, "Duchess, come back."

Duchess stopped and turned. The Dreamspeaker stood at the fence, elegant head stretched over the top. Her eyes were anxious.

"What's the matter?"

Lily shook her head, silky mane flying. "I don't know. There is a shadow on the sun. The earth has gone still under my feet. Stay here. Please."

Duchess snorted and walked down the concrete aisle to the arena. Fresh sawdust had just been delivered and spread on the arena floor, and the stringent scent of pine filled the air. Sawdust was dry and scratchy, unlike the cold puddles in her paddock run, and she knelt and rolled luxuriously for a long moment. As she rolled, something slim and dark caught the corner of her eye in the far corner of the arena, and she jumped to her feet. For a moment, she could have sworn she had seen another horse. A horse or—what? She inhaled sharply, her senses alert, but no scent of strangers came to her. The black fly, with the persistence of its kind, had followed her. It stung again, drawing blood. She reached around to rub the bite with her nose and stood with her ears forward in surprise.

A pile of alfalfa lay loosely stacked in the corner. It was freshly cut, still damp, and bright green. It must have been trucked in, Duchess thought. The Bishop Farm harvest wouldn't be ready for months. An intense craving seized her. She trotted over, plunged her nose into the bale, and began to eat. Grey cobwebs were tangled in many of the leaves, and she ate them, too, the musty taste a pleasant balance to the fresh green.

The pain began quietly at first—a soft, insistent pulse deep in her gut. She snorted, puzzled, and backed up. Water would help. She turned to find it, and a single cramp struck with terrifying force. She whinnied in surprise. A light sheen of sweat sprang on her neck and withers. She lowered her head, patient, as horses are in illness, and waited for the cramp to pass.

It struck with redoubled fury. The blows in her belly tore through her flesh as though seeking air.

She walked restlessly around the arena, breathing in deep grunts. The movement helped. She relaxed a little and moved out in a rhythmic trot.

The pain spiked up through the soles of her hooves. A nail? She stopped, unable to move forward and nuzzled her forelegs. Fear crawled through her and she rolled her eyes in desperation.

Then the real agony struck—relentless and unforgiving.

When the Bishops finally came—and after them, the vet—she couldn't move at all. Foundered, she stood with her forelegs extended, a prisoner of the torment.

When they took her to the isolation stall they made her walk and the pain drove up her legs with each trembling step and she cried out that her feet were bleeding. When she stood finally in the thick straw she bent her head to lick the blood away and found none.

She'd never known such pain, not even at the birth of her foals when she thought her body would burst with the life trying to come from her. That had been a joyful suffering buoyed with the promise of glory to come. This pain was different. Deadly.

The Bishops tried all that men can try. They forced oil through a tube in her nose and a temporary relief came from a tranquilizing shot but it wasn't enough, not nearly enough, and the last she saw of her home was the sad, wise face of the farm collie, Cory, filled with a terrible grief.

So Duchess began her journey on the long Green Road to death.

• 1 •

Sweetwater Ranch

Sweetwater Ranch lay in the hollow of the mountains of Big Sky country, its vast, thinly-grassed range spreading out from the buildings like spokes from a wheel. The ranch's ten thousand acres were fenced with barbed wire strung between hemlock posts, mile after Montana mile.

To the east of the ranch house stretched the hay fields. Pockets of snow lay dimly white on the furrowed acres on this April morning. To the west of the house was the forty acre pasture where the brood mares were kept all summer long. A small stream meandered down the circling mountains here. Sometimes, on nights when the moon was full, making a silver bridge from the stream to the sky, the mares would gather and listen to ancient Tales of their kind and the forty acre pasture became an enchanted place, linked to the heavens themselves by the reflection of moonlight on water.

But now, with dawn only a faint promise on the mountaintop, the ranch lay quiet, the forty acre pasture empty, waiting for the wintering herd to come home.

A stallion appeared to the southern ridge, ears pricked forward, nose testing the wind. He reared, a darker shape against the pre-dawn sky, then galloped down the mountain. He was nimble, his hooves deftly avoiding treacherous slides of gravel and the burrows of the small predators who shared his range. By the Dancer, the magnificent Appaloosa stallion of Bishop Farm, and out of Duchess, the buckskin mare who carried the precious Appaloosa gene in her blood, Sweetwater's Dancing Piper raced to the barns of Sweetwater Ranch. He stopped just out of view of those who lived there year round, and called his herd into a compact mass behind him.

When the call came to bring them home, he'd be ready.

Just before dawn, the lights in the bunkhouse snapped on, a warm glow in the graying night. The bunk house stood a few hundred feet from the corral where the Working cow ponies were turned out in all but the fiercest weather. The Herd chief, a Tennessee Walking Horse named Blackjack, woke from a light doze at the sounds of moving men. He raised his head, ears forward, breath a mist in the chill air. The morning was sweet with hyacinth, crocus and the rainy scent of jonquils. A breeze brought the distinctive odor of range-fed horses somewhere south of the valley; Piper would be bringing the mares in today. New Grass already blanketed the pastures, and it was past time. Ranch routine would change. The slow, dull days of winter were behind them now. Foaling, weaning, the selecting and culling of the horse herd lay ahead, and the challenge of the rodeo.

The dark lifted, slowly.

Blackjack flagged his high set tail—the bones broken when he was a yearling to achieve the sweeping Saddle Seat look, and trotted to the watering trough. He broke the thin skin of ice on the surface with his nose and drank deep. He shook himself and snorted twice.

A three-sided shed sheltered the rest of the Working Herd at the east end of the corral. Three cow ponies ambled out and joined Blackjack. They were all geldings, rough coated against the cold, muscular and fit from long days spent riding fence and herding cattle. They stood shoulder to shoulder: Hank, a grayed out Appaloosa and Blackjack's Second-in-Command; Duke, a white Connemara-Arab cross, and at twenty-two the oldest member of the Working Herd; Alvin, a chestnut Standardbred with one inglorious season as a racehorse in his past.

They turned at the crunch of booted feet on gravel. A ranch hand swung a bale of hay to the topmost rail of the corral, clipped the bailing twine, and scattered the hay along the inside fence. The geldings trotted over and began to eat with the concentrated appetites of those who work hard for a living.

Dawn crept finger by finger over the high ridged mountains surrounding the valley. Blackjack watched the arrival of the sun with a prickle of anticipation along his flanks. The state of the brood mare herd was vital to the survival of the ranch—and to the working Herd itself. If the mares were sound, the foals live and healthy, Sweetwater would prosper.

Abandoned for many years, Sweetwater had fallen into decay until David Bishop, a horseman like his father and grandfather before him bought it to raise cattle and horses. He arrived from his home in the East, bringing a three-year-old Appaloosa stallion to stand at stud, and enough of a stake to start a herd of Black Angus beef cattle. For six years, David struggled with terrifying winter storms, dry summers, and late springs. As the seasons passed, and David's stallion, Piper, proved his worth with a stream of brightly marked Appaloosa foals, the brood mare herd grew to forty strong and the ranch began to pay for itself.

David was prudent, he built slowly and well: barns and stables against the unforgiving Montana weather; wooden hay racks to store the forage grown against the grassless months which follow summer; a rodeo arena; a stout corral; a remodeled bunk house. The ranch house was the only building to remain from the original stake; oak-sided, it was the ranch's vulnerable heart.

But well-made barns and well-kept fences were no hedge against the weather, and the success of Sweetwater was driven by the seasons. In good years, the weather allowed healthy foals to thrive on good forage. In bad, drought, blizzards, floods and heat all took their toll: the weak starved or died of thirst or fell prey to the bear and cougar who roamed their range. The strong bred true so that the breed would survive.

The weather had been kind this year, at least so far, and Blackjack waited, expectant, to see how Piper's band had survived the winter in the mountains.

The sun topped the mountain range, flooding the valley with pale yellow light. David Bishop came from the ranch house to stand on the verandah, a steel triangle in one hand. Meg, the gold and white collie bitch, sat at his feet.

"David's ready," said Duke the Connemara.

David struck the triangle. A pure metallic note

sounded in the morning air. Blackjack scanned the mountain tops.

The ice-pure chime rang again. In the distance, the geldings caught the whispery sound of horses running through the snow.

Piper came down the mountain.

Like his sire, Piper's chest and belly were raven black. Like Duchess, his dam, his muzzle and hind-quarters were the color of wild grass dried by an August sun. An effortless jumper, he took shrubs and fallen branches in his path in even leaps. The mares and yearlings followed, a parti-colored river flowing brown, dun, chestnut, gray. Most of the mares were big-bellied with foal, due to be born in one month's time when the weather was mild and sunny days long.

"Piper!" Blackjack lifted his muzzle in a welcoming call. David whistled sharply from the verandah and Meg pricked up her ears. He gestured, palm up, at the gelding's shed in the corral. The collie raced to the fence, head low, ears back.

"Back to the shed," Meg said to the geldings, "they're coming in here first." She slipped between the boards and circled the Working Herd, crouching a little as she ran. She snapped harmlessly at Black-jack's heels, forcing him inside. Duke, Alvin, and Hank crowded after him and David latched the gate. Blackjack shouldered Duke and Hank aside and pushed his way forward.

"Come and stand next to me," Alvin said peaceably.

The ground shook with the approach of the on-coming herd. Piper swept into the yard, the mares and yearlings bunched behind him. David ran to the west gate of the corral and swung it wide. Clover, the Lead Mare, raced in, her Storyteller, Frosty, close at her heels. Piper swept around the back of the herd at a steady lope, snaking his head low when a mare or yearling broke formation, shouldering them gently into the corral when they turned to run back to the mountains.

The last of the stragglers came into the corral, and the herd milled aimlessly for a moment, finally settling to drink at the trough and nose at the few bites of hay the geldings had left. Piper circled the yard at a gallop.

"Piper, saa, saa, Piper." David held the west gate open for the stallion. Piper bucked in midstride, hind feet flashing to the sun, creamy muzzle down between the polished black of his forelegs. He circled the yard twice, blowing fiercely, then swerved with the speed of a diving hawk into the corral. He raced along the fence. As he passed the geldings shut into the shed, he rolled a dark eye rimmed with white in greeting. David shut the gate, and stood outside, one hand over the top rail. "Saa, saa, Piper," he said.

The stallion slowed to a trot, then a walk, and stopped a few paces in front of him. David extended his hand beneath the stallion's muzzle. Piper lipped the sugar cube and nosed his hand for more.

David swung between the boards, laid his hands on the stallion's neck, ran his hands carefully over the stallion's ears, then down the back of the hard-muscled legs. Piper rested his nose in David's hair, inhaled, then stepped back, nodding his head.

A pickup truck pulled out from a row of hay racks, the bed loaded with cut bales of dried timothy and orchard grass. One ranch hand drove the truck slowly around the outside of the corral, another stood in the bed and pitched forkfuls of hay over the side into the corral. The mares rushed to the hay in a confusion of legs and solid bodies, and plunged their noses in to eat.

"Wait!" Piper ordered. He loped to the hay and nosed it, turning the leaves over carefully. Clover the Lead Mare bit him irritably on the shoulder.

"What danger could there be in hay from men?" she asked. She was a wiry, leopard Appaloosa, brown spots mottling her white coat. A yearling lounged sulkily at her side, the blanket covering his hindquarters a confusion of black and brown spots on white.

"He wouldn't have much else to do if he didn't check out the hay for you," called Blackjack. "Seeing as how he doesn't spend his days hauling some barn-fat man on his back." Piper snorted in amusement, and flicked an ear in Blackjack's direction. He trotted to the shed and greeted the geldings with a courteous inclination of his head. "And how have you all passed the winter?" he asked.

"Well, thank you, Piper," said Alvin. "And you?"

"Well enough," Piper glanced over towards the mares. "We lost one foal to the wolves. Another was born lifeless. And Brownie lay down on winter morning, and walked the Path to the Green Road without pain. It was merely time for her to die. Other than that, it's been a good winter."

Alvin reached over the fence and nosed at a ridge of proudflesh on Piper's shoulder. "What's this?"

"Clover's yearling Rocket is coming into a stallion's heritage somewhat before his time. His play with one of the fillies got a little rough."

Blackjack narrowed his eyes at the yearling eating hay near his dam. "I don't see any scars on Rocket." He cocked his head. "Losing a little speed there, Piper?"

Piper snorted, then said, "Anything *not-routine* here at the ranch?"

"They're setting up for the rodeo tomorrow," Hank said. "And the hands are ready to do the worming and the shoer is here."

"You can smell the dip from here," said Blackjack. "Same as last year."

"Not quite the same," said Alvin, wrinkling his nose. "Did you notice how Meg was this morning? Snappish. Worried. Hustled us into the shed without much greeting at all."

"Who knows why a dog worries?" said Duke. "Foxes in the hen house more than likely. Things are just the same, Piper, except Hank's getting a little better at staying inside the barn. We had that big blizzard a few weeks ago, and even Hank didn't object to being shut in."

Hank twitched his ears. "It was quite a blizzard," he said. "Worse being outside than inside."

Piper nodded absently, his eyes on the mares. "Yes. We smelled it coming, and found the canyon on the west ridge a good enough shelter before it hit. Excuse me."

One of the yearlings squealed and began to kick furiously at the filly eating next to him. Piper trotted over and firmly nudged the two apart, then walked around the corral, lifting his head to scent the air, large eyes scanning the mountaintops.

Satisfied, he went to the watering trough and drank.

"Piper. Welcome home." Meg slipped next to him and lapped the water, a canine courtesy Piper always found odd. Her tall wagged in greeting. "Are all the mares in foal?"

"All but a few. Lady hasn't come into season yet."

"She's an every-other-year-mare," said Meg. "We may not send her back with you this time. David's thinking of using her as a cow pony. She'll join the geldings then and go to work. They could certainly use some help."

"We'll see," said Piper briefly. "She may catch when the others drop their foals and are rebred." He glanced at her. "The Working Herd's Blackjack's responsibilty. He's doing all right, isn't he?"

"What do you think? Some days he's pretty good at what he does—other times not. He wants settling. He gets bored."

Piper moved to the stack of hay. He ducked his head quickly, took a large bite and turned to watch the mares as he ate.

"Relax," said Meg. "Clover's right. You're safe here, you know."

He cocked an amused eye at her. "You and I, Meg, were bred to watch for the *not-routine*."

"Yes, well, we both must watch, nowadays." She sat down and looked back at the ranch house, a worried furrow between her eyes.

"And what is going on that is *not-routine*?"

She worked her forelegs forward and laid her pointed nose on her forepaws. "Something's not right." She rolled her eyes up at him. "I'm not sure what it is. But it's trouble, I can feel it."

"With the men?"

She shook her head and grunted. "I'm not sure." She paused, "We're getting company, you know. This afternoon."

Piper stopped his methodical progress through the hay and looked intently at her. "The vet? Is that what is *not-routine*? Do we have steals-breath here? Or bloody spit? I . . . excuse me."

One of the yearling fillies, suddenly discovering that she was fenced in after a short lifetime of freedom on the range, began running up and down, scattering hay and horses. Piper rumbled a warning. Jessica the Caretaker raised her head and whinnied a sharp reproof. The filly sprinted to the fence. Piper sprang after her. His jaws gentle, he picked her up. She struggled in the stallion's grip. Piper dropped her to the ground and she trotted to the mares with a high pitched squeal.

"Jessica, why hasn't this filly learned the Law of Fences?" Piper's tone was grim.

"I thought Frosty told her," the Caretaker said apologetically. She was young and slender, a Palomino with a gold coat and cream-colored mane and tail. "Come on, you." She gave the foal a quiet nudge. "Listen when Frosty tells you the Law. You can get hurt if you don't."

Piper laid his ears back and raised his muzzle. "Frosty? Come here, please."

Meg settled herself on the ground with a resigned air. The Storyteller, a blue roan with a parrot mouth and a permanently anxious expression, trotted up and hung her head.

"This sort of thing has happened once too often. A Storyteller's job is to teach the Law."

"I'm sorry, Piper, I'm truly sorry, but there's so many foals, you know, and it's hard to keep track of who's heard what." Frosty's lower lip swung loose. "I'm certain I told this one the Law of Fences, at least it was one of the ones who looked an awful lot like this one. Or maybe I told this one the First Law twice and the Law of Fences to somebody else." She stopped, fuddled, and looked vague.

"Perhaps you ought to tell her again, just to make sure."

Frosty ambled uncertainly back to the hay. Piper cocked a grim eye at his Lead mare.

Clover sighed. "I know what you're going to say.

I'm sorry. She's a little foolish. More than a little. If you wouldn't call her on it, she'd do better. She gets nervous when she has to talk to you. But there isn't anyone else in the herd who's anywhere near capable, Piper. They're all young, and David brought most of them at auction. Quite a few are free range mares and they've forgotten the Laws, if they ever knew them. I keep hoping we'll get a Dreamspeaker one of these years."

"How do you go about getting a Dreamspeaker?" asked Meg curiously, getting to her feet.

"Equus sends them, I guess," said Clover, "I'm not too sure, myself. Some herds have them and some don't." She sighed again. "We'll do the best we can, Piper."

"Do you know how the herd can get a Dream-speaker?" Meg asked as the Lead Mare rejoined the mares.

Piper snorted impatiently. "Why this sudden interest in Dreamspeakers, Meg? Does it have to do with this trouble you sense is coming?"

"It might." A furrow appeared between the collie's eyes, and she scratched her side with her hind leg.

"Tell me."

The collie sighed. "I've had these dreams, odd dreams, about horses at a place called Bishop Farm. That's *your* home farm, isn't it? That's where you were born. The dreams have a bad scent about them. If I could tell the dreams to a Dreamspeaker, she might be able to explain them. I . . ." she broke off, and her ears tuliped forward. "Do you hear someone coming down the road?"

Piper raised his head. "It's one of the pickup trucks."

Barking loudly, Meg dashed out of the corral and into the driveway. An old blue pickup truck came rattling down the road and stopped in front of the house. Meg leaped around the cab. David ran out on the porch. A man and an old collie got out of the truck. Both stretched in the pale sunlight. The wind blew their scent to Piper and he stiffened in sudden recognition. Cory. The collie from Bishop Farm where he had been born and weaned. And with him was David's sire, Emmanual. Piper sniffed the air in pleasure.

Meg bellied low and wriggled toward the dog, head down. The old collie stood majestically still, a low growl rumbling in his throat. Their noses touched. Meg's tail flew back and forth in sudden exhilaration. Whining, she leaped into the air. The whine turned to a series of high-pitched yips, and she raced frantically around the yard, passing Piper at the corral gate. She skidded to a halt in front of Cory and touched his nose with her own once more. The old dog's tail moved slowly in acceptance.

David and Emmanual put their arms around one another and walked to the house. The old dog lifted his leg against the truck tire for a long moment, then walked deliberately to the corral. Meg frisked around him.

"Welcome, Cory!" Piper bent his head over the dog's back and inhaled. "It has been a long, long time. It's very good to see you again."

Cory smelled of southern places, where spring was grass that was fetlock-high, where the sun lay on lush pastures. There was a strong scent of other horses, and an odor of long travel. There was an unfamiliar smell, too, and Piper breathed in again, curious.

It was the scent of sorrow, of mourning, of a long and weary time spent howling at the sky. This then, Piper thought, was Meg's trouble. This was *not-routine*.

"Do you remember me?" asked Piper. And he

blew out a greeting, three long exhalations, which meant the herd has met a favored friend.

"Of course I do, Piper," said Cory.

"I remember you well," said Piper. "And I remember my home, and those who lived there." Memory flooded him, of sunshine-filled summers and the soft sides of his dam—of his sire, distant and magnificent in his paddock. And of Cory himself, younger then, his coat a glory of gold and white, his muzzle free from the grey that speckled it now. Cory's eyes, wide, brown, and steady, met his own; the eyes were still the same.

"You know Cory, Piper?" said Meg. "There is a famous Tale about him among us dogs. The Tale of The Collie's Quest." She leaped, whirled and bit her tail. "It's an honor to have him here!"

"How is my dam, my sire?" asked Piper. "Does Pony still tell her own versions of Tales to the weanlings? Does Cissy still drive my dam to distraction?"

Cory looked past Piper at his herd. "Which of these is your Lead Mare?" he asked. "I haven't been introduced."

"We're to be formal then," said Piper, in surprise. He stepped back, and Clover made her way to the fence. She glanced sidelong at Piper, who nodded approval, then sniffed cautiously at the dog.

"Lead Mare," said Cory, in ritual greeting. "I am Cory, of Bishop Farm."

"I am Clover, by Spotted Tango of Staltmarch. I am Lead Mare to the Sweetwater herd, and my stallion is Sweetwater's Dancing Piper. Since our stallion makes you welcome, we mares do, too. This is Flax, my Second-In-Command, Jessica, our Caretaker. Frosty, our Storyteller. The others are unranked."

Cory's eyes swept the herd of assembled mares. "Your Dreamspeaker?" he asked.

"We have no Dreamspeaker, dog."

Cory, who showed no surprise at this, sat down and directed his steady gaze at Frosty. The blue roan looked back, then down at the ground. Her lower lip hung loose, and she wrinkled her eyes at Clover, as if to say, "What now?" Clover gave her a nudge, and hissed, "The introduction!"

"I'm Frosty, by Spotted Tango out of Blue Ice. I'm Storyteller to the Sweetwater mares."

They all waited. Clover nudged her withers, more sharply than before, and hissed, "The stallion!"

Frosty, with an air of missing something, said, "Our stallion is him, Sweetwater's Dancing Piper."

The silence stretched out and Frosty said, helpfully, "That one, over there. The spotted one."

"For Equus' sake," said Clover, embarrassed. "Tell Cory the Stallion's Tale, Frosty. The dog wants to be introduced to the herd."

"I knew that," said Frosty. She switched her tail, squared up and began.

"The Stallion's Tale," she announced. "Long ago, when rivers were few and all the earth was grass, Equus, whose style and shape were glorious even then, was called before the One . . ."

"Oh, Equus, whose coat shines like the moon, whose eyes are like the stars on a night when there is no moon!" sang the brood mares.

They stopped, the chorus over.

"Exactly!" said Frosty, pleased.

They waited. Clover stamped her feet, then sighed and lowered her head. Frosty looked at nothing in particular. Then she said suddenly, and very fast, "Exactly, exactly, exactly." She rolled her eyes and backed up.

"Oh, my," said Jessica. "Oh, my. Let her settle a bit, Clover. She's overexcited."

Piper blew out in what might have been a laugh. "I'll introduce myself, shall I Frosty? If I begin, perhaps you'll remember, too."

"Stupid mare!" said Clover loudly. Then, in an undertone, "But she's kind, Piper, very kind."

"Yes. Well Cory, The Stallion's Tale." Piper squared up and seemed to grow taller in the sunlight. His heavily muscled chest was as black as a crow's wing, his muzzle a soft cream. The familiar Stallion's Tale rang out with power.

"Equus woke to mist and cloud, and the sense of a new light rising.

Equus woke to a fresh-made spring, and the sound of the One's Voice, calling.

'Your future, stallion. What strengths would you ask to lead these Horses of mine?'

'I'd ask you for strength to cover these mares. For speed to leave danger behind.

'I'd ask for wisdom, to teach them your Law. I'd ask for all stallions in kind.'

'Well done!' the Voice cried, 'Your talents shall be: strength; speed; and wisdom. I'll add to these three—

'Courage to stand and fight when you must. Heart to continue when the battle seems lost.'

So we stallions all, at Equus' call, accept the gifts of the One.

To be wise, strong and swift with the One's added gifts, of courage and heart to fight on."

"I call on this courage," said Cory, abruptly.

"It is yours," said Piper, in surprise.

"I call on this heart."

"It is yours."

"I call on your leadership, stallion."

Piper lowered his head, and said, "Ask, Cory. What may I do for you?"

"Courage and heart to fight on," said Cory. "You're going to need both, Piper."

Piper inhaled sharply. The scent which clung to Cory's coat came to him once more: The scent of grief.

"You're in mourning," he said steadily. "What has happened? What's wrong?"

"Your dam is dead, Piper," the dog said. "And the Dancer, your sire, is missing."

CORY

• 2 •

The Traveler on the Green Road

Piper went still. "Tell me," he said. "Tell me how she died."

Cory looked away. "Founder. And colic."

Twisted Gut. The most agonizing death in the horse's world. Piper quivered, and a sound escaped his throat.

"Get on with it, Cory," said Alvin quietly, "bad news is best eaten fast."

"Some one, some . . . *thing* left poisoned alfalfa in the arena. The latch on Duchess' paddock was broken—Pony said it was an accident, but I'm not so sure, the poisoned hay was no accident." Cory licked his forepaws for a long moment; if Alvin noticed that the old dog was shaking, he kept it to himself.

"I was with her when she died, Piper. And she was as brave at dying as she had been in life. She fought it, with everything she had. She couldn't help crying out; we all know what it's like to die that way. The Dancer was locked in the stallion barn. He was frantic. He beat at the stall door, trying to get out to go to her. He heard her scream. And he heard her stop.

"She breathed out one last time. She went still. And her eyes turned from the brown I'd known in life to a bright green."

"The Green Road," said a mare from the depths of the huddled herd, "she walked the Green Road."

Cory groaned as though he had been kicked in the ribs. "The Dancer's old, older than I am and where he got the strength to break open the stallion paddock, Canis only knows. I saw it later and wondered at the strength he'd had. He came into the Big Barn like a thunderstorm, to the stall where Duchess lay. His eyes rolled back to show the white. Foam dripped from his muzzle. He screamed once: 'El Arat!' Then he raced into the front drive, jumped both fences and was gone."

"El Arat," said Blackjack. "He called out for El Arat."

"The Soul Taker," said Duke.

The dog looked away, panting a little. "You have no Dreamspeaker here at Sweetwater, but you remember Lilly, Piper? The Dreamspeaker to the herd at Bishop Farm?"

Cory's voice came to Piper from a great distance. The stallion shook his head impatiently. He had to hear. He had to understand. "A fine mare," he said too loudly. "Very beautiful."

"Something about Duchess' death was unnatural, *not-routine*. Lilly tried to Walk The Path To The Moon to find out what had happened. But the Moon was dark and hid its eyes from us. The Moon will not be at the full until three days from now, and Lilly will attempt to Walk it once again. But that will do us no good here at Sweetwater." Cory paused, then said. "Lilly failed to walk the Path to the Moon, but she is a Dreamspeaker, and you know that all their Dreams are true. She dreamed of Duchess. And this

is why I have come to Bishop Farm." He looked at
Piper, then at Clover. "It is a true Dream, and Lilly
sends her message through me."

"Greetings, from Lilly, Dreamspeaker of the
Bishop Farm mares, to the Storyteller at Sweetwater
Ranch. I had a Dream sent to me by Jehanna,
Goddess Mare to us and our kind, Dreamspeaker to
the Army of One Hundred and Five in the Courts of
the Outermost West, and companion to Equus
himself.

"I slept under a full moon, and this is what came
to me. I was standing by a pool, in a place I have
never been before. The mists rose all around me.
Clouds drifted across the surface of the pool, and
obscured the images there. I looked, and looked
again, and saw the image of a buckskin mare, standing alone and silent. And through the sighing of
a wind I heard but could not feel, came the cry of
a stallion. I strained to hear the name, and faintly,
it came to me: 'Duchess!' the stallion cried,
'Duchess!'

"I woke, then, to the Moon streaming over the
pastures of Bishop Farm, to the shapes of my herd
mates in the darkness. And still that faint cry filled
my ears: 'Duchess! Come to me! Duchess.' "

Cory fell silent.
"She's alive!" Piper said. "They're both alive! But
where are they?"
Cory shook his head. "Lilly believes they are caught
between the Courts above and the earth below. Duchess is lost and must find her way out again. The
Dancer is somewhere near her. Lilly knows that if
she could reach them, she could lead Duchess and
the Dancer out." Cory dropped his ears. "She cannot

leave Bishop Farm herself. She is old and she has a nursing foal."

"I must find her. I have to," said Piper quietly. "So this is why you've come, Cory. I am grateful to you."

"And how will you accomplish that?" asked Cory. "You need to know more before you act." He looked at Frosty, who tossed her head in a bewildered way, as though something were expected of her.

"Well, what is it, dog?" said Blackjack. "I suppose you want Frosty here to Walk the Path to the Moon."

"Yes," said Cory. "For only Jehanna can tell Piper where to find his sire and dam."

There was a shocked silence.

"Only a Dreamspeaker can Walk the Path to the Moon," said Clover. "We don't even have a Dreamspeaker."

"Frosty could try," said Cory. "All Dreamspeakers begin as Storytellers."

"I'm not walking anywhere," said Frosty, planting her forefeet firmly into the ground. "I may forget who I told what Story to, but nobody is going to make me walk where I don't want to walk."

Clover shifted helplessly. "I'm sorry, Cory. And Piper, I'm sorry for you, too. But this is no concern of ours. This Lilly must try again when the Moon is full."

"She will try again, of course, when it's time," said Cory, "but what good will that do? She cannot leave Bishop Farm to tell you what she has seen. And no matter what she discovers, it will not help you here."

"Perhaps I could go to Bishop Farm and ask Lilly myself," said Piper.

"It would take many seasons to walk there," said Cory. "There's no time. And there are too many obstacles to a journey like that, Piper. Men, their cities, their roads."

"Make that dog Walk the Path to the Moon," said Frosty, "not me."

Duke, who had been listening with ears pricked forward, and a look of great interest, said, "What do you hope to achieve in this Walk to the Moon?"

"Jehanna can tell Piper what to do, where he may go to rescue Duchess and the Dancer," said Cory.

"Hm." Duke flattened his ears and walked thoughtfully to a corner of the shed.

"Make Cory walk," said Frosty, again.

Piper snorted in agreement. "Could you try, Cory? You know how it's done. There's more to you than you seem. I can sense it." The stallion looked eagerly at the collie.

"A dog who knows how it's done?" said Clover. "Mares, and *only* mares can Walk the Path to the Moon. And they have to be Dreamspeakers at that. And Dreamspeakers may walk only at the full of the Moon. We're three days from that. We'd have to find a pool of water . . ." She broke off and flipped her mane. "Besides, it's an insult, the very idea of a dog trying it. We shouldn't even be discussing it in this careless way. It's a holy task."

Piper leaned over the fence, his muzzle close to Cory's ear. "Tell me how," he whispered urgently. "*I'll* try it. I must."

Cory's eyes wrinkled at the corners. "It could be very dangerous. Jehanna, the Watcher at the Pool, may not take interference from a stallion lightly."

"It doesn't matter," said Piper. "I have to try."

Cory cocked his head. The morning was wearing on toward noon, and the pale April sun was at its height. "Clover's right. We'll have a few days until the full of the Moon. We'll have time to consider what's to be done. But one thing is clear to me, Piper. I believe you must prepare to leave Sweetwater Ranch to find Duchess."

"The rodeo's tomorrow," said Meg. "What happens when Piper takes a blue?"

"If Piper takes a blue," said Blackjack.

"Piper always takes a blue," said Meg loyally. "In calf roping there's no horse around who's faster."

"You go on the rodeo circuit?" said Cory to the stallion.

"I did last season, yes."

"And the season before that and before that," said Hank. "Blackjack and I go with him. I'm a barrel racer, and Blackjack does exhibition rides." He hesitated, then admitted, "When he's in the right frame of mind. Duke and Alvin stay here."

"Duke's too old, and Alvin's just a plodder," said Clover with slight contempt. "Piper's the important one. When he wins, we all win. And more men come to Sweetwater to buy yearlings and the two year olds because he wins and he's their sire."

"Plodding saved one of your mares," said Hank unexpectedly. "Who went out with David when Lady wandered off and who found her, what's more, in the middle of the biggest storm we've had for seasons? Alvin the plodder did. It was plodding old Alvin who pulled the oat bag away from the puddle." He laid his ears back. "Stallions and mares aren't the only horses who can do great things."

"That's enough," Meg said briskly. "Each horse has its place on this ranch, and each its purpose."

"Baby bucket," said Hank to Clover.

"Barn hound," Clover retorted.

Hank reared, and curled his lip back. Piper, moving quickly, stepped between the mare and gelding and decisively shoved them away from each other.

Meg watched them thoughtfully. "It's Piper who keeps order here, Cory. Piper who sets the value of the stock. Piper who protects the stock in the mountains. It would be a great loss if he left the ranch for even a short while. Sweetwater might never recover."

Clover kicked up her heels and squealed, then pushed two of the mares into a purposeless lope. Piper stood apart, neck arched, thoughtful.

"I'd recommend a little less squabbling, and a little more sense of purpose here," said Duke. The Connemara moved deliberately toward the gate. Alvin stepped aside for him. "We have some decisions to make, it seems. Piper, the story we've just heard from this dog is a terrible one. But all of us, at one time or another, have met cruelty at the hands of men and nature both." He paused, some painful memory in his dark eyes, and then went on. "But these things weren't necessarily due to our gods. They are due to the way of the world. Your dam died one of the most painful deaths for a horse. Founder and colic. And your sire left the farm and hasn't been seen since. These are facts. But all these signs and dreams Cory tells us come from brood mares standing in the pasture at night under a full moon. What we *know*, dog, must be separated from what we believe." He paused, then said gravely, "We live in the belief that all of us here will foot on the Green Road, before we pass on to the Courts."

"I'll bet Hank won't," Clover interrupted.

"But who among us has *seen* the Courts? Who among us know these things to be true, and not," Duke hesitated, "a hope or symbol of what lies beyond this world of men?"

"Dreamspeakers don't lie," said Clover.

"How would you know?" asked Blackjack. "You don't even have a Dreamspeaker, and the Storyteller you've got is too dumb to remember what she told to who and when and why she didn't." He looked at Frosty, whose lower lip protruded in a stupid way. "Geldings should be able to Walk the Path to the Moon," he muttered.

"Even if Cory's tales are true," said Duke, "what can Piper do about it? What can *we* do about it?"

"We can go get Duchess," said Blackjack, flippantly. "I've always wanted to see what's at the end of the Green Road. And Hank's right—brood mares and stallions aren't the only horses who can do great deeds."

"Don't be a fool," snapped Clover. The brood mares rustled behind her with the sound of birds settling on a field of wheat.

"Is there a Green Road?" asked Duke. "And does it lead to a real place called Summer, where we're judged on the worthiness of our lives? I've lived longer than you all, and I have my doubts. I've seen many deaths in my time, as we all have. I've never seen El Arat, the Soul Taker."

Jessica nosed her foal closer to her side, and the brood mare called Tina flung her head up and whinnied. "El Arat," Duke continued firmly, "is a legend, a way to accept death when it's unfair. As for the Dancer's cry of rage at Duchess' death—who among us has not railed at fate in such a way, when a member of the herd has left the pastures of our range?" He sighed heavily. "The Courts of the Outermost West are *here*, in spring when the grass grows high and green, in summer, when the sun grooms our coats with warmth. El Arat is a symbol of the unfairness of death itself. She has no more substance than the Green Road. None of these things are real like this is real." He nosed the boards that separated the geldings from the brood mares.

"Is the sound that a brood mare makes calling to her foal real?" said Piper softly. "Can you touch that sound, or eat it? But there is something in that sound which draws the foal to her side, wherever it may be, or whatever it is doing."

"El Arat's real enough," said Cory grimly. "As real as those scars on Hank's neck. As real as the memory of cruelty Duke has in his past, or the broken bones of Blackjack's tail. I know. I've met her."

There was a long pause. The wind rose and fell again. The herd was silent. Suddenly, Piper stiffened, his stallion's crest held high, the muscles of his chest and shoulders in sharp relief. His ears swiveled forward and his eyes searched the mountain ridges.

"Did you hear that?" he asked quietly. "There was a sound, a howling cry." The coal black hair on his neck and withers rippled. "And the wind is hot."

The mares huddled closer together; Jessica, Flax and Tina turned their hindquarters out toward Cory in a posture of defense.

"I don't hear anything," said Duke.

"I heard," said Clover, shivering.

"I heard!" said Blackjack in excitement.

"So, you've met the Soul Taker, Cory," said Duke, firmly drawing their attention back to him. And, his expression said, I don't believe you for a moment. "When was this? Your grief at your friend's death may have misled you in thinking that you saw this in the barn when Duchess died."

Cory shook his head. The white ruff on his neck bristled. "I do believe that El Arat tried to call Duchess's soul from her at the moment of her death. But I didn't see her there, nor would I have. I'm a dog, not a horse, and your gods have never been visible to me. No, I knew El Arat at Bishop Farm. She was a herdmate of your dam's, Piper. I knew her well before she passed to the Black Barns. She had reason enough to hate your dam, and to destroy her."

"*El Arat*, the Soul Taker, the Goddess Mare of death?" said Frosty (for once remembering clearly). "The mare who walks at the side of the Dark Horse himself? The mare who hunts with the Harrier Hounds? Why should she hate your dam?"

"Because of who the Duchess and the Dancer are," said Cory. He turned to Piper. "You haven't told them?"

"Why should I?" asked Piper simply. "There are many of my line who walk the world of men, now. I was the first of the Dancer's get, but I am not the last. And all horses eventually trace their ancestry back to gods."

"That's very true," said Clover firmly. "All of us go back to our foundation sires and dams: Appaloosa, Tennessee Walkers, Standardbreds, the lot." She added thoughtfully, her eyes on Hank, "As hard as that may be for some of us brood mares to believe."

"Tell them of the Appaloosa Breedmaster and Breedmistress, Frosty," Cory prompted.

"I'm sure I've told you all before," said Frosty. "I know I have. It's the Rainbow Horse, the Spotted Horse he's sometimes called. We Appaloosas call him the Dancer. And our Breedmistress is a mare called Duchess."

There was a very long silence.

Piper moved uneasily under Clover's amazed look. Frosty said crossly, "What?"

"We just never connected the Breedmaster and

Breedmistress to Piper's sire and dam," said Clover faintly. "I mean, it's your job to tell the lineage to the foals and to us Frosty, and you never . . ." She stopped, and shook her head, bewildered.

"Wait!" said Frosty. "This Duchess that you know, Piper. Is she the same?" She rolled her eyes at her stallion and backed up uneasily. "Are you . . . ?"

"I'm not anything except what I seem to be," said Piper. "That's the whole point."

"Why does El Arat hate Duchess?" Jessica asked Cory timidly.

"You all know the Tale of the Appaloosa or you should, since this is an Appaloosa breeding ranch. How Sycha, the first Soul Taker, betrayed her kin to move from the Courts of the Outermost West to live in the Black Barns with He Who Should Not Be Named in The Dark. When Sycha betrayed the Appaloosa, the Appaloosa breed began to die out, and Dancer left the Courts to find the last true mare of the line and breed her.

"El Arat, when I knew her, was a member of Duchess's herd at Bishop Farm, before Duchess knew that her true destiny was to become Breedmistress to all your kind." Cory's expression softened, then he said roughly, "El Arat was beautiful, I remember that. But, she was proud. She would be Breedmistress, and could not. Pride turned to envy inside her. Since she could not reign as Breedmistress at the side of the Rainbow Horse, she decided that she would rule in hell. She struck a bargain with the Dark Horse: she would kill the first foal the buckskin dropped. In return, she would rule in the Dark Barns, a Soul Taker more evil than the Barns had ever known.

"I was there when El Arat failed in her attempted

murder. The foal, Piper, was saved, to become the first of many spotted Appaloosas. I was there when she fled the pastures of her home to the Black Barns below.

"El Arat is real. The Courts and the Barns are real. Piper's task is real. And I have come here for a purpose: to speak to you of Lilly's dream. I believe that one of your mares must Walk the Path to the Moon to discover how Piper may leave Sweetwater to save his sire and dam. If he does not, his dam will remain at the mercy of the Soul Taker."

"No!" said Clover. "I will not allow this. The future is *here*, Piper. You'll go on the rodeo circuit, as you have before. You're the Lead Stallion. You can't forsake us. You heard Cory. The Bishop Farm mares are old. With no stallion, there will be no future for the horses there. You can't leave your duties here."

"I'll come back," said Piper, "Equus permitting."

"Paah! What if you *can't* come back? Cory said that many have been killed in this battle for the Appaloosa breed. What if you're killed, too? What will happen to us? To the foals we are carrying now in our bellies? There may be no foals next season and the season after that. Men won't buy the yearlings if you fail to win in rodeos. It is the way of the world. It is part of the Bargain we horses have with men, that we give them foals and they protect our breed."

"Tell me, Cory," said Duke. "Have you ever *seen* the Soul Taker? I know you have seen an Arabian mare named El Arat. But have you ever seen the Soul Taker? Have you ever Walked the Path to the Moon yourself? Or have you been listening to brood mare's dreams?"

Cory rolled his eye and regarded the Connemara. A memory shook him, and he panted hard, but his tones were steady. "I've seen Anor, the Executioner, take the Dancer by the neck and drag him into the earth. And I have fought Anor's Voice: Scant the Harrier Hound. I have seen him transformed into a skull-eyed creature who would freeze the blood in your body. I have tasted Scant's oily fur in battle." He sat up, trembling. "I carry Scant's mark, here!" He raised his muzzle to the sky and howled. A vivid scar tracked through his white throat like tangled wire through pasture. "I have run from the fanged teeth of the Executioner himself: Anor the Red, the Dark Horse's killer, who feasts on the bodies of his own kind. I have seen all this, and I remember. It is this evil which has captured Duchess now, I am convinced of it. It is this evil that the Piper must fight." He howled and howled again, and Meg, ears flattened, howled with him. The horses stood frozen. Piper flared his nostrils red and snorted.

Cory lowered his head and was silent for a long moment. "Don't you see?" he said finally. "Can't you see what is happening now? It is beginning all over again. Both the Breedmistress and Breedmaster of the Appaloosa line are lost, between here," and he scraped the dirt with his forepaw, "and the Courts themselves. Without the Breedmistress, your breed will grey out and die off. If you are to save your line, Piper, you must save them, too." The collie looked south to the mountains. "The moon is almost full. Three more turns and it will be at its height. We must wait until then, and Frosty must try to Walk the Path to the Moon. Only Jehanna the Goddess Mare can tell you what to do."

"No!" Clover bared her teeth, and bucked briefly in place.

"We have no other choice," said Cory.

"*I* have no other choice," said Piper. "This is what

I have decided to do, mare. I won't be disobeyed. Not in this."

"But what about the rodeo?" said Clover urgently. "Every year when you win, you go on the road. You *must* go on the road, Piper. It's the only way to bring back the championships that make our foals valuable to men. You'll be sent on the road in three days, unless you lose the competition and they keep you here at Sweetwater. And you can't lose, Piper. I've never known you to lose before."

Piper turned and looked at the rodeo arena behind the long barns. The ranch hands were dragging the ground with the big tractor. Several of them worked on the fence, replacing splintered boards with new ones. In the distance he could see one ranch hand in the judges' stand; the smell of fresh paint came to him as he inhaled sharply. Two cowboys emerged from the Long Barn, halters in hand, and walked purposefully toward the gelding shed. The Working Herd would be saddled up and the day's routine go forward as it had in seasons past.

The wind rose cold and brisk. A cloud passed over the sun. Cory howled once more, and the eerie cry echoed in the April air. A faint yowling wail, of hounds hunting in a pack, came in mocking answer.

"No!" said Clover. "No!" She kicked out furiously. Piper, still and massive, moved away from her and searched the sky.

Blackjack, watching them both, stamped twice and blew out. A light sweat shone on his withers.

"About time," Duke grunted. "We should have been grained hours ago."

"What?" Blackjack turned to look at the Connemara. Duke indicated the approaching cow hands with a nod of his head.

"But what's Piper going to do?" said Alvin.

"Not our business," said Duke. "Riding fence, that's our business. I don't want to know what Piper's going to do. It's *not-routine*, the whole thing, messing around with brood mares' dreams."

"Dreams," said Blackjack, "It's got to be more than dreams."

"You'd better hope it isn't," said Duke. "Come on. let's go to work."

• 3 •

A Change In
Routine

Blackjack watched the cow hands approach from the safety of the shed. There was a door in the back wall; he knew from long experience that the Working Herd would be taken out the door and into the Long Barn, where they'd be saddled up for the day's routine. "We should be out on our own," he said, "like Piper, running free in the mountains."

"And what would you do running free in the mountains?" said Duke. "Get yourself and us into trouble I suppose. Now, the ranch stallion's got a purpose running free in the mountains. Guard the mares. Protect the foals. Breed the barren."

"Gas, gas, gas," Hank muttered to Alvin, lifting his tail to prove his point. "He doesn't want to be Storyteller, but he can't help himself from laying down the Law. Go figure."

"Well," said Duke, "work's our duty, and we're a Working Herd."

"Why?" demanded Blackjack, sensing the two ranch hands approaching the shed door. He turned and faced the others. "Why should we stay here and miss all the excitement?"

One of the hands swung the door open. Blackjack blew out, kicked up his heels, and crow-hopped backwards. Hank eyed the hands, then his Herd Chief, and removed himself to a far corner. Duke, with a slightly self-conscious attitude, walked over to the second hand and allowed himself to be led out.

"Saa, saa, Blackjack," said the remaining hand. His arm was crooked behind his back. Blackjack cocked an amused eye at Hank.

"Do you believe this guy? He thinks I can't see the rope."

He settled, outwardly quiet, as the hand approached and slipped the lasso around his neck. "I lull them, you see," he informed Hank and Alvin over his withers, "and *then* . . . He jerked backwards, spun, and ducked out of the lasso.

It was a trick, one of several, which had prematurely retired him from the show ring.

The hand clucked, "Saa, saa," ill-concealed irritation in his voice.

"How mad does he have to get before you shape up?" asked Alvin. There was no irony in his tone, only inquiry, as if he were storing up information for future reference. "I mean, you don't really think that we'll get out of work this morning, do you?"

"Of course he doesn't," said Hank. "And I don't know about you two, but if we're going out on the trail, I'd just as soon have my ration of oats."

"So would I," said Alvin. The hand who had taken Duke into the Long Barn returned and Alvin trotted to him. Hank, too, accepted the lasso and they left the corral.

"Saa, saa," said the hand left with Blackjack.

Blackjack watched Alvin and Hank go into the

barn. He watched the hand, who was beginning to smell angry rather than merely irritated. He pawed at the ground, then studied his left foreleg.

The hand walked up to Blackjack and slipped the lasso over his neck. Deftly, he twisted the rope into a makeshift halter. He pulled it snug, and Blackjack raised his head in mock suprise. "Well, well, well," his look clearly said. "You caught me after all. Clever you."

He nudged the man sharply, burying his nose in the sheepskin-smelling thing that Blackjack theorized was man's equivalent of a saddle, since it covered his skinny back. The hand tapped him on the neck, then slid a lump of sugar under the gelding's muzzle. Blackjack crunched it with elegant movements of his head, nodding up and down, and allowed himself to be led to the Long Barn.

Like Sweetwater's rodeo ring, corral, and hay-ricks, David Bishop had built the Long Barn low and snug against the harsh Montana weather. Winters could be fierce, the blizzards howling down the mountains like some demon rider from the Pit, the summers hot and dry. It afforded protection against both these extremes, remaining cool and airy in the August heat, providing a sturdy bulwark against snow and rain.

The Long Barn reminded Blackjack of his years in the show ring and the stalls which had been his home when he was on the Saddle Seat circuit. He, Duke, and Alvin all had a fondness for it; in their stalls, they ate oats rolled in sweet molasses, and curled up in thickly piled straw when the winds were piercing and the weather bitter. It was a place to which they frequently tried to return—particularly when an inattentive hand was riding them off-ranch for a trip to ride fence or herd stock.

Hank's attitude toward the barn was altogether different. He would walk easily through to the open door, then stop suddenly outside his stall door, all four feet dug into the ground. It took two hands to get him into his stall every morning.

The sugar-carrying hand put Blackjack into the stall next to his Second-In-Command. Hank, his withers damp with the effort of staying calmly inside, pressed close against the wall adjoining the Walker's.

Hank was a greyed-out Appaloosa; he had been brightly marked at birth, with a shoulder-high spotted blanket that quickly began to fade as he grew to yearling height. He had the white-rimmed eye, the striped hoof and the spotted muzzle of the true Appaloosa, but his coat had faded to a dirty grey . . . except for the scars circling his neck and withers.

Blackjack eyed the scars. Although Hank refused to answer any questions, all the members of the Working Herd knew that Hank had been in a barn collapse somewhere. Hank, trembling with the closeness of the roof to his scarred back, pressed against the wall and said, "Do you feel the walls tremble? Do you feel the floor shift underneath your feet?"

Blackjack blew out in a soothing way, three long soft expulsions of air that matron mares sometimes used with foals. "The walls are still, and the floor is solid," he said in answer to this ritual cry. "Your grain's here. Eat." Hank, shivering, walked to his bucket and grabbed a mouthful. He chewed rapidly, eyes rolled back to watch the roof.

"It's safe here," Blackjack said. "Look, see that little cat there? You know what cats are like: *very* careful of their own skin. Would it be here if it didn't feel safe? The Long Barn's a refuge for that cat."

Hank eyed the cat: no more than a kitten and no wider than the belly band on a saddle. It was scrawny, with copper-black markings and a white spot in the middle of its back. "Its eyes are bigger than the rest of it altogether," said Blackjack. "Stray, most likely. And it's come *here* to be safe." He stopped, glumly considering the boredom of safety. One of the hands pulled a piece of beef jerky from his pocket and tossed it to the cat who leaped on it, jaws working between loud purrs.

"There you are," said Blackjack. "Listen to it. If the barn were going to fall, it'd be out of here in a flash."

The kitten grabbed the remaining bits of jerky and raced out of the Long Barn as if pursued by a kennel-full of hounds. Hank grunted hopelessly.

"He never really feels safe unless Piper's here," Alvin said.

"I can do anything Piper can do," Blackjack said confidently. "We all can."

Duke snorted in derision. Alvin blew out in amusement. Blackjack flattened his ears.

"Looks like we'll be riding fence," said Duke after a moment, tactfully changing the subject. "Look at the packs piled in the corner."

"Three days on the trail, maybe four," said Blackjack. He sighed and bent to his grain.

When he had worked well in the show ring, which hadn't been often, he had made an impressive spectacle, and even now, long-haired against the cold, his muzzle and chin unclipped and his feathers grown out, he looked close to majestic. He had the thick, graceful neck and high action of the well-bred Walker, and his long face, if lacking the delicacy of an Arabian or the elegance of a Thoroughbred, was well-chiseled, with a full dark eye and broad forehead. His coat was deep brown, and in some lights, almost black. He wasn't sure what spirit of mischief moved

him to a longing for the *not-routine*; it had kept him
from championships, and ended, as it had for other
geldings, in an ignominious sale at auction. They
were all lucky, he knew, to have been picked up by
David. Things could have been a lot worse.

Blackjack chewed his grain. He thought of himself
and his Working Herd tacked up in the plain horned
saddles that were all Sweetwater could afford for
everyday use, sloping along at the same flat-footed
jog, up and down the mountain ravines. He'd loved
the show ring, the applause, but couldn't take the
discipline . . . and now?

Mule work.

He sighed heavily, then caught Alvin's eye. The
Standardbred blew out with a friendly sound. A ranch
hand was unsuccessfully trying to pull the gelding
from his stall to tack him up—and Alvin refused to
take one step forward.

Blackjack considered Alvin. The Standardbred was
big, close to seventeen hands. He was Last-Ranked
in the herd hierarchy, and obedient and sweet-
tempered with his fellows. His behavior with men
was another matter altogether; he often refused to
stand still for mounting, was obdurate about hoof-
cleaning, and almost always ignored frantic signals to
halt from any hapless novice who got on his back.
This flouting of men's routine was always accompa-
nied with such an air of surprised good nature—"Me?
You want ME to go straight ahead at a walk? Why
didn't you say so?"—that he was rarely punished.
This annoyed Blackjack, who got his share of well-
placed blows when he acted up. He'd have to mention proper Working Herd behavior to Alvin once
more, he supposed. The Herd Chief was supposed to
keep order, make sure the members complied with
men's rules, kept up with men's routine.

Blackjack sighed again. He wished for the *not-routine*.

Hank, trembling, pressed close to the adjoining wall, his grain finished, seeking the warmth of the Walker's solid side. Blackjack rumbled comfortingly. Duke winked gravely at them and chewed his grain carefully. At his age, Blackjack reflected, it was lucky that it was just the Connemara's teeth that were going.

A wave of affection hit Blackjack. So, he wished for the *not-routine*. They all did. But they were a pretty good Working Herd. And they were taken care of, well fed, brushed, and vetted. The men at Sweetwater even put up with Blackjack's tricks which, the Walker admitted in his maturer moments, were an unnecessary pain in the tail. In return, the geldings rode fence, went packing, rode the roundup, and joined the rodeos which would begin tomorrow.

But didn't life hold more exciting things than this?

• 4 •

Rodeo

That afternoon, Piper watched the familiar preparations for the rodeo from a corner of the corral. He pushed his grief deep into his heart where it glowed like a banked fire. He could do nothing now but wait until the Moon had reached the full.

In the midst of the rodeo clean-up, the business of vetting the mountain herd went on as it did each year. Ranch hands led the mares into the Long Barn, where they were checked for injuries and old wounds. David and his men looked into each mare's mouth, sometimes using the large rasp to grind down the sharp edges of teeth worn unevenly by grazing. They checked the mares' eyes and listened to their hearts and wind, alert for the first signs of disease. Each mare was wormed, given a shot to protect her from disease, then dipped in a foul-smelling liquid to destroy the ticks that carried fever.

They came for Piper, finally. David slipped a rope halter over the stallion's ears, snugging the stallion chain across his muzzle with deft hands. Piper flung

46

his head high against the chain, working his powerful hindquarters in a circle, feet stepping high and light. David pulled firmly against the lead rope, and Piper followed him willingly, the understanding clear that David led him only with his full cooperation, that he did not bend to man's will out of fear or through the man-made obedience of geldings.

In the barn, David cross-tied Piper in the aisle between the stalls lining both sides of the large building. The roof shut out the feel of the wind and sky. A new set of scents swirled around him. Leather, oil, and the odor of the dip overrode the natural scents of grass, snow, dirt.

There was concrete under his hooves, and he pawed at it to break its silence. Bare ground told him many things, the shifting of the earth itself sending messages of where his mares were, and what predators stalked his range. Concrete told him little; he could feel the weight of the building settling, vibrations from the ranch hands going about the business of Sweetwater, the beats of a horse walking in a stall.

Attending to all of this, Piper ignored the wasp-sting of the needle, and accepted the paste wormer with no more than a curl of his upper lip. David ran his hands up and down the great sides, pausing a long while to probe the tendons of the steel-spring legs. "Piper," he said, "saa, saa, Piper," and rubbed the stallion's ears.

Piper leaned into the curry comb when David brushed him down. His eye caught David's and held it for a long moment. The man's eye was small, and to Piper, even stranger than the Tales of Soul Takers and Green Roads Cory had told the herd. "Saa, saa, Piper," said David. Piper blew out in response and nudged the man's hairless cheek.

The smell of disinfectant purled heavily through

the air, and Piper wrinkled his nose in disgust. The first time he'd been dipped in the stuff, it'd taken most of the day to get him to step into the trough. It had been a long time ago, at the end of his first season in the mountains with the mares, but he remembered clearly the oily liquid and the odor, which had lingered for days, interfering with his ability to scent the moods of the mares and weather.

There had been a battle of wills over the dip, and David, Piper thought, had won. The stallion hadn't recognized at the time how important the battle had been. It had not been a test of strength; that was not David's way. He'd led Piper to the trough and Piper stood firm, refusing to go another step. David had tied him there and waited, leaning against the stall door and occasionally calling, "Saa, saa, Piper. Walk on," until finally, Piper understood that they would stay there until the moon rose, and he put one foot, then the other, into the trough and endured the stinking rinse.

Piper stood now in the trough without complaint. He was used to it. He and David had a bargain between them: Man serves horse, horse serves man.

The rinse finished, David placed Piper in a stall piled high with straw and shut the door. The ranch hands brought the geldings in to be cross-tied, examined, wormed, then dipped. Blackjack was first, his tail set high, rusty-black coat gleaming in the barn lights. He snorted and jibbed at the lead ropes, dancing sideways down the aisle to avoid the trough. One of the ranch hands slapped him firmly on the withers and he settled reluctantly, stepping into the dip with wrinkled lip.

Obediently, Duke placed his feet where the ranch hands directed, rolling his ears flat against his skull and sneering in a dignified way when the milky liquid slid into his ears. Alvin, whose natural courtesy extended only to other horses, splashed through and walked on without stopping to the far end of the barn. It took three hands to make him stand in the trough and three more to coax him out.

They brought Hank in last. The Appaloosa moved quickly, shivering all the while, starting nervously at the slight shiftings in the building.

"Easy," said Piper through the wire mesh of his stall door, "easy."

"Do you feel the walls swaying? Do you feel the barn tremble?" Hank tossed his head nervously, spittle flying from his mouth.

"The barn won't fall, Hank. And if it should, I'll lead you out."

Hank sighed heavily. He controlled himself with an effort. The ranch hand rolled open the stall door next to Piper, and Hank stepped in. "We stink to the Courts themselves." Hank blew out, the spray coming through the mesh that separated their stalls. He paused, then said curiously, "Do you believe in the Courts, Piper?"

"I believe."

"And what will you do about your dam and sire?"

Piper wrinkled his eyes and glanced sidelong at Hank. "What do you think I should do?"

"Me?" Hank considered. "The Law says that your allegiance is here, to the ranch, and to the brood mares. And Duke came out of the chute in time, you know, when he told you that those things may not be real. But sometimes I wish there were no Laws—or at least, not quite so many. It's terrible Piper, what is happening." He dropped his tone and added, "But it's exciting too." He shook his head. "I don't know what to think. *I've* never actually seen any of those things. And brood mares tend to be resty when the Moon is full, and think up fanciful things."

"Brood mares hold the existence of our kind in their bellies," said Piper. He pawed restlessly at the stall door. "Have you ever seen a brood mare fight, Hank?"

"Fight? Mares fight, of course, I've been in many Working Herds and they're just the same as geldings. But *brood* mares?" He looked doubtful. "They fight among themselves."

"So do you and Blackjack and the others. This year, in the mountains, a pack of wolves stalked the herd; this is nothing unusual, we watch for this. Several of them managed to get a yearling separated from the herd. Clover heard the yearling scream when the wolves attacked it. I was at the other end of the valley, too far away to help. She gathered the entire herd together and raced to the aid of the yearling. When I returned, there was nothing left of the wolves that had attacked the youngster but a few bloody scraps of fur."

Hank snorted, and pawed the stall floor.

"They are tough, brood mares, and they look life straight in the eye. I remember the brood mares at Bishop Farm. They were no different, no less brave, no less inclined to dream than the Sweetwater mares. I believe, Hank, in the story Cory has told us. I believe that Lilly saw what she saw."

He stepped and pricked his ears forward. David was coming to ride.

"So what will we do, then?" Hank stopped. "What will *you* do?" he corrected himself.

David came down the aisle, a hackamore in one hand. He slid open the door to Piper's stall, and the big stallion snorted. The bridle's silver conches gleamed in the barn's light. David slid the bridle over Piper's ears and drew him from the stall. They walked down the aisle together, and Hank called out, again, "What will you do?"

Piper shook his head. "I will do what I have to."

Piper and David walked into the sunlight. It was late, and the sun was going down, splashing red along the mountains like water spilled from a pail. David grasped Piper's mane in his left hand and leaped onto the stallion's back. He settled lightly, thighs firm in the slight hollow between Piper's barrel and withers. Piper tossed his head at the feel of the man on his back, bringing his hindquarters underneath himself, shifting off his forehand.

The visions came back as they always did when he and David rode bareback. He saw what David saw. Felt what he felt. He and the man became one being, neither man nor horse, but an entity that was more than each.

RACE! came the thought, and Piper leaped from a standing halt to a full gallop down the drive. Gravel sprayed from his hooves. He ran with joy, his heart lightened with movement.

The first time David had settled on his bare back, Piper had been startled at the closeness, the sudden contact. David's wiry muscles, his blood and bone, seemed to merge into Piper's back and sides like water into sand. With this merging came a feeling that he was Piper as something else, with senses in the world of both horse and man.

Like all horses, Piper's vision was wide-angled, seeing everything in front of him and behind, except for the space between his eyes and the area blocked by his hindquarters and tail. Now, David's different vision overlay his own, and he saw with this extra sense that the world lay narrow and deep to men. Sweetwater Ranch sprang to strange and vivid life when David rode him bareback.

THE FENCE! David's legs tightened, pushed forward, and flexed against Piper's sides. Piper extended his gallop.

JUMP! David rose slightly, knees and calves digging into the stallion's side. Piper collected himself and pushed, rising over the topmost rail of the fence in a powerful spring. As he left the ground, he lost the sense of communication with the earth and all the messages that came to him from his hooves. He swept through the air suspended, feeling only the man on his back, scenting only the wind. David's knees were steady, his hands low on Piper's neck, the reins loose, and sensitively held. Signals came from the reins, from the blood pulsing through David's own body, from the breath going in and out of his chest. Piper landed on the other side of the fence low and flat, back level. Behind them Piper could see—and knew that David could also see—the man who had come with Cory in the truck on the ranch house porch, the collie at his feet.

EMMANUAL! And with the name, a sense of grief and trouble came from David, and memories of Bishop Farm.

Piper remembered the soft underside of his dam, and her scent on a cool summer evening. He remembered his sire, a massive, brightly-colored presence who was never far away. He heard once more Dancer's familiar low whistle, as clearly as if his sire were nearby. The shapes and sounds of Bishop Farm rose before them both, man and horse, and Piper grieved.

Piper's gallop faltered to a lope, the lope to a trot. He shook his head, the silver conches jingling. David's hands stroked his neck; Piper stopped and pawed the earth. The man leaned along the stallion's neck, his breath in Piper's ears. David pulled the reins up; Piper backed up. The left rein touched his neck; he turned back to the ranch. David nudged him into a trot. They came back by way of the open drive, and

Piper did not leap the fence again, his exuberance gone. They walked to the porch and David drove his weight lightly down. Piper halted and stood still.

David jumped down, and with the contact gone, Sweetwater returned to itself again. Piper shoved his nose against David's back, rubbing up and down, pushing him forward. Emmanual went to the stallion's head, and the two men murmured in low tones.

"Are you well?" Cory asked, ears alert.

"Yes," said Piper.

David pressed his cheek to Piper's heart. His cheek was cool against the stallion's side.

"They don't know whether or not you should ride the rodeo tomorrow," said Cory. "You're not working as well as you usually do, apparently. This is of concern to them."

"The future of this ranch rides with me when I ride tomorrow," said Piper. "How can I be the same knowing that I must decide whether to win or lose? How can I turn on my master and abandon Sweetwater? How can I leave the herd?"

"It is a hard choice," said Cory.

Piper watched the men. David turned and the strange blue eye looked into his own.

"And what does he sense about me?" Piper asked the collie.

Cory cocked his head, listening. "That your mind is elsewhere."

Piper flicked an ear.

The collie looked intently into Emmanual's face, his tail wagging. Then he said, "Emmanual doesn't believe David. He can observe nothing strange or different." The collie sat down. "They've decided you will ride the rodeo tomorrow."

David walked Piper in the corral, opened the gate and slid the hackamore over his head, freeing him.

Piper rolled in the mud and snow, then trotted along the fence, cooling himself. He greeted the mares. Frosty, her jaws working steadily, moved clumsily behind Jessica, with the obvious intention of hiding from him. Clover walked up and welcomed him anxiously, rearing and bringing her forelegs over the back of his neck. Piper nipped her shoulder in reassurance and she went back to the hay, her step light.

Cory slipped through the boards and stood watching the mares as they ate the hay set out for them.

"They foal late here," he observed. "At Bishop Farm, all the foals have dropped by now, and the mares have been rebred. Or at least, they would have been had the Dancer been there." He raised his head and sniffed. "Winter lies here late, too. Do the mares return to the mountains when you ride the circuit?"

"They stay here until the foals are weaned. They're put into the brood mare pasture there, where the stream runs, until the foals have dropped. I return near Longlight to rebreed the mares and then I'm on the circuit again until autumn comes, and the leaves turn from green to gold and red. We go back to the mountains when the leaves fall, and the foals are strong enough to take the winter." He lowered his head and sniffed at the dog. "What would you do in my place, Cory? How would you decide? What's important?"

Cory sat down and scratched at his ear with his hind leg. "I'm not a Pack Leader. My loyalty's to man. That's my job. I've tried to do it well all my life, and except for one time, I've never broken my oath."

"And when was that?"

"It was on your dam's behalf, as a matter of fact. She made me a member of her herd." He grinned, and his tongue lolled pink. "She even made up a special oath for me."

"Tell me exactly what happened," Piper paused eagerly, his eyes dark.

Cory moved uneasily. His hackles rose, perhaps against the oncoming night.

"She left the Farm with your sire, and went to live in the mountains, free, she said then, from the rules and laws of men."

"She broke her bargain with man? And my sire broke the Stallion's Oath?"

"Yes. But you know, Piper, she was abused in her youth, and it was hard for her to trust the Bishops. And as for the Dancer, I don't believe he ever took the Stallion's Oath in the first place. He had been captured in the mountains where he was running wild. Emmanual never did break him to saddle until much later.

"The first time I saw the Dancer, he was locked in a slaughtering chute, the killing tool raised to his forehead. We brought him back to Bishop Farm and then, in the night, when I was asleep in the farmhouse, he jumped the fence and ran, taking Duchess and a Paint mare with him. I had been working hard that day, and I slept hard, and they were miles away before I woke up.

"We searched for him, David and I, and we couldn't find him. David gave up and returned home. I slipped away and followed the scent on my own. I was angry. I felt that my trust had been betrayed, and that I needed to redeem myself in the eyes of my master, and the horses who had remained behind.

"I wasn't sure then, of who he was, or why he had been sent to Duchess in the first place. Then I discovered that when he Walked the Green Road at the end of his life, he would once again become the

Rainbow Horse, Breedmaster of the Appaloosa. I guess I figured that for who he had been, and who he would become, I could make an exception in my loyalty to man. So I joined your dam's herd, and gave my allegiance to both of them. I never regretted it."

"He always seemed ordinary to me," said Piper. "Not ordinary perhaps, but as I must seem to my own foals, remote, large, a stallion to be obeyed. And I know he worked well with Emmanual."

"And no other," said Cory wryly. "But he is the Rainbow Horse, although you have never seen him in that form." He sighed heavily. "It must be hard for you to believe. For both of us, dog and horse, it is the things we smell and touch that we believe in. I would not believe, except for that one time, meeting Anor himself in the mountains." His eyeteeth gleamed in the deepening twilight. "Like Duke, I've asked myself, now and then, if I had had a dream. If it had happened as I believed it. But I have this scar, and on nights when the moon is down, and the sky dark, I remember the scent of Anor's breath, sodden with blood and the flesh of horses. I remember Scant and the Harrier Hounds, their eyes burning in their skulls. And I remember the voice of He Who Should Not Be Named In The Dark. And I know what I saw was true.

"It was a strange winter, that season I tracked your sire to the mountains and lived with the herd. He had picked up another mare in his travels, a Shetland Pony." Cory rubbed his nose reflectively with a greying forepaw. "You'll remember Pony as a great friend of Duchess; she wasn't, not at first. She sold herself to the Dark Horse. To save your dam, and the Paint mare Susie, and Pony herself. Dancer bent to the Dark Horse's will and traveled the Path to the

Dark Barns. Duchess and I took Susie and Pony back to Bishop Farm then, and in the summer, you were born. And your sire, rescued, so they said, from the Final Death by the sacrifice of Sycha the first Soul Taker, returned to Bishop Farm to live out his mortal days."

Sweat patched Piper's withers. "Then what was my sire's sin, that he wanders now, lost, in search of my dam? And what has Duchess done to die as she has, in pain and terror?"

"It's El Arat's work. I don't doubt that. Duchess is destined to be Breedmistress of your kind, Piper. El Arat has never forgiven her that. As for your sire, I'm not surprised that he forgot his duty to man and left to find her. He broke the Law once before to live with her in the mountains. Dancer never endured the Law lightly." He rose to his feet with a grunt. "So. Do you win or lose tomorrow?"

"Either way, there is a loss," said Piper.

"Yes. Well, the sun's gone down, and my bones ache with this cold. I will see you in the morning."

"Sleep well, Piper."

"Sleep well, dog."

Piper and his mares were turned out to the forty-acre pasture to spend the night. The mares were restless, and the yearlings picked up their uneasiness.

Rocket, Clover's yearling, strayed from the nighttime circle down to the stream and back again, until Clover, in exasperation, asked Frosty to tell a Story to settle them. To the herd's surprise, Frosty readily agreed.

"It's been on my mind all day, this Story," said Frosty.

"Or what passes for her mind," muttered Flax.

"I remember this Story very well, and I never told it before, so I'm going to tell it now," said Frosty doggedly. Without the usual preamble, she swung straight into the Tale.

THE TALE OF THE TRAVELLER
ON THE GREEN ROAD

Long ago when rivers were few, and earth's land was grass, the One decreed the Balance. For each good thing in the world of men and gods, there is a counterweight of evil. As there is a heaven, so there is a hell, for how can one exist without the other?

At one end of the Balance lie the Courts of the Outermost West, ruled by Equus, and the Army of One Hundred and Five. Each breed of Horse in the world of men has a Breedmaster in the Courts, and for each Breedmaster there is a Breedmistress.

At the nether end of the Balance lie the Black Barns and all foul things. The Dark Horse with the Twisted Horn reigns here, and his Army are these:

The Harrier Hounds, who never lose the scent, and their Pack Leader Scant.

Anor, the One-Eyed Executioner, who feeds on the bodies of his kind. Scant is Anor's Voice.

El Arat, the Soul Taker, who calls horses to the Final Death.

Between the Courts and the Black Barns lies the Green Road, the Road each horse travels when it leaves the world of men. At the end of the Green Road is Summer, the place of Judgment. Each Horse who travels the long Green Road is judged in Summer. Some Horses take the White Gate to the Courts and live in glory with their kind. Others who have spent their lives in evil are sent to the Black Barns, to await the Final Death. Their souls are locked in the depths of the Black Barn's stalls, never to be free again.

But all horses travel the long Green Road at the end of their mortal lives, and all are judged by our gods."

She paused for the chorus, and the Sweetwater mares sang:

"Move out! When you step on the long Green Road
On your way to Summer's Gate.
Go straight in a line, for there's not much time;
At your back the Soul Taker waits.
Don't step to your left to eat sweet grass.
Don't wander off to the right;
Mist covers the land near the long Green Road
The way will be lost from your sight.
Don't try to return from the long Green Road
To the place where your life has been;
The Soul Taker waits at the Green Road's gate
To carry you off for your sins."

Frosty clamped her mouth shut.
"I don't know why that particular Story came to you, Frosty," Clover snapped crossly. "I'll think twice about asking you again to tell a Tale to the herd. It wasn't very settling."
Frosty shrugged.
Piper spent a restless night.
Stallions sleep in short bursts, alert for danger even in the deepest sleep. But dreams came to him to disturb even this sleep, and the waxing moon lit up the pasture and washed him with its light. Before dawn he had given up on rest, and he was awake long before the final preparations for the rodeo brought the ranch to life.

*   *   *

Sweetwater rodeos were held in a vast open arena surrounded by a one-board fence. Those who came to watch stood on the outside looking in. At one end of the arena was a closely-boarded chute. The calves and steers came from here for the roping competitions, leaping out into the arena when the gate was dropped, running from the cattle prod wielded by the cowboy behind. Calf roping and cutting were two of Piper's talents; standing in the corral waiting to go into the Long Barn, he flared his nostrils at the chute.

One of the ranch hands drove the old tractor around the arena, dragging the earth and smoothing it flat. Piper flexed his hocks, grabbing at the earth beneath his hooves, feeling the tractor rolling the dirt. The tractor stopped, the drag was unhitched, and a fertilizer trailer loaded with sand hooked up. The tractor made its slow rumbling rounds again, dropping the sand evenly over the muddied ground.

The sun rose, and strangers came to Sweetwater. They drove pickup trucks and rigs carrying horses for the competitions. Piper called an occasional challenge at the newcomers but his heart wasn't in it. Questions worried at him like a dog with a rabbit; What will I do? What should I do? Should I lose the competition and perhaps lose everything?

The brood mares were excited, huddling together at one end of their pasture, then breaking into short gallops to race to the stream. They called to Piper, and to the strangers on their land.

One of the ranch hands came and took Piper to the barn where the geldings waited, bathed and brushed. Blackjack gleamed and even Hank's dingy grey coat glowed a little. Piper too, was washed, brushed down, and his mane and tail combed until the hair reflected the sunlight streaming in the open doors. His hooves were trimmed and shod, the farrier making short work with the rasp and clippers, and Piper waited for the rodeo to begin in the stall between Hank and Alvin.

"Do you hear the tremble? Do you feel the walls swaying at all?" asked Hank, moving restlessly in his stall.

"No," said Piper, abstracted.

"I hear it." Hank struck the side of the stall with his hoof. "I want out!"

"We'll get you out if the barn falls," said Blackjack impatiently. "Stuff it, Hank. Piper, have you decided what we should do?"

"What *we* should do?" asked Piper.

Piper's stall door slid open. David came in carrying a horned saddle and a brightly-colored blanket. He slipped the blanket on Piper's back and settled the saddle on top, loosely buckling the cinch and attaching the belly band. The chased silver stirrups bumped gently against the saddle skirts and Piper blew out.

"Do your best," he said. "And leave me to worry about it."

David attached a lead rope to the halter under Piper's chin, and tied the rope in a slip knot to a large ring at the side of the stall. He whistled. A ranch hand came down the aisle to Blackjack's stall. The two men drew the Walker out to the aisle, cross-tied him, and began to brush him down with particular attention to his high-set tail. They clipped the bridle path far down along his neck. The ranch hand polished the show bridle with the sleeve of his shirt, and drew it over Blackjack's head. Three silver and turquoise conches shone on the chain face piece,

matched by the conches on the full diamond breast
plate of the martingale.

"How do I look?" Blackjack curved his neck so that
his chin touched the martingale and his mane flowed
rippling down his neck.

"Like a rooster," said Hank. "Full of yourself and
twice as cocky. You planning on finishing the exhibition ride—or are we going to be treated to the famous Duck and Run Loose trick?"

Blackjack winked, then pranced a little, pulling
against the cross-ties. David slapped him lightly on
the flank and unhitched him, turning the Walker
over to his men. A third hand took Hank from his
stall and the geldings walked down the aisle. David
himself slipped the knot on the lead rope and walked
Piper outside to the rodeo.

Sweetwater was a mass of busy figures in ceaseless
movement. Piper stopped, head up, and took a deep
breath. It was a fine day, the cloudless sky a deep
blue, the sun a pale gold. Men were dressed in shirts
as heavily fringed as a horse's mane, the fringe swinging over intricate designs woven into the brightly-
colored cloth. Most of them wore chaps of deerskin
which flowed down around their show boots. Wide-
brimmed hats shaded their faces from the sun. The
horses glittered more brightly than the men in their
ornate saddles, the skirts thick with elaborate designs worked into the leather. The air was filled with
odors of show shampoo, sweat, and the scent of high
emotions. Piper nodded his head up and down, his
show bridle jingling.

The arena was surrounded with human beings standing, sitting, walking, talking to each other, in a rumble that rose and fell like white water rapids. Piper
strained at the bridle; there were several mares in

season in the crowd of horses around the arena fence, and he trembled with eagerness. David held the bridle firmly. Piper lifted his head and announced his presence with a long deep whinny.

The John Deere tractor raked the arena smooth. Five barrels placed at equal distance from one another sat in the center, and the tractor maneuvered carefully around them. The ranch hand with Hank mounted with an easy swing of his leg and trotted the gelding to the entry gate. Hank, ears up, collected himself with an eager look at the ring.

"He does like to race," Blackjack said to Piper. "Now who's acting like a rooster?"

Hank and his rider loped into the ring, moving in a wide circle around the track just inside the fence. Hank watched the barrels carefully, eyes rolling as his rider took him around the turns. When they reached the starting point, he pawed the ground, ears up, body tensed. The rumble of the crowd subsided, and there was a moment of quiet. A shot rang out, and Hank bolted for the first barrel, feet flying, head low. He swerved into the pocket with a sharp right turn that rocked the barrel forward.

"It's going to go over," said Blackjack.

"No," said Piper. The barrel righted itself, and Hank swept to the second, flowing to the left with a swift, collected movement that anticipated the rider's aids. He left the pocket wide, dust from the arena floor a cloud that reached his belly. He took the next two barrels with the same urgent intensity, his ears rotating forward as he drove into the turn, and flattening against his skull as he pushed off for the next barrel. He made the last turn and in a final, tremendous sprint, raced back to the starting point, his rider's legs pumping high and wide. Hank stopped on his haunches, his tail spilling flat on the ground, forelegs high as his rider drew the reins up and back.

Applause spilled over the fence. Hank relaxed and walked slowly out of the ring. He passed by Piper and Blackjack with a nod. His withers were lightly covered with sweat, and he breathed quickly; otherwise he was calm.

"You were wide on the last turn," commented Blackjack.

Hank rolled his eyes. "There's plenty of time yet, he said, "best ten out of ten, remember?"

The morning rolled slowly on. At the end of the barrel racing class the judge attached a red rosette to the cheek piece of Hank's bridle and the gelding left the arena with proud, deliberate steps.

"You got a blue last year," Blackjack reminded him as the ranch hand walked him past for the final time. "That little chestnut filly beat you by a furlong." Hank flattened his ears. His grey coat was plastered with sweat, and he stretched comfortably when his bridle and saddle were removed. He was happy, Piper could smell it.

Hank nudged his rider with his muzzle, rubbing his face up and down to scratch the wedge between his eyes. "Yeah? Well, my part's over. I get to stand in this corral and watch you work now." He glanced over his withers as his rider drew him to the corral. "I'm going to take a nice long slow roll, and then drink the trough dry, and then take my time eating hay. There might be some left for you—and then again, there might not. Let's see if you get kicked out of the ring this year."

A flat bed truck came into the ring to collect the barrels. The sand was raked once more. David handed Piper's reins to a hand and tightened the cinch on Blackjack's show saddle. He polished the stirrups with the sleeve of his shirt and ran a curry comb through Blackjack's mane and tail. Then he lifted himself into the saddle and settled his hat firmly on his head.

"I ask you," said Blackjack, peering down at his breast plate, "is this going to be something to watch or not?"

"That depends on you," Piper said dryly. The Walker shot him an intense look, then said, his tone unexpectedly serious, "I can do well, Piper. You'll see."

He pranced out into the ring, joining five other horses, each with the high-set tail, flowing mane, and elaborate tack of the Saddle Seat Horse. Blackjack peacocked sideways, and then a rhythmic noise began. The horses settled into single file at the amble. Blackjack's action was high and graceful, his neck curved, his ears forward. His black coat shone in the sun, and his tail floated free with the breeze.

The mare in front of him tossed her head impatiently, jibbing at the double bit. Her mouth foamed pink, streaked with red, and Piper caught the scent of blood. One of the judges waved his hand, and the mare left the ring, disqualified.

David turned his head to watch them leave, and Blackjack side-stepped at the unexpected shift in weight. David's scent of anger came to Piper, and the stallion rumbled deep in his chest. The mare came past him. The rider leading her jerked the bridle, ill-humor in the set of her shoulders and the scent of her body. The mare squealed and jibbed, her mouth filled with blood. She rolled an eye at Piper in appeal. The Sweetwater cowboy at Piper's head patted the stallion's neck, then spoke quietly to the mare's rider. Reluctantly, she pulled the mare to a halt and loosened the bit.

The mare yawned gratefully and snorted the blood from her mouth.

"I'm sorry," said Piper. "It must hurt."

The mare, head down, plodded by without a response.

The rhythm in the air changed from four beats to two, and the saddle horses stepped out in the rack. David swayed easily in the saddle. Blackjack moved laterally, his right fore and hind alternating in perfect synchrony with the left. The file of flashy horses reversed and racked in the opposite direction. The rhythm changed once more, and Blackjack made a faultless transition into a slow, gliding canter, his front feet pumping high, the muscles standing out clearly in his glossy hindquarters.

A wave of applause swept over the arena. Blackjack threw out his chest. Piper rumbled for a third time, in amusement.

At the end of the class, Blackjack walked proudly to the gate with a blue ribbon attached to his bridle.

"Pretty slick, pretty slick," Blackjack said as David led him off to the barn. "Did Hank see that?"

"I'm sure he did."

"And you, Piper. You saw how well I can do when I put my mind to it."

"Yes," said Piper, his tone noncommittal.

"You're up next." Blackjack eyed him speculatively. "Decided what you're going to do?"

Piper fixed his eyes on the arena, and ignored him.

The ring was cleared for the calf roping. The noise of the calves being driven into the chute cut through the air, and Piper listened carefully. There was bewilderment in their calls, but no panic.

Several riders led their horses next to him. Piper looked them over. Baron had come to the rodeo. A Quarterhorse-mustang cross from a ranch to the west of Sweetwater, he was tough and clumsy looking, with a coarse head and a small, mean eye. Piper had come up against him many times in the ring, and lost to him only once, the first time.

Baron saw him, and stretched his neck and curled his lip over his teeth. Piper scraped the ground in response. Two purebred Quarterhorses jostled at Baron's side. One was a newcomer, the other a bay with a perfectly groomed coat and superb definition of the muscles in her chest and forearms. Piper had met her before. She was soft, despite the muscle.

The newcomer flirted her tail. Piper curled his muzzle over his teeth, stretched his neck and breathed out, the proper greeting to a maiden mare.

The mares would lose, Piper thought. But Baron was a force to be reckoned with. The battle to win would be hard fought.

If he wanted to win.

If.

David drew Piper to the double gates beside the steer chute. The calves milled inside, bawling for their mothers, for a drink, for the freedom of the range, for nothing in particular. In the arena, an aged mare with swollen knees and clubbed feet stood patiently in the sun, a Stetsoned rider on her back.

"It's Old Maudie," Baron said in surprise. "I thought she'd retired to pasture last season. Can't keep a good horse down, I guess."

Piper said nothing.

"Now, Maudie's someone to beat," Baron continued, an odor of challenge rising from his body. "You'll be hard-pressed to keep up with her, Piper. I might have a bit of a problem keeping up with her myself."

Piper chewed at the bit. His muscles swelled and tightened.

"Feeling a little colicky?" asked Baron in elaborate concern. "Little tired from spending all that time on the range? Maude and I will give you a run."

Old Maudie shifted from one sore foot to the other. She was ewe-necked, and although she had been carefully groomed, her coat was long and coarse. She yawned, and her teeth showed yellow and worn. Her ribs stood out under the hairy coat, speaking of her aging body's increasing inability to absorb feed and grass.

The calves burst from the chute, bawling with terrified cries as the cow hands moved them into the arena with electric prods.

Old Maudie stiffened as though struck by lightning. Her ears went up. Her hindlegs tensed and she collected in a movement almost too fast for Piper to catch. The calves shot past her and Maude's rider barely kept her seat as the old mare sprang forward, stiffness and age forgotten. Noise from the crowd beat the air like a giant fist. Maude's rider's legs showed daylight, then clapped together to drive the old mare forward. There was no pain in Maude's gallop, and her old knees bent with the springiness of youth. An odor of ecstasy came from her as she charged after the calf, sand spraying from beneath her hooves. The rider wound one end of her lariat firmly around the saddle horn, swaying easily upright as Maude turned and swerved to cut one of the calves from the massed herd. The calf ducked, and raced and ducked again. Maude followed as if an invisible rope linked her to the calf's stubby tail. The crowd cheered, voices climbing over each other like ravens at a kill.

Maude backed the calf into the arena corner, and the rider swung her lariat in a high wide circle. The rope whistled thinly as it cut through the air. The rider let fly, and as the loop sailed past Maude's eye, the old mare skidded to a halt, quarters touching the sand, front legs stiff.

The rope settled and tightened over the calf's head as Maude backed, straining to keep the rope taut. Her rider twisted the reins around the saddle horn, leaped to the ground and raced to the struggling calf. Maude, head high, pulled steadily against the twisting weight at the other end of the rope. In three swift movements, the rider tipped the calf on its back and looped the rope around its thrashing legs. She sprang back, hands held wide to the sky.

The crowd noise swelled to a roar.

The rider released the calf, and it ran to the far end of the arena, where it snuffed at sand. Maude slumped on to all four feet. Her head swung low. Her lower lip drooped. She shifted uncomfortably from leg to leg, her swollen knees flexing a little with her weight. Her rider patted her briefly on the neck, then led her from the ring. She stumbled at the gate, and rolled her eye at Piper.

"Beat that, sonny," she said. And moved on, with an impudent flick of her tail.

Men cleared the ring of the calves and drove the yearling steers into the chute.

David put a booted foot into the stirrup and mounted, settling firmly into the saddle. Piper danced, a familiar excitement in the pit of his stomach. In the arena, the chute opened and five steers stumbled out of the hole, bumping into each other, leaning their heads on each other's backs. Piper flared his nostrils and snorted. They were yearlings, and their heads hung low, heavy with horns, the points trimmed and capped with metal. Piper had seen steer-cutting competitions where the cattle's horns were sharp and uncapped. More than one horse had been gutted when the horns caught them in their vulnerable bellies.

Piper could feel David's excitement in the man's steady hands. He squeezed Piper lightly with both legs; a ranch hand swung open the arena gate, and Piper went through with a high, light step. The crowd receded from his senses; he heard, smelled, and tasted them at a distance. It was just the two of them, David and himself, against the steers crowding each other in the sand.

WALK ON! David's signals were faint, as they always were when Piper was under saddle. The visions never came with the same intensity. Sweetwater did not change with an overlay of David's own senses when they worked like this. It was always, only, bareback, with the two of them and no one else.

Piper was grateful for the distance the saddle created between them. Despite Old Maude and her courage in the ring, despite the tough and aggressive Baron watching them, Piper knew what he had to do.

RUN! The signal was imperative. Piper responded sluggishly.

He felt the rare touch of David's spurs and sprang forward in surprise.

"Plug!" Baron called above the crowd. Piper flattened one ear to show he'd heard, and would remember. He loped toward the small herd of steers.

THAT ONE! David's knees flexed left, right, and

Piper moved obediently, a calf with a white patch on its face directly in front of him.

MOVE! Piper watched the steers, then moved out at a rapid trot. Steers almost always bunched together, with a vague idea of protection through their own mass. White Patch squeezed in the center with a terrified bleat. David drove Piper straight ahead and the steers broke to either side. Exposed, White Patch looked from side to side for escape. Light glinted off his capped horns. The steer fumbled, turned, and made up its mind; it raced clumsily toward Piper, horns aimed at the stallion's vulnerable flank. Piper swerved left, shouldering the steer aside. The steer ran heavily past, and Piper whirled on his hindlegs to follow. White Patch kicked out in midstride, and his hooves caught Piper's belly.

David reached for the lariat, and despite himself, Piper moved his hocks well under his body, prepared to spin and leap no matter which direction the steer would take. A rising need to win hit him like a blow, and he snorted in great regular breaths.

David whirled the lariat high above his head and urged Piper forward. The stallion sprung to a hard gallop, the steer running and dodging in front of him. The loop flew past Piper's eye, and instinctively he stopped, pulling back hard when the loop settled over the steer's head. The rope caught, held, and the steer backed up frantically, shaking its head back and forth, grunting. Piper's haunches swelled with the effort of keeping the rope taut. The girth creaked with the strain, and he inhaled sharply to keep the saddle in place. The rope twisted and swung, the steer doing its best to pull Piper off his feet.

David leaped to the ground and ran forward. Piper

was prepared for the sudden loss of weight, and he shifted over his hocks as David left his back, concentrating every muscle on remaining still. Then suddenly, under the restless mutterings of the crowd, a call came to him.

"Piper!"

Duchess?

David reached the steer, and slipped behind the horns to throw it to the ground.

To keep the rope tight was crucial.

"Piper!" The call came again, from inside his head, from the sky, from the air itself. He trembled. A green mist rose before his eyes.

"Piper!"

David's frail back was to him, bent over the struggling steer.

I'm sorry! he cried silently. I'm sorry!

Piper stepped forward, and the rope swung loose.

The steer thrashed to its feet.

David flung himself to one side. The steer ran past, whirled, and charged, horned head aimed at David's belly. The steer hit him just below the chest, lifting him up and over his horns. David let out a grunt, and fell face forward into the sand.

The silence was absolute. Piper shuddered, and took one step forward. The crowd suddenly broke into a clamor of shouts and whistles.

Piper, his breath short, watched as men ran into the arena. One waved a red shirt at the steer, who stumbled after it with angry bellows. Two more knelt beside David's motionless body and lifted him carefully onto a stretcher. Piper pawed at the sand, once, twice.

A fourth ranch hand led him quietly away.

He would not ride in the circuit this year.

He prayed to his god that his master was alive.

What if I'm wrong? Piper thought. What if I'm wrong?

EL ARAT

Old Dog, New Trick

F rosty the Storyteller, knees locked, belly sagging, slept under the open sky in the brood mare pasture. The rodeo had lasted a long three days, and although none of the brood mares ever competed when they were carrying foals, she had gotten tired just watching all the activity. It was a relief to have the ranch to themselves again, to be turned out in the pasture. The water from the stream was cool and sweet, and she had gotten a good share of the new spring grass.

Most of the men had taken their strange horses and left Sweetwater before dusk. As the stars poked through the sky and the full moon rose, David, moving stiffly, had turned Piper loose with the mares. The mares discussed this as *not-routine* in low voices. Every year before, Piper had left them to ride the circuit. Their eyes slid sidelong to watch Piper walk his guardian circle before they settled down for the night. They murmured in distress; anything *not-routine* was dangerous. "Strange times!" Jessica had said soberly before Frosty dropped into sleep. "Legends walk among us." And she had shivered as though they grazed in a blizzard instead of the mild April night.

"Legends walk," Frosty thought as she dozed.

She liked the brood mare pasture. It held none of the terrors of the open range. The lights of the ranch house shone warm and comforting half a furlong away, and the Sweetwater stream ran nearby with a gentle trickle. Meg the collie roamed on her nightly rounds. Meg's presence, and that of the men and the ranch itself, kept dark thoughts away.

So Frosty slept deeply, her herdmates close by, the clear running stream a quiet rhythm in her ears.

The moon rose, high and full.

Frosty dreamed.

She dreamed that she was asleep in a sweet place in high summer and that someone was calling. She twitched. The call was faint, covered by the increasingly loud sounds of the running water and she strained to hear.

Storyteller! Rise and walk!

Frosty grunted and jerked awake, gazing mildly into nothing, eyes a little puzzled. The moon sailed overhead, its clear light shining straight into the water, the silver light creating an arch from the moon to water and back again. With a dim idea that she was thirsty, she walked to the bank and stepped in. The water was cold, numbing her fetlocks with the sting of sweat bees, and she splashed her feet to warm them, the water sparkling around her hooves. She lowered her head to lip the water, then raised it, muzzle dripping, to look at the eye of the moon.

"You'll freeze your hocks," said Clover, coming up behind her. "Come out of there. What are you doing anyway?"

"I don't know," Frosty switched her tail. "You

woke me up. What do you want? Do the yearlings need a Story? I was sleeping nice, and you woke me up to tell me to tell the yearlings a Story." She looked around indignantly. "And they're all sleeping, anyway. Why did you call me to come and tell the yearlings a Story when they are all sleeping?"

"I didn't," said Clover briefly. She stretched her neck from the bank and took a drink of water. "Come back to the herd. You stand here much longer and you'll catch nose-runs-water and it'll go through the whole herd. We'll never get back to the mountains if there's sickness here."

"Bad for the foals when they drop," said Frosty. "Right?"

"Right, but that's not for a while yet." The hair on Clover's withers rippled. "Not soon enough. We've got to get away from the ranch and back to the mountains. It's safe there. No dogs come and tell us news that doesn't make any sense. We won't go back until the foals have dropped, and it won't be for far too long a time to suit me."

"My belly's pretty big," said Frosty, looking down at her bulk. "Maybe we'll foal sooner than you think."

"That's from too much hay and grass," said Clover. She stamped in exasperation. "Come on."

"I don't know why you should be so spooky," said Frosty. "Piper's going to stay with us this season instead of going on the circuit and I like that. I don't know why the others think it's *not-routine*. It's routine to have him with us, isn't it?"

"It's *not-routine*. And anything *not-routine* is dangerous. You standing in that stream in the middle of the night is *not-routine*. So get out."

"There's a pebble under my hoof," Frosty observed, splashing in the water. "Not in it, but under it. In the water."

"All the more reason to move," said Clover. She reached out and nipped Frosty's flank. The blue roan jumped and squealed.

"SOMEBODY TOLD ME TO DO THIS!" Frosty shouted, moving upstream, away from Clover's teeth. "Somebody told me to stand in this water and look at the Moon. Was it you? Why did you do it? Why am I standing here, anyway?" She looked inquiringly back at her Lead Mare, her lower lip hanging loose.

Clover plunged both forefeet in the soft drift of the bank and bucked in sheer frustration.

"What's going on?" Piper came up to the Lead Mare, moving quietly in the bright night. His coat shone under the moon and it seemed as if the white spots on his hindquarters were fighting free of shadows.

Clover jerked her muzzle at Frosty in mute annoyance. The blue roan was gazing earnestly at the moon. Piper looked up too, lost in thought.

"Come on, Frosty. Back to the herd." His tone was kind, abstracted.

Clover leaned forward and whispered angrily, "Frosty! You're disturbing him and he shouldn't be upset, not after what happened at the rodeo."

"David was hurt," said Frosty, wrinkling her forehead with the effort of remembering. "And Piper's going to stay with us this season, instead of going on the circuit and Flax says our future is ruined. Ruined."

"Hush! David's not dead and it won't ruin us if Piper misses the circuit one season out of many."

"Legends walk," said Frosty, gazing at the moon.

"And so must you," said Cory. The collie, Meg at his shoulder, joined the group at the stream. His plumey tail waved over his back, the tip gleaming white. "Did you have a dream, Frosty?"

"I was asleep."

"Did this someone tell you to stand in the water and watch the moon?" Cory's tone was quiet, at odds with the tension in his body. Piper, his flanks barely moving, stood as if frozen beside him. "Try this for me, Frosty," said Cory. "Just raise your head and say, 'Jehanna! Goddess Mare! Open the Path that I may Walk and seek your counsel.' "

Clover gasped. Frosty rolled her eyes until the whites showed. "Jehanna?" Frosty shouted. "Goddess Mare? ME? Nossir!" She scrambled up the bank and out of the water, ready to bolt. Cory looked at Piper, his ears tuliped forward.

Piper said, "Easy, easy," his tones soft. He shouldered Frosty back to the water, his broad chest heaving with his pent-up breath. Frosty swung her head back and forth, and backed away from Piper's massive body. The bank crumbled under her weight, and she scrambled to stay on dry ground.

Cory flattened his ears against his head. "Here. Watch me. Nothing will happen to you." He moved carefully into the stream, the feathers on his ankles floating in the water. He waded until the water reached his shaggy belly and he stopped. He threw back his head to the Moon and howled, "Jehanna!" He stepped forward, until his body glowed white in the Path the moonlight made. "Jehaaaaana! Open the Path!"

Nothing moved in the dark behind them. The stream trickled on. The moon hung silver and silent.

Cory howled again, his voice lonesome against the mountains bulked around them. "Jehhaaaannnnaaaaa!" The howl trailed away. Far off, a coyote yowled in answer.

Cory began to shiver.

"It won't work," said Clover crossly. "This is sacrilege."

"It must work," said Piper urgently. "Frosty, you have to try."

"This is a business for mares, Cory," said Meg. "Come out."

Cory waited a long moment. Silence settled over them like a blanket. Meg waded in next to the old dog and licked worriedly at his ears and nose. "Come out," she said softly. "You can't help them."

Cory bowed his head, then moved slowly out of the water.

"Come on, Frosty," said Clover suddenly. "If this has to be, a mare will do it, not a dog. Into the stream. Move! Move!" She circled Frosty at a trot, nipping at her sides. Frosty cow-kicked and ran clumsily to the herd of brood mares beyond the banks. Clover whirled and kicked out with both hind feet, catching Frosty in the chest. The blue roan grunted and fell back.

"You're not coming out of there until you say it!" Clover gasped. She cast a desperate look at Piper, then ran forward in increased fury. "You'll do it for him!"

Frosty dug her heels in and trembled.

"Equus save us all!" the Lead Mare muttered. "Jessica! Tina! Flax!" The three mares moved out of the darkness, ears pricked forward. "Stand beside me. Frosty's to stay in the water until she does what she has to do. Frosty, we'll say it with you. Come on!"

The mares stood shoulder to shoulder on the bank. Frosty backed reluctantly into the stream. She backed until she stood in full radiance of light, then stood, head down.

Clover stamped impatiently, then scolded, "All right. Cory, tell us again."

Frosty looked at them miserably.

"Look up, you foolish mare! Come on, Cory!"

"Jehanna, Goddess Mare," said Cory.

Frosty looked at the moon and away again.

"Jehanna, Goddess Mare," the mares said in a ragged chorus.

"Open the Path!"

"Open the Path!"

"That we may seek your counsel!"

"That we may seek your counsel," said Clover, Jessica and Tina.

"What? What?" said Frosty.

"You remember!" said Clover fiercely. "You do it!"

"Jehanna, Goddess Mare, open the Path that we may seek your counsel," Frosty muttered.

The moonlight brightened to a brilliant, painful intensity. Meg and Cory dropped to the ground and shut their eyes against the glow. Frosty shook, turned, and splashed out of the water where she huddled close to Jessica. The Caretaker nuzzled her ears and breathed on her neck for comfort.

Piper gazed straight at the path of moonlight.

The trickling stream slowed, then stopped. The night sounds drifted away. Utter quiet settled over Sweetwater Ranch. The glow from the moon shone so brightly that nothing else could be seen against it. For a brief moment, it seemed to Piper that a gold shape moved within the center. But the light slowly ebbed away, and the animals blinked with the return to a normal dark. The stream ran free. There was a small rustling in the brush nearby.

"Nothing," said Frosty. "I told you. At least I think I told you."

"You did well, Storyteller." The voice was sweet, with a crystalline chime. The scent of flowers and fresh grass drifted through the air, and the night was filled with the smells of deep summer. A gold shape moved in the shrouded dark on the opposite bank and moved into the light.

It was a mare, glowing like a miniature sun, light streaming around her perfect head. She was beautiful, with a slim arched neck and a delicate muzzle. She moved like a maiden mare with floating steps, but her eyes were old, filled with the glowing red light of the sun rising. Only Piper held their steady gaze.

"I greet you, Sweetwater's Dancing Piper, out of Duchess, Breedmistress to the Appaloosa, by the Dancer, the Rainbow Horse, Breedmaster of the Appaloosa."

Piper inclined his head until his muzzle touched his foreleg. His powerful chest and black and cream colors stood out clearly in the flood of radiance from the Goddess Mare.

The mare turned to the collie lying flat on the rocky earth. "Cory, my old friend."

Cory opened his eyes and his tail moved slowly back and forth.

"Ma'am." Clover, hiding behind Piper's massive hindquarters, edged herself into the light. "If we offered any insult to you in our ritual, I apologize. We did not mean offense. We are range horses unused to the ways of the great. But we stand together before you, and welcome you to our herd."

"I did it," Frosty said. "I did."

"Quiet!" said Jessica softly. "And bow your head, you silly mare."

"No need," said Jehanna. "I should bow to you and your mares, Piper, not you to me. I bring trouble with me, and a request." She stepped from the opposite bank and into the stream. Where she walked the water parted. The moonlight flooded around her, so that she seemed to stand above the sandy bottom.

"You will tell us of the fate of my dam," said Piper.

Jehanna nodded. She leaned forward and breathed on the water flowing in front of her feet.

"Watch with me," she said. "I will show you things which few mortal horses have seen before. First, we shall see your dam, Piper, and the place where she is trapped. And then, my good Lord willing, I will show you what has happened in the Courts themselves, after we saw what you see now." She raised her head, and rested her ruby gaze on Piper. "It is better that you see, stallion. You must feel what she feels."

The water whirled with Jehanna's breath. It wound around itself, a whirlpool, and in its center an image formed. The horses leaned forward and saw nothing but a heavy mist. The mist cleared and they saw the head of a buckskin mare. Her eyes were clouded, and her muzzle was gaunt with pain. And by some trick of the Horse God himself, they saw what the buckskin mare saw, and felt what she felt.

She could see it, the beginning of the long Green Road, and she raised her head to call out. The pain in her feet began to ebb. The pain was with her, stabbing through the soles of her hooves like rusty nails, but she stepped out, knowing that the Soul Taker waited somewhere behind, knowing that there was one last race to run before the Green Road and safety. The shivering fits passed, and she walked toward the beckoning green with eagerness. There would be peace and comfort at the end.

The Soul Taker was behind her, slow and evil, a dark coiling cloud to her left. Her soul's name came to her on an evil wind. She shut her ears to the sound with the courage that had made her what she was in life. She collected herself and jumped, soaring broad and long, and stood safe on the misty green road.

The surface was springy beneath her hooves, and she exhaled in relief. The pain in her feet ebbed and disappeared. She breathed out gratefully. Her coat, sweat-soaked from the fits, steamed gently in the cool green air.

Off to the side, the misty Havens lay, ahead, the gate to Summer. She moved forward, head up, memories surrounding her with each step she took. Good memories, that she would take with her to the Courts:

The Dancer, his colors rainbow bright, flying across the meadows like the wind.

Piper, the first of her many foals, struggling in the straw at her feet, spotted coat dark with afterbirth.

Susie, her old friend, waiting at the end of the long Green Road.

And then, a call came to her, insistent, demanding. Her soul's name!

The call came again. She stopped, head high, and tested the air, her ears alert. The Dancer? Not even he knew her soul's name. No one did, but the Soul Taker and the One Himself. Her soul's name. She had passed by the Watcher at the Green Road's Gate, and escaped the Soul Taker's call, and the Soul Taker couldn't travel the Green Road.

Could she?

Her soul's name! Coming from the side of the road, rising from the mists of the Havens. Was her good Lord there, in the mists? Bewilderment in the carriage of her head, the slant of her neck, she stepped from the road into the boiling mist.

And knew, as the mist took her, that she had made a terrible mistake. The mist poked hot fingers into her eyes and ears. The pain throbbed again through her feet. In the distance, she heard the Dancer's frantic cry, and she turned to find her way back. But the road disappeared in the boiling mist, and in the fitful rolling light of the misty havens, the memory of who she was and why she had begun this journey began to drift. As the memories ebbed, so did the pain in her feet; as the memories left her, so did the shivering fits. Her soul passed into the Havens, and she felt her self emptying from her body like water from a bucket.

She had fought so long! She was so tired! She fought against the relief the forgetfulness gave her with the stubborn patience that had made her great. Deliberately, she lifted her forefoot and slammed it against the rocky ground. As the pain leaped high, she remembered: She was Duchess, and she had to travel the Green Road.

"Duchess!" It was the Dancer calling her now. He was above her on the Road, and she struggled to cry out. He had called, and never once in her life had she failed to answer.

"Duchess!"

She moved, groaned aloud and her answer died in her throat. When she stood back on her heels, the pain steadied and began to die. She rocked and hung her head.

"Duchess!"

She stood still.

She forgot who she was, and why she must move.

The pain quieted, went away and her soul fled into the eerie quiet.

Jehanna breathed softly on the water and the vision disappeared.

Piper trembled, his muzzle suddenly gaunt. Cory whispered deep in his throat.

"So," said Piper, "it is the Green Road after all.

Lilly was wrong. I cannot go there, and return to Sweetwater. I must travel the Green Road and stay forever."

"If the Dancer leaves the Road, he will be lost, as Duchess is," said Jehanna, quietly.

"Then I must go and find them both," said Piper. "You must tell me how, Goddess Mare. I cannot bear to see her."

"The Green Road only goes one way, Piper. You've known that all your life. And I would not send a horse along its length before his time."

"What am I to do? What can I do? There must be a way."

Jehanna nodded slowly. "There is. You will see why my Lord has sent me in response to a Storyteller's call—a thing that has never happened before. Stand close by me—and Watch!"

For a second time, Jehanna breathed on the water. This time, the image in the water was of a meadow, starred with flowers, circled by a grove of linden trees. In the center of the meadow was a Pool. Circling its edge stood an Army of mighty stallions: one for each breed upon the earth. Each was a perfect image of its kind: Quarterhorse, Thoroughbred, Morgan, and the rest.

The Army of One Hundred and Five.

The last rays of the setting sun slipped over the horizon in the Courts of the Outermost West and violet twilight fell. Along the banks of the Watching Pool the ranks of stallions stood gathered together to Watch.

Jehanna stood apart, her mane swung over her face in grief. The Thoroughbred stood tall and leggy, long, noble head thrust forward. The Percheron towered massively over his fellows. The Shetland, spotted brown and white, creamy mane falling thickly on his stubby neck, stood next to the shining glory of the chestnut Morgan.

Then a silver light like the moon behind clouds moved among the ranks. The stallions parted, and Equus himself moved to the Dreamspeaker's side.

"Jehanna." The great god nodded, silver eyes reflecting the years of his long life.

"Lord." Jehanna breathed out lightly, twice, as a mare will when she meets a favored stallion.

Equus looked into the Pool, and the sadness in his eyes dimmed their brilliant light. "She waits then, for the Dancer to find her?"

"She has forgotten who she is. The pain became too much for her, and when it left, her soul went with it. She waits, now, not knowing who she is, or where she is to go. She has suffered, Lord, and she held on as long as she could. Longer than I would have, had I been in pain."

"And the Dancer?"

"He travels slowly, Lord. He knows he cannot turn back once he has reached the end, and he will not leave the road without her. And he knows that if he steps from the side of the road to find her, he, too, will be lost."

"Then what shall we do?" asked Miler, the Quarterhorse. "We wait here, while one of our own roams beyond help. This is intolerable."

Equus regarded the images in the Pool. The god placed his foreleg gently on the Pool's green bank. "I cannot call Duchess. She is beyond my help in the Havens. The Soul Taker has no power there, either. Whatever called her from her journey home is beyond the powers of the horse here and below."

Jehanna said, "I suspect, but I have no proof. I've Watched, but I cannot see. You must call El Arat, my Lord. She must answer you. And she will have to tell you what she knows of this matter."

Equus nodded gravely in assent. He walked slowly to the very edge of the Pool. The silver light he carried with him flowed into the Pool and mingled with the Water. He bent his head.

Equus called, softly.

The clear water grew dark.

Equus called again.

The dark water turned black and began to bubble. Steam rose from the Pool and an evil stench tinged the summer-scented air of the Courts.

A black mare rose from the water. She was beautiful, an eerie echo of Jehanna's own gold grace in her ebony head and delicate ears. Her eyes were yellow-green and her lips curled back from her teeth, as a stallion's do when facing a rival in battle.

Hakimar, the Arabian, turned his hindquarters and staled in contempt. The Stallions in the Army moved and swelled in a wave. The Trakehner raised his voice in a battle call.

El Arat spoke, and her voice was like hornets in honey.

"You called, White Fool, and I answer."

"The buckskin mare has been taken from the Green Road into the Havens," said Equus. "This has never happened before, El Arat. You had some part in this."

El Arat dropped her eyelids, and looked sidelong at the god. Smoke trailed in a slow spiral from her nostrils. "And so you ask me? As you saw, White Scum, she slipped by me at the Green Gate. What part did you have in that?"

"Her soul is not for you to take, El Arat," said the Morgan.

"She has not yet been judged in Summer," El Arat

spat suddenly. "How dare you tell me where her soul will walk? She may serve me yet, dung."

"Her soul will live nowhere if she is not pulled from the trap of the Havens," said Equus. "Explain this, El Arat."

"It's no concern of mine, White Fool."

"It's your doing," said Jehanna. She whirled and reared, her hooves flashing crystal in the sunlight. "I don't know what you've done or how you've done it, but you'll tell us. The buckskin must complete her journey."

El Arat opened her eyes. Yellow fire lived in them, and only Equus remained unmoved at the evil in their depths. "I did nothing. I have no more power than you over what happens in the Havens. If she stepped off the path, it was her own foolish doing, not mine." El Arat's long mane floated in the water and she swirled it luxuriantly. "Let her rot there, fool. It's no concern of ours, now. That barren cow can stay there as well as anyplace else." She half-closed her eyes and breathed out. Steam rose in a great cloud from the pool, and the Stallions snorted their nostrils free of the stench. She began to sink back into the Pool and Equus slammed his foreleg angrily against the ground. A great sheet of white light rose into the air where his hooves struck and El Arat hissed in pain as the light struck eyes used to the dark of the Black Barns.

"I watched her step from the Green Road myself," said El Arat. "I don't know who called her. Neither you nor I have any power on the Green Road, White Dung."

"You're forgetting your dark master," said Jehanna quietly. "It is you and I who occupy the opposite ends of the balance, El Arat. Not you and Equus. Or has the Dark Horse turned the reins of power over to you?"

El Arat curled her upper lip. Her teeth gleamed. "My lord," she said evenly, "my own dark lord did not call her name. That task is mine, and mine alone. So do not ask me, White Fool, who has called your precious mare. What was her name among men? Duchess. That was it. Duchess." The malice in the black mare's look was terrible. Miler stepped protectively in front of Jehanna.

"That buckskin." She sank, and only the yellow-green poison of her eyes remained visible in the water. Then, her eyes slitted shut. She disappeared like a snake into a field. A hissing whisper drifted in the air: "Duchess!"

The Waters of the Pool cleared of oil and heat, and where they had been crystal blue, a faint green scum scarred the surface, Equus stood deep in thought.

"There is one other possibility," Jehanna said slowly. "But I will not believe it."

Equus waited, silver eyes grave.

"The Old Mare, the Namer of Names. She is the only other being who could have called Duchess."

"The Namer," said Miler. "But why? When she calls creatures to the Havens they disappear from the world of men forever. It is not the Appaloosa itself which is at risk here."

"Why should she do that?" Jehanna agreed. She stepped to Equus' side and the gold of her coat mingled with his silver light. "And how can we ask her?"

In answer, Equus walked to the water and breathed on the surface; the weeds left by El Arat had grown, and the surface was sluggish.

The Waters did not change with Equus' breath. He curved his great neck and looked at the blue sky arching over the Courts. The wind lifted his mane from his crest, and he called out to the sky with a great, hammer-like cry. The Water stirred, and an image appeared in the Pool of barren rock, broken by a few pine trees scrubby under a clouded sky.

Nothing stirred in the image. Equus murmured. There was movement; one of the rocks shifted, stretched, and shook itself onto its feet.

An ancient mare blinked up at the Watchers. The Old Mare, the Namer of Names.

The Namer's belly hung almost to her knees, and her back swayed concave with the weight of her years. She swung her head slowly, lower lip pendulous. Stiff whiskers sprouted from her chin and nose. She yawned for a long, long moment. Her yellow teeth were worn to stumps, and her rheumy eyes teared a little.

"Who woke me up?" she asked querulously. "Who disturbed me from my nice little sleep?"

"I, Equus, Lord of the Horse. Leader of the Army of One Hundred and Five. I woke you, Namer."

The Old Mare ambled forward and peered upwards. "Equus? Is that you? I'll be. You've changed since I saw you last, sonny. One toe instead of three. You're much, much bigger." She blinked. "Not bad lookin', if I say so myself." She mumbled her lips and said crossly, "I hope you had a good reason to wake me up."

"I do. One of our kind has been called from the Green Road to the Havens. She knows nothing of who she is, for her soul has fled into the mists there. She cannot travel forth to be judged in Summer, as is the Law of the Balance. Did you call this mare from the Road, Old One?"

"Me?" She dropped her head, considering. Slowly, she raised her right hind to her ear and scratched with difficulty. She rubbed her muzzle along her foreleg and her eyes dropped. She snored once.

"Old Mare," said Equus, patiently.

"Eh?" She opened her eyes and raised her head. "Thinking. I was thinking. A buckskin mare? I believe I must have called her. I believe I did." She nodded, as if to say, that settles it, and turned and started up the rocky path to the top of her hill.

"Wait please, Namer." Equus' voice was respectful, but the tones commanding. She turned back reluctantly, and blinked irritably at him.

"Why? Why did you do this? You are the Namer, a member of the Council of the One who Rules us All. A Keeper of the Balance. Why trouble yourself with the fate of this mare?"

The Namer shrugged. "Beats me. I do what I'm told to do. I get word, you see, from the Owl. Now there's a bird that never changes. Not like you, growing up in a flash and not telling me. The Owl comes by, see. He never stays long." She switched her tail. "I ask him about this and that and he just flies around—not much conversation in him, the Owl—and then he tells me, call the Blue Whale, he says, and so on."

"The Blue what?" said Jehanna.

"Call the passenger pigeon, he says . . . and a couple others to call to the Havens, a bear, the spectacled bear, and an ox." She wrinkled her nose. "Tigers is waiting to be called, the white ones. The Owl hasn't heard about them yet, but I expect he will, soon enough." She shook her head, and a little spit flew from the sides of her mouth. "Bird doesn't even stay to chat awhile after that. Just flies off. I ask you, is manners what they used to be, or what? They are not. Paaah! So that was why I called this mare off the Green Road to the Havens. 'Call the Appaloosa.' And I did. Easy enough to do." Her tone was complacent.

"It is not easy for her," said Equus gently. "She is in great pain. And her stallion searches for her. While he is on the Green Road, and she is in the Havens, the fate of the Appaloosa itself remains uncertain."

"Well, that's it, isn't it? The fate of the Appaloosa. I calls them as I'm told to."

"This isn't just," Jehanna cried. "You cannot do this, Namer!"

"Who's that?" The Old Mare craned her head and squinted. "Jehanna, right? I remember you. Arab you are. Pretty little thing. So, sonny," her attention switched abruptly back to Equus. A sudden, sharp intelligence shone in her rheumy eyes. "You know the Laws as well as anyone, being what you are. The only justice is the justice you create for you and yours. So don't talk to me of justice, of what's right and wrong, that's up to you all, as you well know. All I know is I get a recall notice, and I do what I'm supposed to do."

"Namer," said Equus. "A mistake has been made. The Appaloosa breed can't be lost to the Havens. The Dancer's get walk the earth, and serve men's needs. You cannot call the Breedmistress while her foals are still alive and well. You cannot call the Appaloosa to the Havens while they are alive and fertile on the earth."

"Who you telling can and can't?" said Namer. "You telling me? Makes no difference to me, sonny. I was told to call them pigeons, and I did. I was told to call the spectacled bear, and I did. I was told to . . . never mind," she interrupted herself.

"Are you certain it was the Owl, himself?" asked Jehanna desperately.

"Course I am. I'm pretty sure I am." She blinked. "Black isn't he, the Owl? Black all over?"

"He isn't," said Jehanna. "He's white. And only the One controls his flight, Namer."

"Flight?" said Namer. "He has wings, don't he?" She chewed thoughtfully, then said, "What d'ya know? Owls pretending to be dogs, or is it dogs pretending to be owls . . . It's no business of yours, anyways." She shook her head and began to walk up her hill, muttering, "What-now, what-now." Equus watched her go with a despairing look in his silver eyes. Jehanna nosed his side in horror. Equus shook his head. "I can do nothing," he said.

The Old Mare marched doggedly halfway up the hill and without pause turned around and marched down again, still muttering, "What-now, what-now, what-now." She swayed to a precarious halt, and gazed past Equus into the Courts themselves. "You say she has live get here?"

"Yes," said Equus.

"You say there's more than one? And they're all able to bear young?"

"Yes," said the god.

"I don't like being tricked. I won't put up with being tricked."

"A Harrier Hound, perhaps Scant himself," Jehanna said. "You have been tricked, Namer."

"Then you tell the first-born of her belly to come and see me," said Namer. "I see him, smell him, chat with him a bit. If he's who say he is, if he's one of the Dancer's blood, and Duchess, too, then I say . . ." she rumbled and her belly shook in amusement. She peered up, and her yellow eyes were sly. "Then *I* say . . . Okay, you can trot right down the Green Road and get her yourself. You got my permission. And she hops back on that Green Road of yours, and the Appaloosa is okay." She paused. "But I gotta see him, mind. And he's gotta chat with me a while. Now let me *be*, and don't wake me up again, unless it's important."

She walked back up the hill, mottled gray back flabby. She reached the top—and whether she curled into the rocks and went to sleep, or went over the hill to an unknown destination, neither Equus or his stallions knew for certain.

The image faded. The green scum left by El Arat had grown, so that the surface was weed-filled. The waters barely reflected the straight white trunks and green leaves of the linden trees. "The weeds grow rank and thick," said Equus. "Soon we will not be able to Watch."

"The price we paid for El Arat's appearance," said Jehanna. "How soon will it clear, my Lord?"

Equus shook his great head. "I don't know. We must wait."

The stallions of the Army stirred: Hakimar, the Arabian, who was Second-In-Command to Equus, and who guarded the empty space where the Rainbow Horse was to stand next to the god himself, pawed at the Dancer's empty place in line.

"Not yet, Hakimar," said Equus. "Not yet."

Jehanna stepped close to Equus' side. Together, they gazed into the water of the Pool, where the weeds grew more thickly still.

The golden shape stirred in the middle of the Sweetwater Stream, and the Vision in the stream's waters winked out like a light in the ranch house. The Sweetwater horses stood frozen, struck with amazement at what they had seen. The mares huddled close together. Piper stepped forward and addressed the bright gold mare.

"The first-born of her belly," the stallion said. "I am the first-born."

"You are," the gold mare said. "Namer cares nothing for good or evil. She was tricked, as you see, by one whose name we do not speak aloud in the dark. The choice is left up to us, as it is to all creatures. If you choose to find Namer and show yourself to be the first born of Duchess and the Dancer, to be an Appaloosa of their blood, you have a chance to save your dam and sire, and the Appaloosa breed itself."

"Ma'am," said Clover softly, her voice shaking. "Cory told us that Piper's sire is the Breedmaster of the Appaloosa—and Duchess the Breedmistress. If they do not take their place in the Courts, what happens then?"

"The Appaloosa join the others in the Havens, those creatures the Namer has forgotten, who longer exist in the world of men, or in any life that comes after."

"There is only one choice," said Piper. "I see that now."

The gold mare was silent. Piper pawed at the ground, then stood immobile, his sculptured head dark against the brightness of the moon.

"Where do I find the Old One?" he said at last.

Jehanna's voice slipped through the dark like a silver chime. "East of the sun, west of the night and to the Dancer's mountain. In a rockbound place where the pine trees grow sparse. She lives in a stone canyon, growing older in years which are measured in the way water wears rock, a drop at a time. You must leave Sweetwater, and follow the sun where it rises. Until you reach this canyon."

"It's a large world and we are small beings, ma'am," said Cory. "Piper must have help."

The gold shape seemed to nod. Jehanna whispered, "You will have more help than you think. And I will send someone. A guide. Walk on, Piper—

and the guide will come." She raised her head. "What more do you ask, Piper? For you must ask me now. I will not be able to Watch, while the Pool is fouled with the memory of the Soul Taker. You will be on your own."

Piper shook his head slightly.

"Are you certain, stallion? I cannot choose for you. And I cannot help unless you ask."

Piper arched his neck, proudly. "It is my task, and I will do it."

Suddenly, there was a flare of moonlight, a flash of molten gold in its center. The light grew and a mist rose from the stream as its warmth met the chill air. The fragrant wind blew warm, then cold, and the scent of summer flowers faded. The mist spiraled, diffused, and Jehanna was gone with the light which brought her.

The normal sounds of night returned. The stream flowed on its usual course. The stars hung close in the dark sky. Clover stared, and a low whinny escaped her throat.

"I done it," said Frosty to the empty night. "I done it, after all."

• 6 •

Legends Walk

The pure note of the triangle greeted the sun next morning, and Piper responded as he always had to David's imperative call. He herded the mares to the gate in a wide circle, driving them forward, pushing the laggards ahead with his head snaked low to the ground and his ears pinned flat against his skull.

David was waiting at the gate, a bucket of oats in one hand, the triangle in the other. Clover led the mares into the corral. Behind them, Piper slowed to a trot, then a walk, and stopped three paces from David. He bowed his head in greeting, his right fore pawing the ground.

"Piper," said David, "saa, saa, Piper." He carried one arm close to his chest, and turned awkwardly to close the gate. Piper watched as Clover led the mares to the hay in the corral, then he looked at David and inhaled deeply. David's scent came to him, a mingled odor of sweat, the smells of the ranch house, and something else: bandages, like the ones the man had wrapped around the stallion's hock several seasons ago when he had been caught in barbed wire. David put the bucket on the ground and slipped a hackamore over Piper's head.

Piper put his nose in the bucket and ate a handful of oats. He looked into David's strange, sky-like eyes, and his own look slid away. He blew out several times with the sound of a partridge rising, as a stallion does with an injured member of the herd. He nudged David's chest gently, blowing on the bandages beneath the cloth covering David's skin. David's hand came up and he rubbed the sensitive spot at the base of Piper's ears. "Saa, saa, Piper," he said.

The oats were good. Piper wondered how long it would be before he tasted them again.

He wondered if anyone else would be hurt before his task was over.

The horseshoer came that day to attend to the brood mares' hooves. Piper spent most of the day in his stall in the barn, his presence a bar to unruly behavior. The months they all had spent in the mountains had worn their hooves unevenly. Most of the yearlings needed no more than a filing. They were unused to having their feet worked on, and the ranch hands tied one foreleg firmly up to their bellies so they couldn't buck their way free.

The mares, who moved about less than the youngsters, and whose feet grew longer in consequence, had their long toes clipped, then filed. Most of them were used to the horseshoer and stood patiently. A muscular man called Tom, he worked quietly, standing back with an impassive face when the yearlings squealed and tried to buck their way free of the ropes, waiting until a warning whicker from Piper settled them.

How many seasons had he stood guard while men

took care of his herd? Piper swiveled his ears, listening to all the familiar sounds of the farm at once. He moved in his stall, his hooves pressed down against the straw, and he felt the movements that made up the universe of the ranch: hooves, feet, wheels, the feel of bales of straw being shoved across a concrete floor several stalls away.

A small skittering caught his attention, and he raised his head to peer through the mesh. A scrawny kitten, the color of sunlight mottling an autumn forest floor, raced headlong into the barn. It skidded to a halt at the sight of Tom bent over one of the brood mares, then wound around the horseshoer's boots, leaping back with a wounded expression when the shoer waved him away.

"Move away from the mare's feet," advised Piper. "That's Jessica. She's our Caretaker and very good with young ones, but it's hard for her to see you when you're right underneath her."

The kitten, who really, Piper thought, had the fattest belly and the skinniest body he had ever seen, danced sideways in front of his stall and rolled over and over on the concrete floor.

"There's a large rat in a hole beneath my grain bucket," said Piper. "Why don't you see if you can catch it?"

The kitten sat up, and regarded the stallion with his big yellow eyes.

"Are you Piper?"

"I'm Piper."

"The dog, the one who came in the truck and knows how to treat a cat, not like some dogs I could mention who think they *own* the place if you know what I mean, that new dog isn't going to stay much longer and he sent me to see if you was here in your stall and if you are, I'm supposed to go back and tell him and he'll come to see you before he leaves to go home." The kitten rolled over and scratched its back on the concrete. "I'd catch that rat for you," it said, "except that I'm on an errand." It lay motionless on its back, creamy underbelly exposed, and gazed dreamily at the barn ceiling.

"Newton," said Cory, pacing gravely into the barn, "I thought you were going to come and tell me if Piper were here." He caught the stallion's eye and nodded. "And so he is."

Newton leaped in the air and landed on all four feet. "I was coming!" it said cheerfully. "I told you I'm about the best ratter you've ever seen and that's why they should let me into the house to stay instead of out here and Piper saw right off what a good ratter I was and *asked* me to catch this big rat, which I've tried to do already, except that it's the biggest rat you ever seen and twice as fast. Piper promised me some corn from his grain if I did." The kitten crept beneath Cory's long shaggy coat, and peered out from under the collie's front legs at the horse. "Didn't you?"

"Not the most trustworthy barn cat I've ever met," said Piper to the dog.

"Imaginative," said Cory. "And interested mainly in what it can find to eat. It's a stray, and in the week it's been here it's eaten enough for a litter."

Piper looked at the kitten's big round belly. "It seems to have done well enough for itself."

"Rats," said the kitten seriously, "are not the best food for exceptional ratters. Exceptional ratters must have chicken, milk, fish. If they're to be any good at ratting."

"The question is, how well can you do for yourself?" said Cory. "You're setting out on your journey, Piper and you are not ready. There are degrees of truth in the world. This little cat represents one kind. There are many others."

Piper cocked his eye inquiringly.

Cory settled onto the floor with a grunt. "Old bones," he said. "I wish I could go with you, Piper. You will need some advice."

"I do not."

"You do. You were asked last night for questions. You had only one: Where do I go? There are many others. If you do not ask them, you may not succeed. And success is vital."

Piper stiffened. "And what questions should I have asked?"

"Who else seeks the destruction of the Appaloosa breed? Will you be followed? What happens if you are injured, or captured by men on your journey to find the Old Mare? Will there be someone with you to carry on your quest? When will the Pool be clear, so that Jehanna may Watch out for you? You didn't ask these questions, Piper, and you should have."

"I have never needed any counsel but my own."

"Then you are as big a fool as your sire was when he decided to abandon his task and take Duchess from Bishop Farm," snapped Cory. "Stallions! 'He who travels alone loses prey' is a saying among us dogs, and it is a true saying. You cannot exist without the pack. Your own first Law would tell you this. 'A horse is a member of a company, a horse is one with its fellows.' "

Piper, his anger rising, pawed impatiently at the stall floor. Newton, settled between Cory's forepaws, had fallen asleep. At the sound of the stallion's hooves, the kitten sat up and bounded off. Cory watched it go in silence, then said, "Take some of the geldings with you. It will be safer. And if something happens to you, they can carry on."

"The Namer must see and hear one of my dam's blood," said Piper. "And I will not steal from my master here. It's bad enough that I'm abandoning my herd. Don't you know what my loss will mean to Sweetwater?"

"I know," said Cory. "I'm sorry. But you have no other choice, really. And yes, you must reach the Old Mare, that's true. But what happens if you're attacked? You must travel with those who can help defend you. If you are injured, you must go with those who can help you."

"And who would attack me?" Piper's great neck flexed, and the muscles swelled in his chest. His hindquarters, splashed with spots the color of pale sunlight, bunched under his glossy coat. "Who would attack me that I could not defeat?"

"There are many," said Cory flatly. "What the Courts know, the Barns know, too. And I tell you, the Soul Taker has no love for you and your kind. Those she travels with are more terrible than she could ever be: Anor, the One-eyed Executioner; Scant, and his Harrier Hounds."

"Legends," said Piper.

"Legends walk," said Cory. "Last night told you that, if nothing else." The dog raised himself with difficulty to his feet. "I cannot go with you. I'm old, and I would slow you down. Meg cannot. She tells me she has a belly full of pups," his teeth appeared in a brief grin, "and we bear our young more quickly than you horses, Piper. She would not be able to walk with you for more than the turn of the moon. You must take Blackjack, Duke, Alvin and Hank. It is the only way to safeguard your task." The collie shook himself. "I've spoken to them. They are ready to go with you."

"*You* have spoken to members of my herd? *You* would put them at risk?"

"Yes." Cory walked slowly down the aisle to the open overhead doors. "Have you thought about a gelding's life, Piper? They serve only man. There is no great task before them, ever. Think on what I've told you. And ask them, Piper. You are right, if you travel into danger, and I believe that you do, you must take only those who would go with you willingly. You are right to consider their safety. You might also consider their souls." He paused, and looked back to the stallion over his shoulder, his fawn-colored face grave. "Decide soon, Piper. Emmanual leaves for Bishop Farm tomorrow morning. I can unlatch the gelding pen for you this evening. But only tonight." With a nod of farewell, the big dog paced slowly out of the barn.

Piper subsided into thought.

The horseshoer finished Jessica's feet, and the ranch hand led her back to the mares' corral. He sat down on a bale of straw and stretched his arms, waiting. Piper pricked his ears: the Working Herd was coming in. One after the other, Blackjack, Hank, Duke and Alvin were put into the stalls surrounding Piper.

The blacksmith rose and bent again to work, selecting Alvin first. The big horse, his attention on the stallion, moved willingly, to the obvious surprise of the blacksmith.

"Quite a night you had," said Blackjack. "At least, that's what Cory told us."

"I am so sorry, Piper," said Alvin. "This must be a great grief for you. We're ready to help you." Tom pushed gently at his left fore. The Standardbred regarded him in mild astonishment, and kept his foot where it was.

"You know the risks?" said Piper.

"Better a short life than a dull one," said Blackjack.

Tom pushed firmly at Alvin's left fore, setting his shoulder against the Standardbred's side and leaning into him. Alvin sighed, rolled his eyes, and picked up his hoof so suddenly that the horseshoer fell forward on his knees. Alvin nosed him upright, and said plaintively, "Better a life without horseshoers." He straddled his hind legs to better bear his own weight, allowed his hoof to be picked up, and looked at Piper. "This is a wonderful chance, Piper. You must take us with you. Cory told us of the Soul Taker and the others. You will need us!" He glanced at the shoer, and said politely, "Excuse me."

His withers twitched a little, and he slumped heavily against the horseshoer, who fell backwards into a closed stall door, Alvin's leg firmly held at an angle under his arm. "That usually does it," Alvin complained gently. "Usually. Well, there's one more thing . . ." The shoer dropped Alvin's left fore. Alvin plodded forward, dragging the cross-ties with him.

"WHOA!" Tom shouted.

The cross-tie chain stretched to snapping point. The shoer jumped in front of the chestnut and pushed him back.

"I don't get it, Alvin," said Blackjack. "You're just patient as a twenty-year-old Caretaker in the herd, and you're as bullheaded as a . . . a bull, with men. Learn the rules, boy. Learn who's in charge." He rolled an anxious eye at Piper, to see if this earnest message was getting across.

"There'll be no question who's in charge if you come with me," said Piper. "You especially, Blackjack, have to understand that."

"The Stallion's Oath," said Duke. "We remember. We're ready."

"You can't do it alone," said Blackjack. "We stand

by you. And remember the First Law, if not the Stallion's Oath: a horse is one with his company. A horse is one with the herd."

"There may be death or worse," said Piper.

"But we may see Her, the gold mare!" said Alvin. "Think of that!"

"No barns to lock us in," said Hank, "we'll stand under an open sky."

"Legends walk," said Piper. "Are you certain? Do you know what might happen?"

"Legends walk," said Alvin. "We know, and we follow you."

"We'll leave then, tonight," said Piper. "When the moon rises."

"When the moon rises!" said Blackjack.

There was no ride with David that day, and no work in the rodeo arena. Piper and the brood mares were turned out to pasture early. Clover led the mares to the stream to drink, then stood grazing with Jessica and Frosty. Piper paced a wide circle around the herd, noting those mares who were missing. Meg had said some would be culled from the herd to work as cow ponies. This eased Piper's heart a little. The ranch would not be left totally without working horses to ride fence and herd cattle.

His first circle of the evening finished, he went to Clover and bit her gently on the neck.

"Lady, Shawnee and Red have been taken to work the ranch," she told him. "None of them were bred."

"Yes," said Piper.

"The men paid particular attention to Rocket," Clover said with quiet pride. "He may not be gelded with the others next spring. Meg told me that they think he has stallion potential."

Piper remembered the ridge of proud flesh on his

shoulder. The yearling had a lot of courage. And he was fast; he had whirled and struck out both hindlegs at his sire when Piper had parted him from his quarrel with Jessica's filly before Piper could move out of range. The yearling was undisciplined, but he had heart.

He whistled and Rocket, grazing with the other youngsters, raised his head at the call.

"Come here," Piper said.

Looking from side to side, Rocket trotted slowly to his sire.

"I will be leaving the herd," Piper said to him. "Tonight. And you will take my place. You are young to be left as Lead Stallion, Rocket, but I have no other choice. If the men turn the mares to the mountains before I return, you must watch, as I watch and protect the herd from danger."

Rocket moved his ears forward in surprise. Clover went very still.

"Do you understand me?"

"Where are you going?" asked Rocket.

"To save my sire and dam."

Clover plunged both forefeet into the earth and flung her heels to the sky. She whinnied shrilly. Piper kept his gaze on his son.

"I must do this thing. And if Equus is willing, I'll be back."

"You can't!" shouted Clover. "You can't! You are breaking the Law of the Herd itself!"

Rocket snorted at his dam. "Hush, mother," he said firmly. He swung his head back to Piper. "This is something you have to do?"

Piper nodded. "If I'm—late—returning, and if you should take the mares through the winter . . ."

Clover screamed again, with fury and without hope.

". . . if you should take the mares through the

winter," Piper repeated, "remember that the wolves travel in packs, and that they will run the weaker horses down if you don't keep the herd close together. And take care when the wind comes from the northeast—it carries storms with it."

"I will," said Rocket.

He moved to Clover, who turned her hindquarters to him, trembling with anger. "I'll be back, Clover, and things will be as they were before."

"You'll be back, and things may or may not be as they have been before," she said. "You risk everything for this!"

"You saw what I saw. What would you decide?"

Clover's breathing slowed, and her head dropped. After a moment, she said, "I would do what you've decided to do, Piper. That doesn't mean that I like it, or that I approve." She rolled her eyes to white half-moons and whispered, "Or even that I will accept you as Lead Stallion when you come back. I cannot forgive you this."

"I'm sorry," said Piper. He approached her and nosed her withers, licking her coat and nipping gently at her ears. "Farewell, Lead Mare."

She moved away, calling to her mares and bunching them together. They stood in a half circle, hindquarters out. Piper looked at Rocket, who nodded uncertainly. Moving hesitantly, the yearling walked in the first part of the guardian circle around the mares. The moon shone on his back, and he moved in shadow and light. The farther he went from where Piper stood, the more confident his strides became, until he was trotting, head up, nose lifted to the wind.

Piper walked to the pasture gate and waited. His heart carried pain and happiness. He was leaving his Master, his heritage and life as a leader of horses in

the world of men. He was going toward a true life in
the wild, as his ancestors had before him, without
men, without the Bargain that held him and his get
safe against the uncertainties of the wild. He raised
his head to the sky; the moon was sailing high and
white, no longer at the full. Its light paled against
the stars beside it, and shone over the high-peaked
mountains, a beacon to light the way.

There was a flash of warm light at the ranch house
steps, and Cory came out to open the door; it shut
behind him, and his white ruff gleamed silver as he
loped the half mile to the pasture gate. He came up
to the stallion, and without greeting him, tugged at
the rope looping the gate closed. The gate swung
free and Piper stepped through.

"Make certain the mares don't get out," Piper
said.

"I'll let the men know that you're gone when
you're safely off. They'll come and close it then."

"Good," said Piper. "Where are the geldings?"

"Still in the corral. Come with me."

Blackjack stood with his head over the fence, Duke
at his shoulder. Hank and Alvin were dim shapes
behind them, eating hay. They, too, came to the
fence when Cory and Piper approached. Blackjack
called out to them, a long, drawn-out whinny, and
Piper responded.

"Do you pledge yourself to the Stallion?"

"We do!" the geldings cried.

"Do you pledge yourself to the herd?"

"We do!"

"Then come with me, and follow."

"We go with you, and follow!"

Cory rose to his hindlegs, grunting a little with the
effort. He took the gravity latch in his teeth and
drew it back, his expression sorrowful. He kept his

paws against the gate and turned to look at Piper. "I did this once before," he said. "I let El Arat loose to stand in the pond at Bishop Farm and Walk the Path to the Moon. Disaster followed that breaking of man's law."

"And the saving of the Appaloosa," Alvin said. "There is no good without evil to balance it."

"There is no evil without good to balance it," said Piper.

Cory dropped to all four feet and stepped aside. One by one the geldings stepped through the gate.

"I was glad to see you again, dog, after all this time, and despite what news you brought us," said Piper. "You'll carry this news to Bishop Farm?"

"Yes," said Cory.

"Greet them for me, Pony, Fancy, and the others. Lilly, especially. The Dreamspeaker." He lifted his head to the mountains, and a night breeze stirred his mane. "Will Lilly tell you the end of the Tale? We may never meet again, dog, and I want you to know if I succeed."

"She will. May the wind be at your back." Cory stepped aside.

Piper leaped into a hard gallop, straight to the mountains. Hank, Duke, Alvin and Blackjack fell into line behind him. The five horses raced down the drive and past the brood mare's pasture. Rocket and Clover stood at the wire fence; Clover raced inside the wire as close to Piper as she could get without hitting the fence itself. She dropped to a trot at the end of the pasture, turning to follow the wire as it circled back to the stream. "Take care," she cried out, "return to us!"

Piper shouted a challenge to the mountains ahead, black against the deep blue night. He whinnied again, a farewell, and cries from the ranch house answered him. David and Emmanual ran out to the porch, their figures tiny in the distance.

The insistent call of the triangle pulled at Piper, and he shook his head as he ran.

"Piper!" David shouted. "Piiiipppppeerrrr!"

Piper bucked in mid-gallop and kicked his heels to the sky.

• 7 •

West of the Sun, And to the Dancer's Mountain

Blackjack rolled luxuriously in the new spring grass. They had stopped to rest in a sheltered pocket of the valley. The meadow was green here, and the clover high enough to eat. The unprotected sides of the mountain had not fared as well, and up until now, they had pawed through melting snow to last year's grass in the days they had been travelling free.

"Nice day," said Duke. He looked up past the mountain peaks to the sky; the blue was patched with grey-white clouds which augured snow, but the sun shone yellow and the wind was warm.

"It'd be nice if we knew where we were going," said Blackjack, hauling himself to his feet. He shook himself thoroughly, and dust rose from his coat. " 'West of the sun and to the Dancer's Mountain.' That's pretty general, Piper. Which way today?"

Piper, standing on a slight promontory with his nose lifted to the breeze, turned and leaped down to stand behind the others.

"West and further west."

He kicked up his heels and broke into a ground-eating lope; the others straggled behind him.

Blackjack jostled Duke amiably, and the Connemara flicked his ears back. "This life suits you," Duke said. "It suits all of you."

Alvin, trotting along with his tail flagged and his action high, raced for a few strides out of sheer delight.

Hank snorted and swung his hindquarters into Blackjack's flank. The Walker bucked in place, then lengthened his stride and swept past the other geldings to run at Piper's side.

Duke, puffing a little, trotted farther and farther behind, finally moving into a gallop to keep up.

They ran down the slope of a valley which lay tucked between the foothills of the mountains surrounding Sweetwater. The scents and sounds of the ranch lay far behind them, and Piper felt only the life of the wilderness beneath his feet. He rotated his ears as he ran, listening hard. He breathed in, reading the air: snow due in a few days and rain; a herd of deer with one stag some furlongs away; the trace of a pack of wolves; partridge, pheasant, and other birds; the faint odor of a ranch in the upper part of the valley. But nothing else. No mare, old or otherwise, was within the distance of his nose, ears, and sensitive hooves.

He swerved to the pines which ringed the base of the foothills.

"It'll be slower going in there," said Blackjack.

"Duke needs a rest," said Piper.

Beside him, Blackjack stopped and inhaled sharply. "Do you smell that ranch nearby?" he said. "I can't tell from the wind, but there's probably mares there. There's an odor of horse, at any rate."

"No. She won't be where men stay," said Piper briefly.

"Where, then?"

Piper shook his head. They slowed to a walk as they approached the pines.

"Keep within scent of each other," he said. "We're headed straight west as the sun falls, and I don't want us to lose each other." He pawed cautiously at the snow drifted at the base of the scrubby pines. "And watch out for holes."

"Does Galwayne's groove still run the length of our teeth?" asked Blackjack of no one in particular. "Come on, Piper, we're not weanlings who have to be coaxed along."

"The groove disappears in aged horses," said Alvin, helpfully. "Neither youngsters nor aged horses have the groove."

"No!" said Blackjack sarcastically.

"You won't grow much older if you don't keep your bit between your teeth," said Piper. "Watch the burrow!" He moved swiftly, his powerful shoulder knocking Blackjack away from a fall of snow. The Walker's hind feet broke through the crust and the snow caved into a hole the length of a foreleg.

"Snap!" said Hank. "They put horses down for broken bones. Excuse me, Blackjack, but I'd rather follow Piper than you." He shoved his way past the black Walker and took his place immediately behind the stallion.

The woods were filled with the rustling, green-scented noises and smells of the wild. Piper moved easily through the trees, head up, ears rotating constantly.

"Once in a while, the big cats rest in the lower branches of trees like this," he said. "You'll smell them long before they're a danger. The scent's like no other I know of. Bears, now, you'll hear them long before you smell them, they're so clumsy. They're about as quiet as a boulder falling down a hill. Other than that," he stopped, sniffed intently, and then moved on, "there's not much to worry about."

"Other than where we're going," said Duke grimly.

Piper laid one ear back in amusement. "There's that. We'll find a clearing soon, and stop to graze and rest. There are some things I need to show you about defense."

"I'm feeling younger all the time," Blackjack said to the air. "Much more of this, and I'll be nursing again."

"We can learn," Alvin protested. "We've never spent time in the mountains without men. At least I haven't."

"Men certainly know a lot about protecting themselves," said Blackjack. "Men's noses are about as useful as a dog with a muzzle full of skunk."

"Well, I think we need all the help we can get," said Alvin. "I'd like to learn how to fight."

"YOU!" said Blackjack. "That I'd like to see. Alvin the Warrior leading a charge against a bear, or a mountain cat. Maybe you're right, Piper. He needs help for certain."

"We should be getting other kinds of help," said Duke. "Cory told us the Goddess Mare said she would send a guide."

"Was she very beautiful, Piper?" Alvin asked. "Was she gold, as gold as the sun in August? I would like to see her. Not to speak to, just to look."

"She was very beautiful. As to her color, it was hard to tell. She was as bright as the sun, and her voice was sweet. I couldn't see her shape."

The trees grew more thickly together as they proceeded up the mountain. The horses walked carefully in single file.

"What color she was makes no difference," Black-

jack said, "as long as she sends that guide that Cory
mentioned. If she doesn't, we'll be as old as the Old
Mare before we find her. It's taking ages to get
through this stuff."

Piper led them at a steady pace through the re-
mainder of the day, breaking for frequent grazing.

At midday, the pale April sun reached its height.
They stopped to water at a mountain stream. The
wind had changed, and as the geldings drank, Piper
tensed and tried to read it: a storm, with the wind
from another a quarter?

"What's wrong, Piper?" asked Blackjack.

Duke, cropping a patch of orchard grass, paused
and lifted his head. Hank pressed close to Alvin,
trembling. The grey gelding inhaled the wind suddenly; his eyes rolled white, and he began to breathe
in short, sharp bursts. Froth came from his muzzle.
He scrambled back a few paces and screamed "FIRE!"
The scars on his neck and withers stood out in sharp
relief. He plunged to the edge of the clearing,
panicked.

Piper moved with the speed of a diving hawk. He
raced long and low to the ground, head down, ears
pinned back. He crashed into Hank and reared, bringing both forelegs down on the gelding's neck. He bit
down hard, muscles straining, and shook Hank back
and forth. Hank screamed again, a different note in
his cry, and sprang away from Piper's teeth. The
stallion whirled and his hindquarters smashed into
Hank's flank. The gelding stopped, sweat trickling
from his withers.

"Fire," he whispered. "Barn fire!"

"It's a long way off," said Piper in low tones.
"Stand still and scent the wind."

Hank, one eye rolled back to watch Piper, inhaled
slightly.

"Furlongs away," said Alvin. "And you're safe here, Hank."

"Some aren't," said Blackjack, his own muzzle lifted to the air. "There's blood and burned flesh in the wind."

"Enough!" Piper ordered. "You recall that ranch on the far side of the mountain we passed this morning. The fire comes from there. It's too far away to harm us."

"What if the woods catch fire?" asked Duke practically.

Hank looked wildly around, then met Piper's stern eye. He stood still with an effort.

"It's too wet for a forest fire," said Piper. "There's snow all through these mountains yet. Look at the sky, Hank. Rain or snow or both are coming. There are no fires in the mountains in spring."

"Just the same, we'd better move away from here," said Duke. "That fire smell is coming from the west, Piper. We'd better head back and around the mountain to pass by it."

Piper nodded. "Hank, stay between Alvin and Duke. Walk on, now, quickly."

He led them steadily on at a rapid walk until the sheer repetition of movement dried the sweat from Hank's coat and dulled the terror in his eyes. Blackjack loped easily along for several furlongs, then murmured, "It's unusual to have a fire this early in the spring, Piper. Do you think it was meant to turn us from the path to find the Old Mare?"

Piper considered this for a long moment. The smell of burning drifted far behind them now, and all of them breathed a little easier.

"Why would you think that?"

"Cory told us of El Arat's desire for revenge against your dam. We've all heard Tales of the Soul Taker,

and the mischief she's already caused the Appaloosa.
Perhaps . . ."

"Perhaps what?"

"Perhaps this is a warning."

Piper snorted. "We have the protection of the
Courts. We'll soon find a guide to take us to the Old
Mare."

"I hope so," Blackjack murmured.

Piper showed his teeth. "So do I."

The sun dropped in the west and the horses circled back toward the sunset. Night came on quickly,
as though a blanket had been drawn over the sky to
hide the daylight. The trees thinned out and finally,
as the first stars shone pale in the twilight, Piper led
them to a clearing and announced that they would
stop for the night.

They ate, and the cold crept up on them. After
they had grazed and rested, Piper drew the geldings
together to show them how to fight.

"There are warrior moves to learn. I will show
you, as my sire showed me, under the Eye of the
Moon at Bishop Farm.

"There are three things a stallion learns," said
Piper, when he had the herd's attention. "The first is
this: if the mares and foals are in danger, and the
odds overwhelming, you must run and take them to
safety.

"The second: once a fight's begun, it is to the
death.

"The third: we, as members of an honorable breed
in the world of men, are generous in victory and
proud in defeat."

Piper trotted in a wide circle, his black and white
coat shining in the starlight. His mane flowed over
his neck, and his finely chiseled head was silhouetted
in the dark. "This is the Snake. It is used to move

the herd quickly out of danger. When you are herding mares and foals, you do not bite to wound. You do not kick to injure. If you use the Snake to chase the enemy from your territory, then you bite to wound and kick to kill."

"Have you ever killed another being, Piper?" asked Alvin.

"I've never killed another horse. I have, in my time, been forced to drive coyote and wolves from my range. And then I've killed, yes, but only to save the herd. Watch me now, and learn."

He sprang into a gallop and circled the clearing. The second time around he brought his head low to the ground, ears pinned flat against his skull, teeth bared. He raced into Blackjack, who leaped back with a startled cry.

Piper whirled, striking low at Blackjack's fetlocks. A loud whinny rumbled in his chest. Blackjack ducked away from the others, and Piper drove him to the edge of the clearing, shaking his head back and forth in a swift, weaving movement.

When Blackjack bolted left, Piper's teeth forced him to the right. As Blackjack ran in the opposite direction, Piper reached out, his neck impossibly long, and snapped at Blackjack's right rear hock. Blackjack collected himself and kicked out with both hindfeet. Piper dodged and feinted forward, his teeth closing harmlessly over the Walker's croup. Blackjack turned and blundered backwards into Duke.

"Do you see?" said Piper, as he halted in front of the herd. The furious activity had barely disturbed his breathing, and except for a light sheen of moisture on his neck, he appeared unruffled.

"Yes," said Alvin. "That was very good, Piper. I guess we can all do that."

"Very well, now. I'll demonstrate the Bear. Alvin,

walk towards me. Then rear up on your hind legs and strike at me with your forefeet."

"I don't want to hurt you, Piper," said Alvin. "Why should I?"

"Do it, please," said Piper. "Walk on, Alvin."

The big chestnut sighed, and moved obediently. At seventeen hands, he was the largest of them all. He reared, and his body blotted out the stars. Piper trotted forward and reared to meet him. The stallion's stippled hindquarters glimmered in the starlight. His hooves reflected the thin light of the new moon. Alvin crashed toward him, and Piper brought his forelegs down over the chestnut's withers. He twisted his head in a swift movement, and bit the vulnerable spot beneath Alvin's jaw.

The Standardbred shouted in surprise. Piper bore down firmly. Alvin jerked sideways, his whinny strangled in his throat. He began to gasp for breath. Piper's great hindlegs gouged the earth and he pushed Alvin back with the force of his body. Alvin's forelegs lifted off the ground from the pressure of Piper's chest against his.

He gasped for air.

Piper released him, and fell to all four feet. Alvin staggered into Duke, who nosed him thoughtfully.

"You bite down hard on the spot under the jaw," said Piper, "hard enough to tear the flesh open. The life blood pools there, and once you have torn it open, your enemy is down for good. A horse that's down is a horse that's already set one hoof on the Green Road."

Alvin, troubled, gazed at him.

Piper's stern gaze softened. "You must bite hard and hold fast," said the stallion. "And when the enemy drops to his knees, you'll taste blood. It is an evil taste, and you'll want to let go and spit out the foulness of it. You can't." He nudged Alvin gently into the center of the group, then cocked his eye at Hank. "Come out, brother, and I will show you kicking."

"We already know how to kick," said Duke. "Thank you very much, Piper. I thank that this is enough for one night."

"Show me how to kick," Blackjack demanded exuberantly. "Now!" The Walker burst from the herd like a calf from a chute, heels flung to the sky. "Ride on, Piper!" he shouted. And he squealed like a bucking bronco, "Rodeo! Yah!"

The geldings were infected with a reckless, mischievous spirit. Hank crawfished across the clearing as if a bucking band were strapped around his belly. Duke pawed at the ground and squealed.

"EEHAH!" Alvin screamed, crowhopping across the clearing. All four feet bunched together and his back arched into a perfect bow. "EEHAH!"

Piper leaped into the chase, his head low, his lip curled in the Snake. He raced side by side with Alvin, then shouted, "The Thunderbolt!" He spun on his forelegs, and kicked out with both hindfeet, gauging the kick to narrowly graze Blackjack's chest. As his hindfeet touched ground, he sprang ahead in a tremendous leap and kicked out rapidly with his right rear leg. The kicks whizzed harmlessly past Blackjack's ear.

"The Rabbit!" Piper cried. He turned again and raked his left forefoot lightly down Blackjack's side, from poll to stifle.

"The Hawk!" He leaped high again, and bit Blackjack lightly on the poll.

"EEEE!" Alvin shrieked. The chestnut ran forward, and kicked out with his right rear leg. "The Rabbit! The Hawk! The Thunderbolt!"

Suddenly, Piper went still, his attention focused on the pine trees with fierce intensity.

"Quiet!" Piper roared.

The geldings were startled into silence. Blackjack stepped to the stallion's side. "What is it, Piper?"

"Smell that? Hear that?" He indicated the copse of trees at the end of their clearing.

Blackjack inhaled deeply, then said with a flicker of excitement, "Another horse." He paused. "Not a mare though. And Piper . . ."

"I know. I've never smelled such fear in my life."

"He's hurt, too," Alvin observed, blowing out.

Piper took one step forward, then another. "Come out," he called firmly. "We won't hurt you."

"Join the warrior clan," called Alvin. "Whoever you are, you're probably a better fighter than all of us geldings put together."

A shadow moved on the grass, and a gelding stepped out of the pines and into the starlight. He was a bay, with rusty black mane, legs and tail. He stood over at the knees, and had a short back and narrow chest.

"Not a stayer," said Blackjack. "What's the matter, fellow? You're not afraid of us?"

The gelding froze. There was a faint sheen of sweat on his withers and his eye rolled white. He vibrated silently, so that his shadow shifted back and forth in the dim light cast by the new moon.

Piper moved cautiously around the bay, sniffing deeply at his ears, croup and sheath. He stepped back, head held to one side.

"What happened to you, horse?"

The gelding stood silent, shaking. Only his eyes followed Piper. The stallion reared, and brought his forelegs gently down across the gelding's back. He bit the bay lightly on the nape of the neck, then pulled away.

"I'm stallion here," he said. "I'm Sweetwater's Dancing Piper, out of Duchess by the Dancer." He swung his muzzle at the others, and one by one, they each inspected the bay as he had done. Duke whirled and kicked out with his hindlegs, his hooves grazing the gelding's quarters.

The newcomer trembled but stood still.

The Working Herd stood shoulder to shoulder, and Blackjack said, "I'm Herd Chief. My herd name is Blackjack, out of Highstepper by Tennessee Dream."

He stepped forward and nosed the bay gelding. "There is a smell of burning here, Piper, and a wound."

"Yes," Piper murmured. "Duke?"

"Sir Duke, out of Bog Trotter, and my sire's not known. I'm unranked."

"Calvin's Cross, by Calvin's Springtime out of Speedster," said Alvin. "I'm the Last in Line."

"And I'm Beecher's Spotted Glory," said Hank, "without the spots, as you may have noticed. I'm by Spot On out of Gloriana. I greyed out, but I am an Appaloosa, like our stallion. I'm Second-In-Command in the Working Herd." He snorted, then said, "Are you all right?"

The bay shifted uneasily on his feet. After a moment, he raised his head.

"Is there water nearby?" he whispered. "I'm very thirsty."

"On the other side of the clearing," said Duke. "It's a little stream, and there's a sheet of ice on the top that you'll have to break. Would you like me to show it to you?"

The bay started forward, then stopped, eyes wide. "There is no fire there, is there? Do you smell fire?"

"No," said Piper. "There's no fire here. The only smell of fire comes from you. You were hurt."

With an abrupt movement, the gelding stretched his hind legs. Alvin walked up to him, and looked at the underside of the bay's belly. He blew out softly in concern. "That is a nasty burn underneath. Duke and I will take you to the water. It's deep enough for you to stand in, and it will help the pain."

The bay nodded, and moved with difficulty. Duke and Alvin walked on either side. Blackjack and Piper followed, Hank lagging at their heels. They reached the stream and Alvin struck the frozen surface with his hooves. The ice broke with a crack. Dark water welled up. The bay ducked his head and drank for a long moment. He finished, then raised his muzzle slightly from the water and stood with his head low.

"Why don't you wade right in?" said Alvin. "It might help."

"It'll be cold," said Duke, "but it will feel good on that burn." He nosed a slide of ice, then said thoughtfully, "Maybe he better not. The pieces of ice might bump against the wound and make it bleed."

"You were burned in a barn fire," said Piper. "We smelled it some furlongs back."

The bay shook his head, eyes clouded. "It must have been a fire. I don't know. I don't remember."

"And your name, your breeding? We have greeted you properly, you must now greet us." Piper was gentle, but firm.

The bay hesitated. "My name . . ." He trailed off, and looked into the water as if an answer might lie there.

"Can't you stop that . . . quivering?" said Blackjack. "It makes me shiver just to watch you. What's the matter, anyway? Your nose should tell you we mean you no harm."

"I smell fire," the gelding whispered, "only fire."

Hank rumbled sympathetically. "I know what it must have been like." For some reason, he sounded cheerful. "I can assure you, fellow, the fear will pass. I was never in a fire, but a barn collapsed on me and my stable mates, and for the longest time after I could feel the ground shaking, when I knew it wasn't, really. You'll stop smelling fire, soon enough. Piper, tell him there is no fire."

"There is no fire," said Piper. "Only the cool air and the meadows and the stars. There is no fire."

The bay inhaled. His trembling slowed.

"Well, let's graze a little," said Alvin. "You get some food in your belly and you might remember your name."

"Not so fast," said Blackjack. "Should we welcome him to the herd just like that? We don't know who he is or where he's from. He could be from anywhere, from the Dark Horse himself."

"Surely not," said Duke. "No horse survives a barn fire without some terrible effect. I'm not surprised he can't remember his name. It's obvious he's from the barns of men, anyway. His feet are trimmed, and his mane and tail have been pulled. You are not a wild horse, are you, fellow?"

"I . . . don't know."

"Well, I'm sure you are not. I've met a few in my time, and they are very different. They smell like grass and wind. You smell of oats. Underneath the fire smell, of course."

The gelding's shaking grew stronger.

"Don't remind him," said Hank. "We could give him a herd name. We could call him Shaker."

"He's not joining the herd," said Blackjack sharply. "Not until we know where he's from."

"The Third Law, Blackjack," said Duke. "No horse shall be turned away from his fellows."

"The Second Law, Duke," Blackjack said. "Each horse shall know his name, and so shall his fellows."

"I am from west of the sun, and from the Rainbow Mountain," Shaker said, as though recalling a dream.

Alvin and Hank snorted in excitement. Blackjack plumed his tail in surprise.

"The Goddess Mare," said Hank excitedly. "She's sent us a guide. She told us she would, and here he is. Welcome, Shaker."

"You think so?" said Duke with a doubtful look at Shaker's upright hocks and ewe neck. "Piper, what do you say?"

"That this gelding couldn't find his way out of a corral with no fence, that's what he'll say," Blackjack muttered. "If this is a messenger from the Goddess Mare, then I'm a donkey."

Duke nudged him, and the Walker quieted. Piper looked steadily at Shaker. The bay kept his eyes lowered. He raised them once to the stallion, then his gaze slid back to the water at his feet.

"We can't turn him away," said Piper. "How could he survive out here alone with that wound in his belly?"

"He'll slow us down," said Blackjack.

Piper ignored this and said to the bay, "West of the sun and from the Dancer's Mountain. Is that where you are from, Shaker?"

"I don't know," the horse admitted, miserably. "I can't remember."

"The wound's on his belly, not on his legs. He can walk just fine," said Alvin. "I don't believe that he'll slow us down, and I vote to have him join the herd." The Standardbred took a bite of grass and added reflectively, "Besides, he might remember who he is if we keep him with us. And perhaps he is a guide, after all, and got caught in that barn fire on his way to meet us."

"Does he want to join us?" asked Hank. "We should ask, you know, since we may be headed into danger."

"That's true," Alvin said. "Do you want to join us, Shaker? We are on a journey, a mission, to rescue Piper's dam and sire. She's lost her way on the Green Road, and we intend to put her right again."

"The Green Road goes one way," whispered Shaker, his eyes rolling. "Do you set foot on it to save her?"

"No. We travel to find the Namer of Names, the Old Mare of the Mountains. She will tell us how to . . ."

"We may travel into danger," said Blackjack, rudely interrupting. "Don't tell him everything, Alvin. How can you trust a horse who doesn't know who he is or where his herd is from? I'll accept him if I have to, but I don't think he should know any more than he needs to know."

"If he takes the herd oath, he'll be loyal to me, even in the face of the Final Death itself," said Piper. "The horse who fails his oath is damned forever to the region of the soulless."

"Make him take the oath then, before you tell him everything. You take too many risks, Piper. You're too trusting." Blackjack swung his hindquarters around in irritation. Piper regarded him thoughtfully and said, "Blackjack," and the Walker faced the herd again, his lower lip tight against his teeth.

"If he takes the oath, he's bound to the herd, and we are loyal to him as he is to us. If he takes the oath, he'll have to go where we go, unless some man arrives out of the skies to take him somewhere, and that isn't likely to happen. If he doesn't want to go with us, he'll still have to, despite the danger. What's fair?"

"None of it's fair," Blackjack said, with a shade of worry in his voice, "you tell me what's fair."

"Perhaps we could lead him to the safety of some man's barn," suggested Alvin.

"Time," said Blackjack shortly, "there is no time. Oh, the Black Barns take me if I'm not the biggest fool in nature. The Soul Taker herself may follow us to keep us from our task, Shaker. It is she and her kind who may bring danger to the herd. Would you still travel with us?"

Shaker, bewildered, looked from Blackjack to Piper and back again. "I think I must travel with you," he whispered. "I believe that I must."

"This is our guide," said Hank. "It must be, and he's met with an accident and has lost his memory. We must take him with us."

"The oath," Piper said. "Well, Shaker?"

"I don't remember," said Shaker. "I don't remember the oath, I remember fire. I remember a stall and fire at my belly like a hungry cat." He shut his eyes and shook like a birch tree in a storm. "The fire came up from the floor and sprang at my eyes. She came. She came and let me out." Gradually, his shaking slowed. "She helped me."

"Jehanna!" Hank said joyfully. "Did you see her, Shaker? Was she gold like the sun?"

"She was gold, like the fire," said Shaker. "She was in the fire, and she set me free, and I promised."

"I'll help you remember the oath, Shaker," said Alvin. "Come on. I, Shaker."

"I, Shaker."

"By an unknown mare, and an absent sire, pledge myself to the herd of Sweetwater's Dancing Piper."

Shaker repeated this, with further urging from Alvin, and then all the horses sang together:

"By the Court's clear light,
By Equus' eye,
By the Wise Owl's Flight,

By the One who is Wise—
We pledge ourselves to the herd!"

The horses squared up and stood shoulder to shoulder.

"Though the holes run deep
and the fences run high,
Though the grass grows short
and the water runs dry,
Though the Dark Horse himself throws death in
our eyes,
We pledge ourselves to the herd!"

"To the herd," whispered Shaker. And the sound drifted eerily in the thin air.

"Come on," said Duke practically, "let's eat."

Dawn rose and stretched like a slow gray cat on the hills. The sun was hidden and the clouds that had promised rain and snow the day before now gathered with intent. The herd ate and drank again and prepared to move out. The graze and the rest had done Shaker good. In the full light of day, the others saw that the barn fire had burnt the ends of his coat, as well as charred the furrow in his belly, and he looked like a leopard Appaloosa, all random spots. As they walked west, his eye cleared, his head came up, and he said that perhaps, yes, he knew where they were supposed to go. "I don't recall anything before she, praises to her name, led me from the fire, but I do believe I might know the way to the Old Mare. That sticks with me, somehow, like someone calling me from far away." He stopped abruptly, and his nose went up. "Do you smell anything?" he whispered. "Do you hear something crackling like hens at a bag of feed?"

"You're fine," said Hank soothingly. "You got out, and there's no fire here—only trees and air and meadow, right, Piper?"

Piper flicked his tail, his attention on the day ahead.

"It's a fine morning, and we know what we have to do," said Piper. "Let's move out! Lead on, Shaker!"

The bay shifted from one foot to the other. Piper pawed at the ground impatiently, turning up the earth. Shaker rolled his eyes.

"Just relax," advised Duke kindly. "Your nose will tell you where to go. Breathe in, and think hard."

Shaker inhaled obediently. He lifted his head, and gazed at the mountain. He moved cautiously up the mountainside. Duke, Hank and Alvin fell in behind him. Piper and Blackjack trotted near, circling at a gallop when their faster pace led them too far away from Shaker's methodical progress. The morning wore on, and the horses climbed higher and higher, the sun beating down on their backs and heads.

Here, in the upper regions of the mountains, the air was thinner and the sun beat down with insistence. At midday, with the sun at its height, they stopped to rest by a clear blue lake. They all drank, and began to graze. Blackjack cropped grass for a short while, then moved to Piper's side.

"Are you sure that this Shaker knows where he's going?"

"I'm perfectly sure that he *doesn't* know where he's going."

"Then why are we following him?" asked Blackjack in exasperation.

"You haven't realized it?"

"Realized what?"

"Shaker's been guided by a pair of foxes. I don't know if he knows, but every time he strays from this upward trail, the foxes move in to close him off. He's been keeping a steady distance from them and the distance never changes. When they move too close, he moves away. And they've been travelling in a steady line to the top of the mountains."

Blackjack looked at the mountainside. The lake waters slapped gently against the gravel shore. A clutch of hawks were nesting in the barely green branches of an oak tree. He could feel the normal life of the mountainside under his hooves. He inhaled sharply twice. "I can smell the foxes. But what makes you think they're guiding him?"

"A fox's territory is small. They've long passed what would be a normal boundary."

"We should flush them out and find out who they are and where they come from," said Blackjack testily. "I can't understand you, Piper. Why trust them?"

"Perhaps you're right. We should question them." Piper raised his head and whistled sharply. "Duke! Alvin! Move out to the left of those trees." Duke and Alvin looked at each other, then obediently trotted to the high side of the pines clustered near the lake. Shaker turned his head in bewilderment, and stopped grazing.

"You go to the right," Piper said to the Walker. "If they break for the open, head them towards me. Take Hank with you."

"What are you looking for?" called Duke.

"Those foxes. I want to talk to them."

"Those foxes there?" Alvin narrowed his eyes against the sun. "There's two, a dog and a vixen, I think, if the wind tells me right."

Shaker shied nervously. Hank and Blackjack loped to the other side of the pines, and Piper galloped up to the trees and stopped.

"Come out," he ordered.

There was a flash of red and dun in the shadow of the pines. The horses heard the pad-click of clawed paws on the rocky ground, and two slim bodies slipped through the trees. The dog was a bright autumn red. The tip of his tail, snout and feet were rusty black. The vixen at his side was smaller, and colored like dried grasses in a drift of melting snow.

"Gather behind me in an attack circle," Piper ordered. "Hindquarters out, ready to kick." He looked at the dog fox; the fox looked back steadily, panting a little. His eyes were a clear deep gold with fine black lines radiating from the center. The vixen beside him squeezed her eyes shut, then rolled over on the ground, her white underbelly exposed. She waved her paws in the air, then looked at the horses, upside down. Her muzzle was rounder and less pointed than her mate's and the mask on her face shadowy dark and ill defined, as though she had rolled in dust before her colors were dry.

"Well, Basil," she said in a high-pitched growl. "Horses, like she said there would be. The big one's spotted, too. I told you, didn't I? Admit it for once. I was right. If we'd followed the spoor you'd chosen, we would have found goodness-knows-what. A bear maybe. We would have been chomped up by this time, no doubt."

"Quiet, Dill." The dog fox crouched in the grass, and raised glowing eyes to Piper's. "Females!" he said and squeezed his eyes shut in amusement. "She's sharp, Dill is. I'm the first one to tell you that. And she does like to rub it in. But we found you, and that's what matters." He sat up proudly. "We've been guiding you the right way, and that matters, too."

"*I* found you," Dill corrected him snappishly. She leaped up, rolled in mid-air, and landed on Basil's back. She grabbed one black tufted ear and worried it back and forth with deep little growls. Basil barked and twisted, sinking his teeth into her ruff and pulling her off his back and onto the ground. He put his paw on her neck and she bit it. In a flurry of squeals and barks, they rolled over and over in the grass. They broke apart and crouched, snarling at each other. Suddenly, Dill stiffened, her eyes wide. She wriggled low in the grass, then sprang high. Basil leaped to meet her, and they crashed together with a soft thud. There was a flurry of snaps and growls, and Dill rolled free. "That was a rabbit!" she shouted. "You stupid fool. I was about to get a rabbit for you! I wasn't playing! And you made me miss it!" She yipped furiously.

"Stop this!" said Alvin. He moved forward and stepped between them. Dill pawed at him, and he nudged her gently back.

"A nice juicy rabbit," sulked Dill. "A delicious rabbit."

"That's enough," said Piper. "Who told you to find us? And why are you guiding us?"

"That's for us to know and you to find out," said Dill.

"We just do what we're asked to," said Basil. "At least *I* do." He glanced narrowly at his mate.

Piper snorted authoritatively. "And what were you told to do?"

"To find a spotted stallion . . ." said Dill.

"And the horses he travels with . . ." said Basil.

"And bring them to the right place at the right time," said Dill. "You're spotted and you're a stallion and you're travelling with other horses and so we're doing what we were asked to do."

Alvin rejoined the circle of geldings behind Piper. Blackjack said in an undertone, "Did she scratch you? Did she draw blood?"

The big Standardbred shook his head.

"Lucky for you. They might have the summer madness for all you know."

"If you mean rabid, we aren't," said Dill tartly. "Thank you very much. But we *are* short of time, so let's go." She jumped to her feet and bounced a short way up the mountain.

"We might as well," said Basil, getting to his feet in a more leisurely fashion. He picked up a paw and examined it closely. "DILL! I've got a THORN!" He followed his mate at a bounding hop, limping abruptly when she turned to look over her shoulder. He held the forepaw up and waved it weakly. "A thorn! I knew it. When you pulled me through those teazels like a mad thing, I told you I'd pick up a thorn, and I did."

"Pssh! We're late enough as it is. I'll pull it out when we reach her. Come on, you lot, don't just stand there like a bunch of moony cubs. Follow me!"

"Come here, please," said Piper firmly. "Here!" He struck his foreleg imperatively into the ground. "Sit down!"

The foxes looked at each other, shrugged, and sat down in front of the stallion.

"Don't get too close," warned Dill.

"Equines," agreed Basil. He wrinkled his muzzle to show his sharp teeth. "Grass eaters."

"Explain this," said Piper. "Who are you? Why have you come? Who sent you?"

"We were sent," said Dill patiently, "to lead you west of the sun and to the Dancer's mountain. And when we do, we can go back to our den and get on with our lives. So let's go!"

"Go! Go! Go!" Basil yipped.

"And who was it that sent you?" asked Piper patiently.

"Who did send us, Dill?" asked Basil plaintively. He looked at Piper and said confidingly, "All I know is, she gets me out of the den and tells me we have to find you and take you to a place where, frankly, no sane party would go, if you ask me." He paused, wrinkled his snout and said, "Tell us Dill, who sent us?"

"A gold mare?" said Alvin hopefully.

"Quiet," ordered Blackjack. "Don't give them anything to guess on."

"I received a message," said Dill primly.

"Was the messenger gold like the sun?" said Alvin. "Did you see her?"

Dill bit furiously at her brush, looked up, and said, "It was . . ." she grinned at Basil, "another fox. Quite good looking. He said if Basil wouldn't go with me, *he* would."

Basil growled.

"Just kidding. Just kidding. No, it wasn't a fox and it wasn't a gold mare. It was a bird."

"An owl perhaps?" asked Piper, his eyes gleaming, "A great bird with a snowy face and horns?"

"I know what an owl looks like," said Dill. "It might have been an owl. Or a kingfisher. Does it matter? It does not."

"It wasn't any of these things, was it, Dill?" said Duke gravely. "There was no messenger—but a message. You had a dream."

Dill opened her gold eyes wide.

"A dream!" Basil yipped. "You dragged me through teazel for a dream!"

"What if I did? It was a true dream. We're to take these horses to the Old Mare, and we will." Her eyes narrowed to thin gold slits. "I dreamed we were to take you to the Old Mare and that's what we'll do."

"At last," breathed Piper softly.

"What do you mean, at last?" said Blackjack sharply. "What about Shaker? How do we know who to believe?"

"Shaker doesn't remember anything," said Hank. "The foxes know who we're supposed to see and why."

"And so does the Soul Taker," Blackjack said in low tones. "What the Courts may see, the Black Barns may see. How do we know who to believe?"

"It doesn't seem likely Jehanna would ask a pair of foolish foxes to take us to the Old Mare," said Duke.

"Thank you very much," said Dill.

"Shaker doesn't seem a likely choice either," said Blackjack. "I say we get rid of all of them and find our own way."

Piper shook his head. "Perhaps Jehanna has sent both to guide us."

"Since when have meateaters and grasseaters walked together?" demanded Blackjack. "I say charge the foxes and get it over with."

"Just try it!" said Dill. She lay nose to forepaw, then leaped and disappeared into the brush. Basil went after her. "Catch us now!" caroled Dill from somewhere deep in the trees. There was a crackling sound of dry branches. Her sharp little face peered out from beneath the branches of a pine tree. She pulled back as quickly as she appeared, and the horses heard sibilant whispers. After a moment, Basil's head appeared from the thickest part of the tree.

"We'll just follow along, like we have been," said Basil. "We'll let you know when you stray off the path." He cocked his head at Piper. "That one there," he pointed his muzzle at Shaker, "doesn't really remember what he's supposed to do. We've had to keep correcting him all morning. We'll just continue on the way we have been."

"I'll catch them," said Blackjack. "I'll get rid of them once and for all."

"No," said Piper. "Whoever sent them for whatever reason, I'd rather have them under our eye. They know more about our affairs than I would like."

"More than they should," said Blackjack. "We'll have the whole mountain know where we're going."

"You think we should creep in secrecy to the Old Mare, Blackjack? You don't doubt that He Who Should Not Be Named In The Dark knows of this mission? Well, neither do I."

Blackjack flagged his tail in frustration. "You believe we are protected, don't you? You think that because you saw a strange mare on a riverbank at the full of the moon, and heard a tale from a collie too old to remember when he had his last dish of food that we're safe from any harm. That we'll escape the Black Horse himself."

"I believe the Courts protect us, yes."

"I believe in saving your legs to carry your mane and tail," said the Walker bluntly. Dill looked at them over Basil's furry shoulder.

"Basil," she said, "this big black horse doesn't

trust us. He thinks us sly. Tricky. Foxes who'd grab a hutched rabbit rather than run an honest hunt through the fields." She grinned suddenly. "You're right about that, horse. I've tasted many a fine pet in my time. But my dreams don't lie. And this Black Horse that you tell us of—he is a Master Liar, is he not?" Her grin disappeared, and Basil added soberly, "He is like the Poacher, Piper, this Dark Horse."

Piper wrinkled his forehead in question.

"You know, the Poacher," said Dill. "Takes the cubs in the Dark. You can hear him on evil nights by the chime of his spade on the rocks."

Duke blew out and shook himself.

"We do not belong to the Poacher, or us to him," said Dill. "We follow the Snow Fox and his vixen." She opened her mouth and her tongue lolled pink. "Of course, you have only our word for this, Piper the Appaloosa, Piper son of the Dancer and Duchess the buckskin mare. How can you trust us? You can't. But if you think that poor old Shaker here can lead you where you want to go, then our task is at an end. You decide, Piper, whether you believe that I had a dream from your gods, and whether this dream is a true one."

"Don't believe them," said Blackjack. "We'll find the Old Mare on our own."

Piper raised his head to the sky. "They've left us a choice, Blackjack."

"So?"

The stallion arched his neck. The glossy black of his hindquarters gleamed. The cream of his muzzle shone silky. "Those who have turned their souls to the Dark Barns would not allow us to choose, Blackjack."

"Those who turn their souls to the Barns would trick us into believing we had a choice."

"It's decided," said Piper. "Dill, we'll follow you to the Old Mare."

"Such a favor," said Dill. "Come then. It's not far."

BASIL & DILL

• 8 •

The Namer of Names

Clouds darkened the sky, and the snow and rain which Piper had sensed in the air the day before began to fall. The path the foxes followed wound to the upper reaches of the mountains, and the horses began to blow heavily in the thinning air. They moved at a walk, placing their hooves carefully in the rocks, stretching and scrambling to move upward. Duke began to sweat, and a white foam stained his withers and flanks. Blackjack, with his long legs and high action, was awkward among the rocks and boulders. His wide hooves gave him good purchase in the gravelly pockets, but he slipped on the sheer granite. He laid his ears flat along his head and moved doggedly along, glossy black coat matted with sweat and dust.

The rain was mixed with snow, and as it fell, it made patterns on the horses' coats. The rain continued and the patterns blurred and merged together, so that except for their size, they all began to look alike, a mixture of muddy, dusty and damp hair.

Only Piper moved easily on the rocky trails. He

swept his head from side to side, blowing out in satisfaction once or twice. Blackjack flickered an ear towards him and Piper said, "It's looking as it should look."

"And how is that?"

"Like the Old Mare's Mountains we saw in the Sweetwater stream."

Blackjack, picking his way through a slide of boulders and dead branches, didn't respond.

The foxes trotted on, agilely slipping their way up the mountain. The bright red of Basil's pelt became a flame to follow in the deepening twilight. Finally, at the crest of a ridge, Basil sat down and peered over the edge, his ears pricked forward. A gust of wind ruffled his coat, and he turned to Piper, his yellow eyes bright.

"It's around here somewhere, the Old Mare's den."

Piper tested the air. "I don't smell anything. Nothing unusual."

"Then we'll have to wait for her." Basil worked his forepaws forward and settled into a hollow in the ground. Dill slipped to his shoulder and curled against him.

"There's nothing here to eat," said Hank. "How long do we have to wait?"

"Perhaps we should try calling her," Alvin suggested. The Standardbred's look was eager. "Shall we?"

"If you like," said Piper.

Alvin raised his muzzle and let loose a ringing whinny. It echoed off the mountainside, and the world fell silent.

"How can she live here if there's nothing to eat, nothing to drink?" said Duke. "Are you sure this is the place, Basil?"

The fox grinned, and worked his way closer into the ground.

"I knew there was something wrong about this," muttered Blackjack. "These foxes have brought us to the top of the world, Piper. How can we get away if we're attacked? There's nowhere to go."

Piper looked back the way they had come. Far below them, the lake they had left at midday glimmered dull grey in the steady rain. He walked to the ridge, stood next to the foxes and peered over the edge. The mountain fell away in an abrupt, sheer drop, a waterfall of stone. Far below, a thin river meandered through the canyon, black rocks poking up from the surface of the fast-running water like men's fingers.

"I think we should leave, right now," said Blackjack.

"No," said Shaker, "we stay here."

The bay shivered in the rain, the singed hair of his coat standing stiffly out from his chest and barrel.

"That's the most convincing reason of all to leave," said Blackjack. The Walker backed away from the bay, teeth bared, ears flat. "Come on, Piper. I don't like this place at all." His haunches collided with a large boulder immediately behind him, and he pawed the ground. "I don't see how a mare could live here, much less an aged mare."

"That's because I'm staring straight into your butt," said an ancient, crabbed voice. "If you could peer up your own backside, sonny, you might see something of interest. Then again—you might not."

Blackjack sprang away from the boulder to Piper's side. They all looked at the stone, astonished.

There was a slow, grinding movement, and the shape they had mistaken for a boulder in the deepening twilight moved, unfolded, and an ancient mare stood on the mountain top. Her lower lip hung loose. Whiskers bristled from her chin. Her belly sagged; she was so swaybacked that the horn of any saddle placed on her back would have been level with her croup.

Her eyes were sharp, at odds with her knobby knees and clubbed feet. She shuffled forward and darted a look at Blackjack.

"This'll teach you to take me for granite, sonny." She swung her head and regarded Piper. "So. What are you all up here for? It's a lonely place for horses from the world of men. I don't get too many visitors, I can tell you that. Men, once in a while, who come here by mistake, so I just ignore them and stay asleep. Horses, now, and foxes, that's a different matter. Been too many visitors here lately." She sighed, "You want something? I don't have it. You come to see somebody? It ain't me. You lost? You can go down or go down, take your choice."

"You don't know me, ma'am," said Piper. "But I have been sent here to speak with you."

"*You* have!" She peered at him through her sparse grey lashes. "You're a healthy looking young stallion, if I do say so myself." She drew her lips back from her teeth, and chuckled a little. "But I'm all past that, you know. Wouldn't be proper."

Piper arched his neck. His crest curved high and his mane blew in the wind. "I came as a messenger from the Courts," he said. "I have a message from Jehanna, the Goddess Mare to Equus."

"You do. Well, now, you haven't got the look of the Courts about you—you look like you come straight from the world of men. Things changed there since I visited last? They taking mortals now?"

"No," said Piper. "I came to talk with you of a mistake that has been made, and to ask you to right it."

"I don't make mistakes, sonny. Leastways, not often. And I don't take kindly to young sprouts telling me things. Making demands. Nossir."

"Ma'am," said Alvin humbly, "we would ask you to listen just for a moment to what Piper has to say. We've come all this way to speak with you—please don't turn us away."

The Old Mare switched her tail, and mumbled her lips.

"You could at least listen," said Blackjack. "Events are occurring without your knowledge, ma'am. Events you may not like, once you hear of them."

"Someone's not telling me something? That Owl hasn't been around much, I'll give you that. Well then, make it quick. I'm going to sleep soon. Night's coming on and I don't stay up much past dark."

"You spoke with Equus himself some suntimes ago," said Piper. "Do you remember, ma'am?"

"Equus. Yeah, I guess I did. He was complaining about something. A buckskin mare who's in the Havens. He said I shouldn't have called the Appaloosa to the Havens. That she had live get upon the earth."

"I am one of those get," said Piper.

"You are. Well." She ambled closer. She stood against Piper's bulk, small but somehow powerful. "Spotted hide in the right places," she muttered. "And the muzzle's right, with them pink spots around the dun." She looked at Piper's feet. "Striped hooves . . . lemmee see your eyes, sonny." She peered up, her breath grassy and sour in Piper's muzzle. "White sclera, dark brown pupil. You're an Appy, alright. Blame it." She stepped back, considering. "You whole?"

"Yes," said Piper, "as you should be able to scent, ma'am. I am a stallion, not a gelding."

"You got foals on the ground?"

"Yes," said Piper arrogantly. "Many."

"Don't get puffed up with me, pal. How many?"

Piper shook his head. "Each spring, I breed mares.

Only a few from my herd fail to catch. And most bear the foals to term."

"They all Appaloosas?" She wrinkled her muzzle, and her teeth showed blunt yellow. "Don't you tell me that all of 'em are Appy's. I won't believe it."

"Almost all," said Piper. "All bright-colored at birth, and most do not grey out."

"And your name, stallion."

Piper drew himself up. Despite the dark and the rain and snow, his spotted hindquarters gleamed. "I am Sweetwater's Dancing Piper. Out of Duchess the buckskin mare. And by the Dancer, known as the Rainbow Horse, first in the Army of One Hundred and Five."

"You have the look of him," the Old Mare said unexpectedly. "And of that buckskin, too. A sweet thing she is—was, I should say."

"Then you will call her from the Havens, ma'am, so that she may set her hooves on the Green Road, and come to the Courts in safety."

"Whoo-EE," said the Old Mare. "Aren't we something. Aren't we the tough guy."

"You must, ma'am," said Alvin, gently. "You said yourself that if the Dancer's foals are alive and well upon the earth that a mis . . . that Duchess should take her place as Breedmistress to the Appaloosa in the Courts of the Outermost West."

"You were there, at the Pool?" said the Old Mare. "I don't remember you at all. Not at all."

"I heard of it, ma'am," said Alvin simply. "Everything you spoke and told Jehanna is held fast in my heart."

"Well, now." She softened and her eyes crinkled a little. "There's a lot of fuss over this-here buckskin mare. You realize that, don't you? A lot of fuss. I got a visitor last week about this very matter." She wrinkled her muzzle and coughed a little. "Thing is, this visitor asked me to keep this mare in the Havens. This visitor said I was right all along to call that mare off the Green Road and into the Havens. Said not to worry if anybody shows up tellin' me different."

"What visitor was this?" said Piper. His heart thumped in his chest, and his muscles tensed. "Where was this visitor from?"

"Oh—here and there." The Old Mare looked vaguely into the darkness. "There was this bargain struck . . ." She shook her head. "You horses. You are such a pain in the tail. I guess I'd better show you what's been happening while you all have been coming to see me."

"So you did expect us," said Blackjack under his breath. "You do know who we are."

The Old Mare flicked an ear in the Walker's direction. "Come with me. Not all of you—no." She regarded the geldings for a long moment. "Piper, you come, and you, pal, the big black one. Follow me round this rock. There's not enough room for the rest of you and I hate to be crowded. Won't be crowded, as a matter of fact, so the rest of you stand there and wait for us. Dill—you keep an eye out on 'em and don't let 'em wander around loose. Might fall off the mountain." She nodded her head authoritatively at Piper and Blackjack. "Come on, boys. Don't stand there looking stupid." Moving more swiftly than Piper thought possible, she disappeared into the dark. Hesitantly, he and Blackjack followed.

She walked ahead of them in the darkness, stumbling over rocks, muttering and stopping now and then to grumble "What now, what now, what now," in glum irritation. She led them past a sudden upward thrust in the rocks, and there in the side of the mountain was the mouth of a cave, glowing a quiet green in the wind-whipped dark. She bulked against the light and went in, Piper and Blackjack at her heels.

The light in the cave seemed to come from the granite walls themselves. A thin coating of green plants grew up the walls, disappearing into the darkness. Piper couldn't sense where the ceiling to the cave began; the currents of air told him that the roof was far above them. A slow trickling of water reached him, and he gazed curiously around. On the far wall, a waterfall slid almost noiselessly into a pool.

Blackjack whinnied eagerly and moved forward, ready to drink.

"Don't do that," the Old Mare snapped. "That's my water. It helps me sleep and it keeps me young. I ain't about to share it with the likes of you. It's my pool. It's where I Watch and where I Name. You stay away from it." She switched her tail and said gruffly, "There's water outside for you. I'll show you when we go back. But this wouldn't be good for you—trust me. Now," she grunted, and shifted heavily on her feet. "You come up beside me and watch, and keep your questions to yourselves, mind. I probably shouldn't be showing this to you anyways."

"Then why show us at all, ma'am?" said Blackjack. "Why not just call Duchess from the Havens, and let us go home in peace?"

"Because I don't think you can go home in peace, that's why. I can't call this mare *onto* the Green Road. That little Arab Jehanna will have to do it. But I can *release* that buckskin. But you gotta do something for me in return. And believe me, it isn't for me anyways—it's for you."

"I don't know what you mean," said Blackjack.

"Then shut up, so you can learn something."

"This visitor you had—the one that said Duchess

belonged in the Havens," Piper said. "Was this visitor from . . . some place other than the Courts?"

"You're not as dumb as you look."

"But not from the world of man."

"Nope. You got that right too. This visitor," she smacked her lips, "this visitor told me I was right to call this buckskin mare. I like to be right." Her head dipped low and she breathed into the rippling waters of the pool. "I don't know if I like to be right this time, though. Watch, you two, and you tell me if you think I'm right."

THE VISION IN THE POOL: The Gathering

Bruise-struck sky, shot with lightning, hung over the wasted earth. Grass was sparse here; what patches grew were sickly and yellow under a chancey sun. The rest was sand, fine-ground, that stung the eyes, insinuating into ears and mouth. A trail snaked through the land. Pocked with holes and muck, it steamed in the fetid air. On the far horizon, the Black Barns swelled, red fire in the distant open door.

Three gates barred the desperate looking road. The first and third were shut.

Nothing moved in the desolation surrounding the gates. At the second, a thorn tree grew over an oily Pool; at the Pool stood a black mare.

She was beautiful, with a dished muzzle, and finely carved head and slender legs. When she moved, shifting slightly in the sand to Watch the troubled water, it was with the graceless movements of a soul long dead and rotting.

El Arat. The Soul Taker. Once Dreamspeaker, and now demon with eyes that reflected death.

El Arat stood at her Watching Pool and breathed on the muck-filled surface. An image appeared, slowly, and she blew out in satisfaction. A buckskin mare stood stiff, unseeing, in the middle of a swirling green mist. "Move," El Arat whispered. "Just once, for me."

The creamy head swung blindly, ears swiveled forward. The buckskin lifted one foreleg, and set it down again and the mare's entire body stiffened with the shock of pain. Brief awareness flared in the mare's brown eyes, and a high-pitched cry sounded once.

"Stand then," El Arat hissed. "And forget, once more, I will pull your soul from you like a bridled bird. Soon."

She breathed out sharply, and the image disappeared into the sulfurous depths of the Watching Pool.

El Arat moved from the Pool's crumbling banks and stood underneath the branches of the thorn tree. The path that ran by the Pool smoked in the dry air. Stagnant water stood in the holes left by the passage of many claws, hooves, paws and feet. El Arat inhaled deeply, despite the choking stench. She had grown used to it.

"Mistress." Scant, Pack Leader of the Harrier Hounds, crept out from behind the thorn break. His body was gaunt, the ribs high and stark beneath his coat. His eyes gleamed dull red in his skull head, and his tongue rolled long, rotten with carrion and dried blood. He licked his lipless mouth and grinned. "It is time. My Master calls you. Come."

El Arat raised her head to the sullen sky, and flicked her tail insolently. Scant's skull head hung heavy on his whippet's frame. Where he walked, black flies circled, clustering at the base of his tail, crawling at the corners of his lipless grin. "It is TIME!" he howled. "The moon is dark, and the sun behind the clouds."

El Arat drew her muzzle over her teeth. "I'll be there—when I wish it. Get out. And take your companions with you." She flicked her long black tail at the flies, then snapped like a striking snake. She spat a fly out with an explosive PAH!

"He calls you now, mistress." Scant paused, then hissed. "If you would like an escort, my hounds will be glad to accompany you." He yowled once, twice, and once again. An eerie chorus came in answer, and the ground heaved and settled beneath his clawed feet.

El Arat tossed her head, mane flying in the still air. Even she feared the Pack in full cry. She struck out suddenly in a vicious kick. The Hound ducked away. "Walk on before me, Scant. You will play none of your tricks behind."

Scant ran ahead on the stinking path, taking care to avoid the steaming holes.

"And what is it he wants from you, the Master?" Scant threw over his back. "What plans are moving forward, Soul Taker, that he demands to see you now, when the moon is down and black?"

El Arat looked at him briefly, and he slunk close against the road, his belly dragging. El Arat's eyes destroyed her beauty; slanted in her elegant head, their color was that of a muddied stream.

They walked on to the Black Barns, the heat hanging over the land like a woolen blanket. They approached the Third Gate; it swung open, and El Arat looked uneasily over her withers. "Anor is loose?" she asked.

Scant grinned. "There was a call from the Pit this morning, charmed one. He went in answer. As to where he might be right now—" They rounded a twist in the road, "—why there!"

El Arat stopped in mid-stride. The Executioner

stood in the middle of the road, his hindquarters facing them, his bulk barring the way. He was a dull red, the color of a crusted wound, his body ropy with muscle. His head was down. His clawed feet held a horse's body fast against the dirt. El Arat heard the tearing, sucking sounds of a large carnivore, feeding. She closed her eyes to slits, and made a wide circle around him. The hot-copper scent of blood struck her as she passed, and she wrinkled her nostrils shut.

Anor swung his head up in a dazed satiation. One yellow eye gleamed at her, the other was empty, crusted shut from an ancient wound. His sharp teeth dripped blood, and something worse.

"Anor lost that eye because of you, did he not?" Scant mused as they trotted past. "I do believe, o beautiful mare, that he's never forgiven you that." El Arat snorted. Scant grinned, "Makes you anxious, doesn't it? Makes you nervous."

Scant sidled close to her. "Anor speaks through me and me alone, Soul Taker. He tells me things—and I? I may or may not pass them on. We are a force to be reckoned with, I and my pack . . . and the Executioner.

"Ally yourself with me, Soul Taker. Tell me why you are called to Him. Tell what transpires between you. Together, we can do much, you and I and the Red One." His eyes glinted up at her, and El Arat's hindquarters bunched with the effort not to kick.

"You cannot do for me what He can," she said. "Move out, carrion, and save your schemes for others."

Scant slid out of kicking range; he looked up and sat down.

They had reached the huge overhead doors of the Black Barns.

The Barns towered high and dark against the sulfurous sky. The doors were open against the furnace heat. Beyond the open door stretched pitch black darkness, broken by a fiery glow at the distant end. To the right of the barns lay the desert of the Soulless Legions, to the left snaked the Path to the Pits, strewn with the bones of creatures who met the Final Death at Anor's teeth and claws. The mouth of the Pit gaped wide and dark; two spotted ponies struggled up the grade, pulling a cart piled high with stones. They were patched with sweat, and their ribs sprang high through their staring coats. A skeletal Legion rider drove the cart. He pulled the ponies up with a muttered curse, the twisted wire snaffled their mouths spraying thick blood on their muzzles. He bowed to El Arat, who turned away, then reached down and pulled a lever underneath the cart seat. Stones emptied from the back of the cart in a noisy heap. The driver jumped to the ground, took a widemouthed shovel, and began to reload the stones in the cart. One of the ponies sighed and sank to its knees. Its companion sniffed at it incuriously.

"UP! UP!" snapped Scant. The hound sprang forward and raked the fallen pony's flank with his claws. It struggled to its feet. El Arat turned her back. She struck at the threshold of the Black Barn's door with her hooves; the red light from its depths dimmed and flared again, and she and Scant stepped in.

Silence held the Great Aisle, complete and total except for a rhythmic, massive sussuration, like the breath of a giant beast. El Arat's eyes accustomed themselves to the hot dark.

On either side of the Great Aisle were stalls of iron oak. Small barred windows were set high into each door. The Souls were here, locked in. They made no sound at all as El Arat and Scant passed by.

The aisle ended in an immense three-sided stall. A dark cloud roiled inside, fire in its center. The giant breath came and went, came and went, hot against El Arat's cheek. Scant bellied low to the concrete floor beside her, whining.

El Arat danced forward, eagerness and fear in her gait.

"The moon is dark," said El Arat. "And I am here, Lord."

She waited. The fires burned steadily in front of her. She shifted a little. Her hooves scraped on the concrete floor.

"Mare!" The fire flared up and down again. The Voice which came from it was calm, slow, and evil. "Tell me how the world goes by."

"Well, Lord," said El Arat.

"The buckskin mare has joined us at last? I do not see her before me."

El Arat flattened her ears at the deceptive mildness in the tones. "Not yet, Lord," she said.

"She tried to call the buckskin's soul again, just now," said Scant. "And she failed, as she has failed before." Scant crawled eagerly forward. "I heard her. Each time El Arat calls the buckskin's soul to join us here, in your domain, the mare moves. And each time she moves she remembers that she is Duchess, and her soul retreats from El Arat's grasp. I do not think that this black mare of ours will succeed in her plans to bring Duchess and the Dancer here to you, Lord. Let *me* set upon this buckskin mare with my pack, and bring her here, so that you may seek your proper revenge for the insults this breed had heaped upon us all."

El Arat moved like a striking snake, sinking her teeth deep into the Hound's mottled neck. She shook Scant back and forth and he howled with a sound like nails on slate.

"Enough!" the Dark Horse said.

His fires flared high, and in their light, he moved, a dead shadow. El Arat dropped Scant to the floor and faced her Master.

"This plan you have, Soul Taker, that we may rule the horse in the world of man—you assured me that it would work." The voice dropped to mock-pleading, "Take me, O Lord, you said, and give me twin foals. They will grow, Lord, and where there was only one Soul Taker, there will be three—and no horse will be able to escape our Call." He paused. There was an ominous silence. "I gave you a single task, Soul Taker, to get that buckskin mare here, in front of me. To find that spotted fool the Dancer and ruin him!" A sudden burst of flame shot to the ceiling, and thick smoke bellowed upward. Scant hid his skull's head between his paws. El Arat looked steadily into the inferno. "And instead, we have plots. Changes. Petitions. You have not obeyed my Order—yet you come to me and ask for more? Ambition, El Arat, is not a talent I encourage. And it seems you have a talent for ambition."

"I managed to get the Namer of Names to call the buckskin off the Green Road, did I not?" El Arat asked. Her tones verging on the insolent, she pawed the aisle. "And the Dancer himself wanders on the Green Road near her, and he will not leave her." She lowered her lids over her eyes and looked straight into the flames. "It should take little effort to have the Dancer pass into the Heavens to find her. And when he does—when he does, the entire Appaloosa breed will be lost." She laid her ears against her skull, and her eyes gleamed a fierce yellow. "And at last you will be revenged, Lord."

There was a restless shifting in the heart of the flames.

"You would not have tried to trick me, Soul Taker," the voice asked mildly. "You *could* not try to trick me, Soul Taker. Could you?"

"No, Lord. You asked to have the buckskin mare caught, and so she is. You asked to have the spotted horse destroyed, and so he will be. He will not leave the Green Road without her. But why stop at merely this? It is a small thing to force the Dancer from the Green Road and to the oblivion of the Heavens." She stepped eagerly forward, "We can . . . *you* can rule where you should rule, all horses in the world of man. If, as you have promised me, where there was one there shall be three. I come to you Lord, to ask you to take me as a stallion takes a mare. For if I bear twin foals, they will be born Soul Takers. No horse can escape our Call. We will surround the dying and bring them home."

There was a deep, dark silence. The Dark Horse laughed. The laughter filled the Barns, spiraling up to the leaden sky, spreading the breadth of the desert wastes.

"As we agreed. Where there is one, there must be three."

Scant looked sidelong at El Arat. His tongue flicked out between his teeth. El Arat stepped forward. The banked fires rose in a brief flare, and for a moment, the black mare's eyes shone a clear brown and she looked as she must have been as a maiden mare, young, innocent, with a blameless life before her.

Fear and desire shook her, took her, as a fox takes a rabbit.

She walked slowly into the Dark Lord's pen.

Scant waited.

The hushed roar of the Dark Lord's breathing quickened.

El Arat screamed, in such pain even Scant froze where he stood.

A burst of flame shot high, and the Dark Horse stood revealed in the center of the blast, massive and cold in the midst of flame, his body covering the agonized mare.

The flame died.

Silence settled like a cloak.

El Arat stumbled from the pen in triumph, her hindquarters splashed with blood.

"Where there is one, there must be three!" she cried.

"What's this?" Scant howled. "What's this?"

"And so it has happened, mare. There will be two fillies born to you, if Scant and his Pack do not get to them first. If you succeed . . ." The dark clouds in the Dark Lord's pen rolled. "Then we shall rule as we have never ruled before. The White Fool shall bow before me yet!"

"Not if the Dancer travels the Green Road to the Courts," said Scant. "There is that little matter to be taken care of, Lord."

The flames dimmed and glowed dull red. "This is true," the voice said slowly, consideringly. "You make me promises, El Arat. You must deliver the souls of the Appaloosa Breedmaster and Breedmistress to me. Here. Soon."

El Arat bowed, her mane flowing over her withers. "I will, Lord. I promise."

The fire rose in a sudden burst. A tongue of flame leaped from its center. It licked Scant's forepaws and the hound screamed and scuttled backwards. It curled around El Arat's neck, and she stood unmoving. The smell of singed hair filled the air. El Arat stepped calmly backward. Scant licked his forepaws with a keening whine. The floor beneath their feet began to shake, and a thunderclap burst over their heads.

"BACK!" the voice cried.

The rumbling died as a storm does when it passes in the distance. El Arat and Scant walked down the great aisle. As they passed the iron-bound stalls, a faint scrabbling followed them, the sound of blinded creatures seeking their way to freedom.

Even the sullen daylight was better than this, and El Arat breathed out in relief when she and Scant reached the overhead door.

The pit ponies were gone, dragging their load of stones back to the Pit. Anor was gone, as well, and as they passed the Third Gate, they saw that it was shut. The torn body of what once had been a chestnut mare lay to one side of the gate.

El Arat walked slowly back to her Pool, Scant trailing behind.

"So you carry young Soul Taker," he said. "Young—and great hopes for them."

"Get out," said El Arat briefly. She swung her hindquarters to him, ready to kick, and the Hound slid away and grinned.

"Twin fillies, no doubt." He yawned, the corrupt flesh of his tongue flaking onto the sandy earth. The flies rose around him in a small cloud, then settled in his ears. "And what will their names be, El Arat? I must tell my Pack."

El Arat gazed into the dark water of her pool, and did not reply.

Scant edged nearer, and peered into the water's depths. "Do you see them?" he said.

El Arat shook her head.

"What will you do? How do you plan to get the Dancer to join her in the Havens? You fooled the Namer once . . . can you fool her again?"

"I do not need the Namer of Names to do what I must do," said El Arat. "Not that it's any concern of yours, hound."

She raised her head and whinnied long and loud.
The cry rose up and passed into the distance.

They waited.

A drumming came from the desert wastes. The
sound of many hooves shook the air. Dust rose in a
yellow cloud from the desert south of the Black Barns.

"The Legion!" hissed Scant. "The Legion rides!"

The ground shook. Legion Riders appeared from
the bowels of the cloud. Skeletal riders, dead white
hair flying, red eyes blank, set astride the Soulless
Horses. The animals galloped without spirit, heads
down, completely obedient to whip and spur.

El Arat watched them come, her eyes half-closed.
"Their ranks will swell by thousands, once my foals
are born," she said. Her tones were low and guttural, a thick satisfaction in her voice. "Each horse
in the world of men will ride with them. Soon. Very
soon."

Scant turned his head to face the on-coming horde.
El Arat, seeing her chance, kicked him swiftly in the
side, and the Hound rolled yowling to the edge of the
Pool. The waters rose to take him, and he shrieked,
leaping to the safety of the bank. He shook himself,
then slunk to the patchy shade of the thorn trees.

"You foolish piece of dung! You're sending them to
chase the Dancer from the Green Road?" he spat.

"Oh, yes," said El Arat.

"The Green Road goes one way," he growled.
"You are a fool. It takes the living from the world of
the men. Those who walk it are dead. You'll lose the
entire Legion in your drive for revenge. He won't be
pleased with you, I guarantee it."

"But the Legion, Scant, is dead already." El Arat
walked forward to meet the First Rider, her tail
flagged high in triumph.

*   *   *

The Old Mare breathed on the Waters of her stream with a quick burst of angry air. "Tricked," she said grimly. "Tricked! Me, a member of the Council of the One."

Blackjack and Piper stood frozen, looking into the imageless waters.

"Can you believe this?" the Old Mare demanded. "Cheek, I call it."

"I cannot," said Piper. "I cannot believe that the One would allow the balance to be overset like this. How can this happen?"

"I don't mean that, sonny. I mean—the nerve of that black cow. I ask you. Things are not what they used to be. They are not." She switched her tail, coughed once, then cocked her head sideways at Piper.

"The Balance," said Piper, urgently. "The Law of the Balance. What is good without evil to Balance it? What is evil without good to shadow it?"

"Why do you think you were allowed to see this?" said Namer sharply. "I don't open my Pool to every cocky stallion that wanders up here, you know. You're smack in the middle of this, Piper. And you got it in one guess: that dark devil is trying to challenge the Balance. Can you believe it? The nerve! The nerve!" She worked her lips in irritation.

"Well you know, or you should, kiddo, that we all can't do much to save you—you gotta do it yourself. 'What is good without evil to Balance it? What is evil without good to shadow it?' Like it or not, Piper, you're the good guys, and if you decide to do something about this mess, then maybe you can save your breed. If you don't—looks like those stalls in the Barns'll be chock-full."

Piper turned to face her. The dim green light of the Namer's cave revealed the splendid lines of his haunches, illuminated the graceful curve of his powerful neck.

"Of course I will do what I can," he said. "You must tell me what to do."

"I can't tell you what to do," the Old Mare said sharply, "that's the whole point. I can give you some information which could help you, but you gotta do what you gotta do without any direction from me, or from anyone else on the Council."

Piper bowed his head. His eyes were large and dark. A fierce anger burned in them. "Very well. Give me the information."

"You tell Jehanna it's okay by me to walk down the road and call Duchess to the Courts. I seen you, and you look pretty healthy." She stopped, mumbled her lips together and muttered, "And I don't like being tricked the way I was. So, Jehanna reaches Duchess before these Riders do, and she and the Dancer will be all right."

"And if she doesn't?" asked Blackjack quietly.

The Old Mare shrugged. "Up to you."

"This was your mistake, Namer," Blackjack persisted. "Why don't you fix it?"

"It wasn't a mistake, it was trickery!" the Old Mare shouted. "We don't intervene. You know that. It's the Way of the One. Your destiny belongs to *you*—not to me. We start things. We finish things. You change them, if you can. Now you shut up and listen. Duchess and the Dancer try to walk the Green Road on their own with them Legion Riders after them, and they won't get far. Jehanna's gonna need some help."

"The Army of One Hundred and Five," Blackjack said. His breath quickened in excitement.

"Maybe. That's up to the Courts. You leave the

Courts unprotected, and anything can happen. But you want some information, I'll give you some. Now," she settled comfortably on her feet, "there's something else I can tell you." She rolled her eye at Piper, who was staring unseeingly at the cave walls. "You listening?"

"Yes," said Piper. "Yes."

"Good." She leaned forward and whispered in his ear. Piper jumped and his eyes showed white. Sweat sprang up on his withers. "That there's that damn fool's Name," she said. "You walk into the Black Barns, stand in front of him and Call him that—he's gonna disappear into the Havens like a mouse swallowed by an owl."

"Are you crazy?" shouted Blackjack. "Walk into the Black Barns? We'll be called to the Final Death ourselves!"

"Not if you sneak," said the Old Mare. "And not if you don't get caught." She plodded forward and nosed both of them ahead of her. "Out, now, and back to where your pals are waiting. I don't have all day and all night to stand around gabbing to you."

Piper, his expression grave, walked out of the cave. Blackjack followed. The Old Mare's voice floated past them. "Turn at the large stone and you'll find them others waiting for you. Go on!"

Piper hesitated, turned, and looked back.

"Old Mare!" he said.

Where the mouth of the cave had been was solid rock, a faint green glow to its surface. Piper rose to his hind legs and struck at the wall of stone.

There was no answer.

He stood for a moment, then nodded to Blackjack. Silently, they walked back to their herd.

It began to snow hard, smothering the ground

with large flakes. Piper and Blackjack came around
the boulder leading from the Old Mare's cave, their
heads and necks powdered with the rapid accumula-
tion.

"What happened?" Hank demanded. He sniffed
Piper's withers. "Did she tell you anything? Will
Duchess and the Dancer be all right?"

The wind rose, driving snow into the horses' eyes
and ears. Hank sneezed and shook himself.

Basil rose to his feet. "Did she tell you where we
have to go next?" He bounded through the snow to
Piper's feet. "Did she show you the way?"

"We have to get off this mountain," said Piper.
"Blackjack?" He nodded to the gelding, who turned
to go down the mountain. "We'll stop at the lake.
There's grass and water there, and shelter from this
wind."

"What did she *say*?" Dill hesitated. The vixen
peered up into Piper's face. Her brush lowered
abruptly. "Not too good, hah?"

"Leave him alone until we get down the mountain," said Basil. "You do go on, Dill. He'll tell us
when he's ready."

The trip down the Old Mare's mountain was slippery, cold, and miserable. Piper, silent, was patient
as Duke cautiously tested his footing on the slick
rocks and stood by as Shaker picked his way through
the buffeting wind.

They gathered at the gravel shores of the mountain lake, and stood in a semi-circle with their heads
down and their tails against the gusty wind. The wild
night wore to a close, and Piper, sleepless, stood
deep in thought while the others dozed.

Near morning, the wind dropped, and the brief
storm left as quickly as it had come. The air warmed,
and the snow melted rapidly. Piper left the protec-

tive circle of the herd to go to the lake for a drink. The water was clean and wild, tasting of fish and a pleasant seasoning of dirt. It was cold, and he took short swallows.

He blew at his reflection in the water; it shattered, and re-formed, distorted. A black face appeared near his in the waters of the lake, and he whirled, ready to strike out. Blackjack leaped out of range of his hooves.

"It's just me, Piper."

Piper settled and looked across the lake. The sun crept over the horizon, ray by ray, like a freshwater crab climbing a steep bank.

"Three Soul Takers, and my dam pursued by the Riders of the Legion," he said.

Blackjack nodded, a glint in his eye. "But we know the name of He Who Should Not Be Named," he eagerly burst out. "Think of it, Piper! What mortal horse has ever had the chance we've got? To walk to the Black Barns themselves! To destroy them—forever!" His entire body trembled with eagerness. Piper turned to him, surprised at the energy, the desire for action.

"Piper!" Blackjack looked around, noting that the others were at a distance. He lowered his head and whispered into Piper's ear, "Piper! This is a chance for glory! It will never come this way again!"

"A chance for glory?" said Piper. "Death itself waits for me, Blackjack. The Final Death, perhaps. I cannot take the others with me. I've thought all night about what to do—I must take you with me, Blackjack, and for that I ask your forgiveness. But Duke, Alvin, Hank—they must return to Sweetwater."

"Don't you think you should ask *them* what they want to do?" said Blackjack. "You've no need to ask forgiveness from me, Piper. I would follow you no matter what you said to me. But the others. We cannot deny them this chance."

"You saw the road to the three Gates. You saw the sky—the very land itself. And you looked into the face of the Soul Taker—into the face of evil. And we both saw the dark clouds which surround him, the Dark Horse. We didn't even see the Pit—or hear the cries and whinnies of those who suffer there. Push your imagination further than thoughts of glory and the approving glance of a gold mare, Blackjack. Look at what I am asking you to do."

"Pah!" Blackjack scraped the ground with his foreleg, and looked at Piper sidelong. "Better to die on my feet than in my stall—or on the road in a trailer to another horse show."

Despite himself, amusement colored Piper's voice. "You would have made a brave, if foolhardy stallion, Blackjack." He sighed heavily. "We must tell them of the dangers." He raised his head, then whistled. Hank and Alvin shook themselves awake, and walked down to the lake. Shaker, who had been standing with his eyes fixed on Piper at a distance, trotted forward. Dill and Basil bounced up from the temporary den they had made for themselves in the rocks, and ran to sit at Piper's feet.

"Are you going to tell us what the Old Mare said now?" asked Alvin. "Are you going to tell us if Duchess will be safe?"

"No one is safe," said Piper.

And he told them of the vision he had seen in the Old Mare's Pool.

"This can't be true," said Duke. He was clearly shaken, seeming smaller than ever.

"It's true," said Piper. "And this is what I've decided. I must take one of you with me. There's a better chance that we'll make it to the Great Aisle of the Dark Barns if there are two to carry this task forward. The rest of you must return to Sweetwater. We have three weeks until the moon is full again; it should only take you three days to return to Sweetwater. You must ask Frosty to Walk the Path to the Moon and tell Jehanna what has occurred.

"Blackjack and I will travel to the Black Barns." He looked down at the foxes at his feet. "Basil and Dill know where the Dancer's mountain lies—and it is there that we will find the entrance to the Black Lands. They must guide us there, and then they can return to their home den."

"I want to go with you," said Hank. "What kind of gelding would I be if I deserted my herd in time of trouble? Alvin and Duke can go back on their own."

Piper sighed. "You haven't seen what we have seen, Hank. You have little idea of what waits for us. It is unimaginable."

"I don't care," said Hank. "I'd rather travel with you than go back to Sweetwater and stay in a stall for the rest of my days."

"The Black Barns are worse than any stall in any barn of men, Hank," said Piper quietly.

"We won't end up in the Black Barns," said Hank cheerfully. "You know the name of the Dark Horse, Piper! What mortal horse has ever had this chance!"

Piper looked at Blackjack. The Walker gazed knowingly back. "Are you certain, Hank?" he said.

"I'm certain."

"And I," whispered Shaker. "I must go with you, too."

"You?" said Piper. "No, Shaker. You took the herd oath, to be sure. But these circumstances are unusual. You must go back to your home. Forget what has happened here."

"I have no home," said Shaker. The trembling, which never entirely left him, even in sleep, increased so that he shivered like an aspen leaf in a storm. "My home is burned, and my brothers dead." He moved forward, and said urgently, his voice hoarse, "You don't understand. They call to me, my brothers. I left them in the fire. I left them, and freed myself. Their voices follow me while I stand here with you. I will never be free of them. Not until I redeem myself. I must travel with you, Piper. Do not abandon me to these voices. Do not abandon me to these dreams of fire." His eyes rolled, and Duke moved forward and breathed comfortingly on the bay's back.

Piper raised his muzzle at Alvin and Duke. "The two of you must go to Sweetwater," he said sternly. "Do not ask to go with us. I cannot allow it."

"It doesn't need two of us, does it?" said Duke. "Alvin can go on his own. And I can go with you."

"No," Piper shook his head decisively. "Two of you must go for the same reason that I need another with me. There is too much danger to trust the task to one horse alone."

Alvin stood with his head at a stubborn angle, the same look on his face that he had when he refused to let men pick up his feet for shoeing.

"Don't give me that look," said Piper. "You'll go, Alvin, because I tell you to. I am Lead Stallion, I don't have to remind you of that." He flexed, and the sun glinted on his black neck.

Duke and Alvin looked at each other. Alvin sighed, and dropped his head submissively. He peered up at Piper from his lowered brows. "What if we go to Sweetwater, give the mares the message, then catch up with you?"

"Too risky. We aren't sure when we'll reach the Dancer's mountain—or whether or not we'll even get past the First Gate. You'll go to Sweetwater, and stay there." He took a step forward, and said, "You must understand how important this task is, both of you. The Old Mare will be of no help to us here on in. It is not the way of the One. And Jehanna cannot Watch for us in the Pool. We are in control of what happens now. It is on our backs that the fate of my dam and sire rest. It is I and all of you, who will bear responsibility for the fate of the horses in the world of men. Go back to Sweetwater, and wait for the full moon. Tell Jehanna that the Legion rides, and will reach the Green Road soon."

"I will see Her," said Alvin softly. "Very well. Duke and I will go." He drew his teeth back over his upper lip. "You'll return to Sweetwater, Piper, and tell us everything?"

"Yes," said Piper, "if the gods are willing and we achieve what we must."

The sun was shining brightly now, and the sky was a clear-washed blue. A breeze sprang up and brought with it the scent of spring.

"Basil, Dill," said Piper. "You're willing to show us where the Dancer's mountain lies?"

"Oh yes, we agreed. We knew before we came that we'd have to go there," said Basil. "Are we ready, now?"

"You'll come back," said Duke suddenly. "You'll come back to tell us the end of this Tale?"

"You bet," said Blackjack.

Duke and Alvin, with a farewell glance over their withers, moved slowly down the mountain, to the east and Sweetwater.

• 9 •

The Road to Hell

Piper watched Alvin and Duke trot away from sight, a steady purpose in the set of their heads and hindquarters. The wind blew their scent to him long after they had disappeared. His heart lightened; they would be all right. And once they reached Sweetwater, how could Jehanna fail to answer even little Frosty's confused call? He stood in thought, visions before him.

"Are we ready now?" asked Dill. "The sooner this is over, the better it is for me. I'm not even sure that we should be going with you. It's spring, and we should be getting back to settle down in our den. There'll be cubs later on, you know, so let's move!" The vixen scrubbed at her face with her forepaw, then yipped commandingly for Basil, who had left the horses to hunt for their morning meal.

"How long will it take us, Dill?" asked Blackjack.

"It is west of the sun, and to the Dancer's mountain," said Piper. "We've come west of the sun in search of the Old Mare . . ."

"And the Dancer's mountain is perhaps three turns

of the sun from here," said Dill impatiently. "BASS-SIILLL! Where is that dog? If he doesn't show up soon, I swear I'll leave without him."

"Without me?" said Basil thickly. He popped out of the brush at the lake's edge, a dead rabbit in his mouth. "So I'll eat this myself."

Hank wrinkled his nose in disgust, then rolled his eyes at Blackjack. Shaker gazed dully ahead.

"Rabbit," said Dill, turning the body over and over with her nose, "rabbit. Couldn't you have caught a mouse? You know I don't like to eat this much in the morning." She looked accusingly at Basil, who began busily licking his forepaws. "You *did* catch a mouse! You did! And you ate it yourself." She boxed his ear with her forepaw, the rabbit unheeded beside her. Blackjack, stepping delicately, removed himself upwind.

Basil, cowering under his mate's buffets, rolled his eyes accusingly up at her. "*Rabbit* you said yesterday. That I couldn't catch a rabbit. Well, I've caught a rabbit and if it's too much for you to swallow all at once, *I'll* eat it."

Dill pranced forward and picked the rabbit up daintily between her jaws. "Never mind," she said primly. "It'll do." She settled herself comfortably on the ground, dropped the rabbit and began to chew noisily.

"Would you mind doing that somewhere else?" asked Hank. "It's pretty disgusting."

Dill narrowed her gold eyes to slits. Her tongue lolled. "Well!" she said. "So you think you're going where you're going without seeing a little blood? This is normal, natural, perfectly acceptable behavior for foxes, you. But if it's just too much, why let me know. I would think, however, that someone your size would have a little more backbone." She opened her eyes suddenly. "You're going to need it!"

Basil, with a bored grunt, darted forward, snatched the rabbit, and raced off to the pines. Dill squealed and raced after him.

"We'll be back!" Dill shouted. "And then we'll be ready to . . . ungh!" She crashed into Basil. They rolled over and over and vanished into the trees.

"Only three turns of the sun from here," said Hank. The flesh on his withers rippled, as though a cold wind blew from the mountain. "I don't understand. How can we just expect to walk to the Black Barns? If we can do that, why can't we just walk to the Courts and tell Jehanna herself what we've got to do? Why is the only entrance here in the mountains? And why should it be so close to Sweetwater?"

"Cory told you some of the Tale of the Appaloosa," said Piper. "Part of that Tale only direct descendants of Duchess and the Dancer know.

"When the Dancer assumed his earthly form, he descended from the Path to the Moon in these mountains. It is here, or near here, where he first set foot upon men's earth. You know the Law of the Balance. For each evil in the world there is an opposite good, for each good, an opposite evil. The Dancer came here from the Courts, and he left from here for the Black Barns.

"When the Dancer left Bishop Farm with Duchess, he broke the Law, and tipped the Balance. The only way to right this wrong was to sacrifice himself to the Dark Horse. Anor the Executioner came for him out of the earth and drew him down again. There has been a way to reach the Black Barns ever since from the world of men. And a way to leave the Courts and set foot in these mountains."

"He returned from the Black Barns, didn't he, and

then went on to the Courts?" said Blackjack. "Was it through this way?"

"He did not return to the Courts from here. He travelled the Long Green Road, as we all must. As to how he left the Black Barns, I don't know."

"Did he fight his way free?" asked Hank.

"I believe he did," said Piper, "with Sycha, the First Soultaker, at his side."

"He got the Soultaker to help him?" said Hank. "I don't suppose we'll be that lucky."

Piper thought of El Arat, of her beauty, of her evil eyes and graceless movements. "No," he said after a moment, "I don't suppose we will."

"The Green Road goes one way," whispered Shaker suddenly. "Its entrance is wherever horses die. It is everywhere," he looked around slowly, his eyes bleared, "and nowhere."

"Thank you very much," said Blackjack sarcastically. "This is a great comfort to all of us, and a positive way to begin our journey."

"We'll begin our journey by staying alert—*all* the time," said Piper. "I'll lead, and Blackjack, you bring up the rear. Hank and Shaker stay in the middle. Stay away from thick stands of trees. And if you see or smell anything unusual—run."

"Unusual," said Hank. "Like what?"

"Strange smells. Shapes which don't belong in the forest. Sounds which make no sense. Follow me, and no one, nothing else. We'll graze together, drink together. Don't ever lose sight or smell of the herd. And if I tell you to do something—do it."

"Or what?" asked Blackjack.

Piper looked at him, his dark eyes filled with the memory of what the two of them had seen.

"So let's *begin* our journey," said Dill. Her sudden reappearance made the horses jump. Hank ran for-

ward and reared at her, his hooves landing harmlessly in front of the vixen.

"Now, now, now!" she scolded. "Come on, you
lot. Move out!" Basil close at her heels, she ran a
little way up the trail to the Old Mare's nest and
leaped in the air. "We go up this way, and then west
by west," she yelped. "Move out!"

"West by west," said Hank, bemused. "How can
we go west by west?"

They climbed steadily all that day and part of the
night. They walked carefully, ears up, noses to the
air. The normal sounds of the woods resolved into
strange whispers, and misshapen shadows seemed to
lurk just out of their range of vision. When they
paused to graze and rest, Piper drew Blackjack aside.

"I've been thinking as we travelled today. I must
send Hank and Shaker back."

Blackjack swiveled his ears forward. "Why?"

Piper looked up at the moon. It was sliver-thin, its
light shadowy against the brightness of the stars. He
said slowly, "Dill's right. They are going to see a lot
more blood where we are going. They are moving to
a terror they can only guess at."

"And their hearts may fail them?" guessed Blackjack. "I don't think that's a decision you can make for
them, Piper."

"It's not their hearts I fear for." Piper turned and
looked at the two geldings. They were engaged in
mutual grooming, a practice of trust and affection in
any horse herd. "It's their innocence that will destroy them. Their minds are what I tremble for." He
turned his gaze on Blackjack, his eyes dark and piercing. "You've been around a lot—you rode the Saddle
Seat circuit. Have you ever known a horse whose
mind has been broken through cruelty? Through
fear?"

Blackjack moved uneasily. "I suppose so."

"We all have. Before your time, when Sweetwater was just me, and two mares, and a herd of yearling heifers, David was given a gelding from an auction house. He believed, I think, that he could bring it back to health." The stallion shook his head. "The horse had spur scars on its flanks, white saddle sores on its back. It had no fear for itself at all. No love, no feeling. It ate by himself, stood by itself, did whatever the ranch hands asked of it and no more. Its soul was gone, Blackjack. Wherever it had come from, when it had been broken to ride, its spirit had been broken, too." The stallion stood in the dark, the whites of his eyes gleaming in the faint reflection of the stars. "What they will see and hear will break them. Death is not something any of us in this herd fear. There are no cowards here. But what we saw in the Namer's Pool—that's worse. No glory waiting at the end, just days and nights of . . . nothing."

"You've told them. They know what to expect."

"It's still a Tale to them. And as a Tale, it is not real. Duke's the most honest of you all, you know. He doesn't believe. The Tales are not real to him. The Tales are not real to Hank, or Shaker, for that matter, because they *do* believe, in magic."

"Well, then," said Blackjack practically, "this isn't real to us either, is it? And if it isn't—if what lies ahead is beyond all our imaginings, we could be wrong."

Piper stared at the ground. He took a bite of grass, then dropped it. "I suppose so."

"It's not like you to be uncertain, Piper."

The stallion sighed. "These are uncertain times." He moved, as if he had made up his mind. He lifted his head and whinnied. Hank and Shaker trotted over, heads pushed forward inquiringly. Dill and

Basil melted out of the darkness and sat near Piper's feet.

"We will sleep, soon," said Piper. "And I want you each to guard the herd in turn while the others sleep. I'll sleep first, then Blackjack, then Hank, then Shaker. But before we sleep, I have a Tale to tell you."

"A story!" said Basil. "Good." The foxes settled expectantly.

"Are you good at Storytelling?" demanded Dill.

"Hush, Dill!" Basil said. "It doesn't matter."

"It matters," said Blackjack. "And he's very good."

Amusement flickered in Piper's eyes. "Thank you," he said gravely. "This is the Tale of Equus' choice. Sometimes it's been called the Tale of the Blind Pony. I prefer the former."

THE TALE OF EQUUS' CHOICE

Long ago, when rivers were few and all earth's land was grass, Equus left his place in the Courts to mark out the domain of the horse in the world of men.

He was young then, and curious, and had asked many questions of the One, some which were answered, some which were not.

He left his spoor in the mountains, hills and valleys of all of man's domain, for the One had decreed that the horse was to serve man, in all ways, in return for man's care of the breeds. One day, he came to a valley shorn of grass, under a leaden sky.

The farms were barren, the fields close-sown with stones. The city streets were narrow: in some, the sun beat down on the roads like a hammer, with never a relief from heat; in others, the buildings were built so high that the sun never blessed the road at all, and the men there walked in darkness.

There had been sickness here, and greed, and Equus, saddened, thought that he would pass by the city in the night so that he would not have to see the suffering of any creatures of the One, man and horse alike.

"This is not wise," his heart told him, "for this is part of the world, and your task is to see what you will see. And a stallion does not turn his face from anything in this world or the next."

So Equus passed through the city and saw much that grieved his heart, much that caused his soul to cry aloud for pity. He called on the One—and the One answered only, "What is there is there. Each has made his choice."

Equus passed from the city to a barren field, and found a blind and ancient pony tied to a withered oak. His coat was muddy with dung, and he was balding in places. His hooves had never been trimmed, and they curled up at the toes in sickly moons. An empty water bucket lay sideways at his feet, long dried. There was no hay to be seen, and indeed, the pony had eaten all he could reach of the withered oak, so that great patches of the wood were chewed from the sides of the tree.

"Oh, pony," said Equus sadly, "how long has it been that you've been tied here, neglected and starved by men?"

"Long," said the pony, swinging his head at the sound of Equus' voice, "very long." His tongue, swollen from thirst, protruded from his lips, and he had difficulty speaking. Equus bent his head and kissed the pony's muzzle, gently. "You will come with me, now," he said, "and drink from the stream in the Courts of the Outermost West. You can graze in the pastures of the Blessed Brood Mares. You will never hunger and thirst again, and you may move freely about the Courts, for there are no ropes to bind you there."

The pony blinked and said, "It is my time, then, to Walk the Green Road?"

Equus looked closely at him, at the cracked and peeling lips of his muzzle, the white clouds in his eyes, the belly swollen with starvation. But the spark of mortal life still lived in the Pony's eye, and Equus knew he could not take the wretched creature with him, for no horse Walks the Green Road before its time, such is the Law of the One.

"My master comes for me some mornings," said the pony. "Walk on, stranger, and let me be. I will Walk the Green Road when it is time."

"I will break this rope and free you for this man has served you ill," said Equus, growing angry.

"Other men may not. Evil comes, evil goes. It is our Bargain with Man, isn't it? That we must serve them no matter how they serve us? Is this not the Law of the One?"

Equus thought a moment, and he said, "What if, pony, I were to take your place, and serve your master for you? You could run free, and the horse's Bargain with your master would be fulfilled."

"My word is all I have now, stranger. All I am. If I allow you to release me, will I have not broken my word? Will I ever earn the right to be judged as worthy in Summer, and find my way to the Courts of Equus himself, blessed be his name?"

"I will disguise myself. Your master will never know the difference."

Hope sprang in the pony's blind eyes, but he said, "He beats me with a whip."

"I see the scars," said Equus.

"I thirst," the pony said, "enough to die of it."

"Then I, thanks be to the One, may meet you sooner on the Green Road than later," said Equus.

"Very well," said the pony. And so they exchanged places, and the pony set hoof on the road to freedom and Equus stood in his place, tied to the withered oak.

The sun rose, the heat fell on the land like a wool blanket, and Equus felt hunger. Thirst. And when the pony's master finally came, with a bucket of scum-filled water and a twist of musty hay, he beat Equus with a willow whip so that his hide was crossed with rivers of welling blood.

Equus' world grew dim about him, and then altogether black. Like the pony, he lost his vision from starvation. His hair flew in great patches from his glorious white coat. His knee bones ached.

One night when the moon was high, although Equus could not see it, the pony returned, smelling of clean water, tasting of sweet grass.

"Is it time for you to Walk the Green Road?" asked Equus. "If it is, I can be released."

"Not quite," said the pony. "But if you wish, Equus, I will exchange places with you again."

Equus pushed temptation from him as a bird pushes its young from the nest. "I cannot," he said. "I gave my word to serve your master, and now I am in the same trap you were in. Oh pony, it is not wise to interfere with the ways of the One. I will wait until your time has come."

"YOU WILL WAIT NO LONGER," said the pony in a voice that held all of the earth around, and all that's above and beneath it. "YOU WILL COME WITH ME NOW." Equus, blind and staring, dropped to his knees, for he knew he was in the presence of the voice of the One.

"Evil comes," said the One, "and because of you,

Equus, evil shall always go. As long as the horse keeps faith in the Bargain. As long as the horse keeps faith."

And Equus returned to the Courts to live in glory ever after.

"Well for goodness sake!" said Dill indignantly. "What kind of half grown tale is that? That pony should have ripped its master to bloody pieces, that's what I would have done."

"You're a creature of the wild," said Piper. "We are creatures of men."

"Well, I mean to say, it's not fair, is it?" muttered Basil. "I ask you!"

"It is our justice," said Piper. "It is our code. We obey—and find our reward only in the Courts themselves."

"Most horses are never faced with this choice, however," grumbled Dill in disgust. "For the Spade's sake, Piper, what a test. What a Tale to tell your herd mates!"

"I want them to go back," said Piper.

"I'm not afraid," said Hank. He faced Piper, his eyes clear. "And neither is Blackjack. But Shaker here, now perhaps Shaker would consider going back to Sweetwater. Not because you are afraid, Shaker, or that you think you might make the wrong choice, but because you haven't yet recovered from the barn fire. You give yourself time to rest. Leave now, and you can still catch up with Duke and Alvin."

"I will never recover from the fire if I go to Sweetwater," whispered Shaker. "Don't plague me with choices, horse. I must let my voices go. I must free them. They must leave me, or I will go mad."

A furrow appeared between Hank's eyes, and he bit Shaker gently on the poll. "Well then," said

Hank, turning to face his stallion once again. "We're ready when you are."

They slept briefly and their dreams were troubled. Piper dozed, woke, and dozed again. In the morning, Basil and Dill led them up the mountainside, "west by west." They climbed all that day and the next, stopping only to graze and sleep in a granite pocket poorly sheltered from the chill night wind. The moon shone dim and diffused behind a heavy cloud bank. The breeze carried strange odors and odd signs, and once or twice, they found a dead crow in the forest. A whispering came to Piper, voices that called to him just below the level of his senses. While the others slept, he stood guard, restless, head up, nostrils wide, ears pricked forward, listening.

Those who face the Dark Horse die.

Did the voices call to him? Was there a sound slipped among them that called only to him?

Those who face the Dark Horse die.

On the third day, just before dawn, the wind dropped and the clouds overhead thickened to an opaque veil. Piper circled the travelling band restlessly, at an impatient trot. The earth shifted, rumbled beneath his hooves, and he felt the movement of many horses climbing upward several furlongs away. He nudged Blackjack silently, nodding to him to stand guard, and walked through the rocks to the origins of the sounds the ground had sent him.

He climbed down a short gully, then up again to a high ridge. He stood there, his patterned coat keeping him invisible against the night sky, and looked down.

Men and horses were coming out of the earth below him.

They walked out of a gaping hole. From the mouth of the tunnel in the earth came the banked coal light of fire. Each horse and rider emerged and carried the glow beyond the yawning cave. Illuminated with the eerie flames-which-were-not-flames were skeletons of men's bones covered, held together, by a tough, leathery covering of skin. Piper snorted in soft revulsion; the skin had the scaly look and scent of snakes. Each rode a horse. Piper watched, and his heart pulsed strongly in his chest. The horses were somehow alive and not alive. Piper could scent hair and bone, but it was of creatures long dead, struck by a hot sun perhaps, so that blood and muscle were dried away, leaving nothing else. The horses' eyes were dimly red, and Piper knew, without knowing how he knew, sightless. They walked in time together, so that as they streamed from the tunnel mouth—a hundred riders and more—the hollow sound of their hooves began as a whisper, then rose to a four-beat boom.

The wind stirred all around Piper as he stood there, bringing him the scents of creatures long dead, who moved as if alive.

The only sound was the scrape of a hundred hooves on stone—ONE!

Striking like a giant hammer—TWO!

A lifeless train of souls—THREE!

The Soulless Legion Riders—FOUR!

Piper willed himself to stand and be silent.

As each of the Legion Riders gained the lip of a burning hole, the red glow they carried with them died. They became men and horses like those Piper knew from the world of rodeos and ranches. Alike, except that on the quarters of each horse, a brand smoked in the cool spring air, a black crescent like the hole the half moon would leave if it fell from the sky.

His mark. The Dark Lord's mark. And these were his demons, sent out in the world of men.

Piper drew back from the ridge. His hooves sent a pebble rattling down the crevasse. It bounced and lay still.

The Lead Rider drew rein, raised his head and turned, seeking the origin of the sound. The great muscles in Piper's hindquarters clenched and he fought the impulse to leap down and attack them with teeth and hooves. The Lead Rider scanned the ridge, eyes glowing red in the skull-head. Soulless eyes. Eyes of the damned. The fiery gaze swept past Piper. The Rider raised the claw of his hand and gestured forward. The Legion disappeared, cloaked in the guise of mortals.

The clouds in the sky overhead thinned, became transparent, and the weak-lit moon shone down on the empty valley. Piper's teeth gleamed. He rolled his upper lip back from his teeth and stifled the war cry that rose in his chest. A night bird's cry rose and died among the stars. Below him, the orange-red fire in the hole died back and the tunnel mouth grew dark.

Piper turned swiftly to get the others.

"So, you found it," said Dill after a swift upward look at his face. "The First Gate."

"There was a rumbling in the earth," said Hank. "Was that it?"

"The Soulless Legion, sent off to search for us, I suppose," said Piper. "We'll slip through the First Gate now, before they discover they've followed the wrong trail."

He stopped and bent his great head to the vixen's. The rising sun turned his coat to glowing speckles. "You may leave us now, Dill, you and Basil. Thank you for your guidance."

"Just did what we were told to do," said Basil gruffly. "Time for us to get back to our den, Dill, right?"

Dill looked from horse to horse, ears flattened against her silky head. She growled deep in her throat, "Off with you, off with you. *Quietly*, mind."

Piper bunched the geldings closely together and led them back the way he had come. Shaker inhaled sharply as they approached the entrance. The hole steamed a little in the cool mountain air. There was a scent of rotting flesh.

"It smells bad," said Hank, "but it doesn't look too bad." He pawed doubtfully at the lip of the tunnel. Gravel spilled beneath his hoof and cascaded down. They listened, waiting for the stones to hit bottom.

They waited a long time until the rattling stopped.

Shaker stiffened and turned to look over his withers at the calm green mountains behind him. "Did you hear something?" he whispered. "Are we being followed? Is there a guardian at this Gate?"

"There's time for you and Hank to turn back," said Piper, his eyes on Hank. The grey gelding stared at the tunnel entrance, muscles quivering. His eyes rolled back, and he controlled himself with an effort. "I'll manage fine," he said. "The roof's pretty high, and it's not like a barn, is it? No splintered wood to cut us, no nails to drive into our backs."

It was Shaker, surprisingly, who reassured Hank. His constant trembling stopped, and he moved with a certain self-possession. "I'll be with you, Hank. I won't leave your side, and this looks like a good sturdy tunnel to me. Not like a barn at all."

Dill panted, seemed about to say something, then busily scratched one ear.

Blackjack poked a cautious foreleg at the tunnel mouth. "Except for the smell, it looks okay to me."

"Let's go," said Piper decisively. "Blackjack, I'll lead. You bring up the rear." He set foot on the path that led below. An oily scum puddled beneath his hoof as he moved forward, and he wrinkled his lip in disgust. He walked calmly into the tunnel, the dark immediately swallowing the black and cream of his hindquarters. Hank, with a swift, upward glance at the lowering roof, followed quickly. Shaker crept close, crouched a little, and scrabbled down after Hank, oily gravel slipping down the graduated slope. Blackjack stopped and looked back at the two foxes. Dill's bright eyes closed in a double wink. "Watch out for guardians left behind," she scolded. "And mind your rear, horse."

The air stank of sulphur and worse. The walls of the tunnel closed about them like the walls of a grave. The gravel slid sideways beneath Piper's hooves as though numberless worms moved slyly beneath the muck.

They walked silently. The pure sky of the mountains vanished quickly. Hank snorted at intervals, clearing the scent from his nostrils, until Shaker's warning nudge silenced him.

The tunnel wound deeper and deeper into the earth. The air grew warmer. A steady wind sprang up, its currents laced with buffets of intense heat.

They travelled on without speaking until they lost all sense of time.

The tunnel twisted to the right and Piper stepped around the bend. The others heard his voice, quiet and deep. "Halt, all of you." He backed up and turned to face them. "The tunnel forks here. Both ways lead down."

The others looked back at him.

"Perhaps we should split up," said Blackjack after

a moment. "Two of us could go down each way. Then we'll come back up, meet here, and decide."

Piper shook his head. "Too dangerous."

"Would . . . they expect two intrusions?" whispered Shaker. "We might have an advantage if we split up."

"Good point," grunted Hank. He kept his eyes fixed on Piper, looking to neither side.

"Let's look," said Blackjack.

The geldings crowded close behind Piper and walked cautiously around the bend in the tunnel. To their left, the tunnel sloped sharply down. Heat swelled up from its depths like that from a blacksmith's forge. To their right, the tunnel was wider, but the ceiling dropped abruptly.

"We'd have to crawl along on our forelegs to get through that," said Blackjack. "I vote to go this way."

"Into the fire?" whispered Shaker. "Not into the fire!" His trembling broke out afresh, and Hank, his attention diverted from his own fear of the narrow spaces, nipped him comfortingly on the withers.

"We need Duke, or Frosty or someone to tell us the Tale of Gates again," muttered Blackjack. "I'm trying to remember . . . Something—something, where the Dark Lord waits. Something—something at the Barn's First Gate . . ."

"Fence of Fire at the Barn's First Gate," Shaker said, then, "Do you hear them, my herdmates, calling me?"

"Stop," ordered Piper. "You're right again, Shaker. 'Fence of Fire at the Barn's First Gate.' This way."

They filed to the left, moving slowly, aware of the deathly silence around them, feeling the heat from below. The tunnel twisted sharply once more, and Piper stopped so suddenly that Hank cannoned into him.

Blackjack shoved his way through the others and peered over Piper's withers.

"We're here," said Piper. He stood hock deep in the muck that piled the floor, ears pricked forward.

Before them was the First Gate.

It was made of flame, and as they watched, it arced before them with a sudden roar, the flames spilling high, masking what lay beyond.

Shaker shrank against the tunnel wall, his coat running with sweat. "NO!" he gabbled. "NO!"

They watched the flames silently. After a moment, Piper backed up into the tunnel. The flames died back.

"The guardian of the Gate is flame," he murmured to Blackjack. "Watch." He moved past the maw of the hole and the flames flared high. He retreated, and the flames died to banked coal.

As the flames died, they could see beyond the Gate of fire: a vast, desolate land spread before them like an infection.

"The Black Barns," said Piper. "There, on the horizon."

At the southernmost reaches of the desert before them sprang a set of buildings, familiar in their shape, frightening in their size and color. They sprang up against the pustular sky, blacker than their blackest dreams. To the east lay a vast stretch of desert— where the Soulless Legion grazed—to the west they saw the rim of the Pit itself.

"Well, what do you think?" asked Blackjack in a practical voice. "Jump over the coals? Or should we walk alongside and see if there is a way through?"

Hank and Shaker huddled together, and looked from Blackjack to Piper and back again.

Piper moved forward, nose against the ground.

The flames leaped up, and he walked in front of them unmoved.

"Here is the scent of creatures running." His muzzle wrinkled in distaste. "The scent ends here." He indicated a spot several feet from the burning fence. "All must jump it, to get in or out."

"Perhaps the second path in the tunnel leads to a safer way in," said Blackjack. "Shall we go back?"

Piper scanned the reaches before them. "We've been lucky so far. There's nothing out there but desert sand and thorn trees and the Barns themselves. If we enter here, we'll be able to work our way to the Third Gate by hiding in the thorn breaks, and moving through the open spaces after dark. We have no idea what the second way may hold." He stamped decisively at the ground. "We're wasting time. I'll go first, then Hank, then Shaker, then you." He made a small circle at the trot.

Hank scraped his forelegs nervously in the ground. "I'm not much of a jumper."

"You will make it," Shaker said softly to him, "you must."

With a sudden, powerful thrust of his great hindquarters, Piper leaped the fiery fence. The red flames glowed against his hide, turning the creamy spots to livid red. The fire struck sparks from his flying mane, and for a long moment, he hung suspended in a magnificent arc over the Gate. He disappeared into the wall of flame, then there was silence, except for the roar of the fire.

Hank scraped nervously at the ground once more.

"Come!" Piper called from beyond the Gate. "Hank. To me!"

Hank drew breath and moved out in a clumsy canter. With a grunt, he jumped the Gate, fire licking at his belly. The scent of singed flesh floated in the air.

"Shaker!" came Piper's imperative call.

Shaker gasped and turned back to the tunnel mouth.

"No, you don't!" said Blackjack.

"You don't understand," whispered Shaker, "you don't."

"I do," said Blackjack kindly. He nipped the bay's quarters, forcing him to the Gate. Shaker's eyes rolled white, and he began to breath in a heavy, regular rhythm.

"*Madness*," thought Blackjack suddenly. He'd seen it before, in horses used to the range who had suddenly been penned in. "Jump blind!" he shouted.

Shaker squealed like a rabbit in a snare.

"Jump!" Blackjack whirled and lashed out with both hindfeet. Shaker backed into the fire, screaming as it snaked towards his flanks. Blackjack plunged forward. "Quiet! You'll wake the dead!"

The bay turned, panicked.

"Jump blind," Piper ordered in a low-voiced call. "Shut your eyes."

Shaker made a hopeless sound, a cross between a groan and a sob, and jumped. Blackjack sprang with him and the two horses landed on the other side. Shaker keeled forward and lay curled on the ground like a foal just dropped from its dam. "I can't," he said, "I can't. I shouldn't have come with you."

Piper nipped him gently to his feet. "Mind him,' he ordered Hank.

He stepped to Blackjack's side, and they looked into the valley of the dead land, where no mortal horse had ever been before.

It lay sullen under the swollen sky, the thorn breaks thick along the sides of the road that led from the ridge where they stood to the Barns. There was an oily glint among the trees about halfway along the road, and Piper inhaled deeply. "Water, of a kind," he said. "We'll make for that spot as best we can. We'll need to drink, and soon, after that heat."

Blackjack pushed his lower lip out in a frown. "Where is everyone?" he asked Piper in a low tone. "Somehow I thought there'd be . . . things waiting for us."

"They lie concealed," said Piper grimly. "Have you ever stood on Sweetwater mountain and looked down into the valley where we winter over? It, too, appears to have no life. But bears wait in the caves, cunningly hidden. Mountain lions disappear during the day to holes among the rocks. There's nothing apparent to the eye, but . . ." He stiffened, the muscles in his neck standing out in sharp relief. He inhaled the air and pawed at the fetid ground, his hooves seeking messages from the dead earth.

"Yes," murmured Blackjack, "two horses, maybe more."

A sudden clatter of rock made them whirl. Three skeletal riders came from behind a large boulder, mounted on horses that were no more than bone and skin. Blackjack looked into their dead red eyes and quivered.

"Legion Riders!" cried Shaker. "The Soulless come!"

"The Bear!" shouted Piper, leaping forward. "Move out and attack!"

Hank and Blackjack charged, forelegs glinting in the sullen light. Piper raced in front, head twisted sideways in the Snake. Hank and Blackjack took the Riders left and right of center; Piper's teeth closed on the foreleg of the rider in the middle. He bit down on bone, and jerked his head sideways. The horse fell with the sound of old bones rattling. Piper sprang back, spitting dank hair. Beside him, Hank

and Blackjack battled on with grunts and cries. The
Legion Riders and their mounts fought in an unnatural silence.

Piper dived at the horse who had fallen beneath
the Snake; his teeth found the vulnerable spot beneath the jaw, and he bore down relentlessly. He
broke through the leather-tough hide to bone. Instead of blood, a balloon of poisonous air filled his
mouth and lungs. He leaped back, coughing. The
horse collapsed under his feet. The Rider, tangled in
the dead bones and hair of his mount, turned his
skulled head to the sky. The red fire in his eyes died
and he lay still, sockets staring up at the murky sun.

Blackjack drove his enemy flat against the flaming
Gate. The Rider, flames licking up on either side,
swung his head blindly. His horse scrabbled awkwardly, four legs splayed. The whip descended with
a "crack". The horse jumped away from Blackjack's
fierce hooves and ran clumsily past.

Hank planted two powerful kicks into the last Rider's side. Horse and Rider fell and rolled in a tangle
down the rocky side to the road that twisted into the
valley.

The escaping Rider hit his mount with a boney
fist. His mount leaped clumsily over the tangled
bodies of his herdmates and galloped down the road.
The horses watched as the Rider slowed to a trot,
then a walk, and disappeared into the thorn trees.

"Victory!" cried Blackjack. "Victory!"

"It may alert the others," said Hank urgently.
"Quiet!"

"We don't need to move in stealth!" said Blackjack
exuberantly. His tail flagged high and he pranced
forward. "We routed them! Did you see? These Soulless Legion Riders cannot fight! They're Tales to
frighten foals, nothing more!" He reared his hindlegs

and whinnied again. The cry spiralled up to the yelow sky.

"Hush!" said Hank. "You're behaving like a fool! Piper, shut him up!"

"Yes," said Piper. "The Legion left these three behind, we don't need to fear them. But stop and listen, there may be others."

The stallion stood still, his head lifted. A faint yowling disturbed the air, almost too faint for the horses to hear. "The Pack," said Piper grimly. "The Harrier Hounds."

"Furlongs away," said Blackjack, his head cocked to one side. "And with more of the Legion back there in the world of men . . ." He nodded to where the tunnel's mouth gaped at them beyond the Gate. "We can reach the Black Barns before the Pack picks up our scent. Come on! It's not far."

"Too easy," whispered Shaker. "That road leads to the Pit. If we travel that road, we travel to the Pit. There is a Tale about the Pit."

Blackjack looked at him. "We should have made you Storyteller, Shaker. What can you tell us about the Pit?"

Shaker, hesitating, finally shook his head. "I hear the Tale, too faint for me to understand it. The voices of my herdmates cry from its depths." He hung his head, desolation in his eyes.

"Tell us," said Piper quietly. "So we can discover how we may rescue them, if we can."

"No rescue," said Shaker. "No hope. It is a place of toil. All are harnessed to pull the carts which are never empty, but always loaded with a weight three times what a horse can pull. They draw the carts up, then down again. There is no mercy in the Pit." He looked at Piper, his eyes tragic. "And no escape."

"I vote we move on," said Hank uneasily. "This is

upsetting Shaker, and Equus knows we have enough in our buckets at the moment. The sooner this is over, the better."

"We'll move out," Piper promised. "But listen to me. Pay attention to me. Shaker is right. This has been too easy. I don't trust it. You must follow me closely, and stay with the herd, all of you. We'll move quietly, and we'll provoke no more battles. This is a matter for stealth. We will run if we are attacked, and stand only when we are forced to fight. We must reach the Barns.

"This is our task. The honor and glory of battle must be set aside for this. Do you understand?" He moved close to Blackjack and looked deep in the Walker's eyes. "You, Blackjack, do I have your oath?"

"You do, Piper." He looked directly back at his stallion, his gaze clear. "And you're right, we must accomplish this by stealth. And to do that, there is one thing you must do before we move on."

Piper curved his neck in surprise. "What is it?"

"You must tell me the Dark Lord's name. So whatever happens, one of us will still have a chance to reach the Black Barns and destroy him."

Piper's eyes clouded. He sank his nose to his chest. "There's a lot of danger in that, Blackjack. *I* will reach the Barns."

"What if you don't?"

Piper flung his head high. He stood a little apart from the others. His coat glowed with his colors in the dull light. His finely chiseled head was still, his face immobile. The heavy muscles of his chest flexed slightly as he breathed. Finally he said, "If one of the Dark Lord's creatures learns his Master's true Name— that creature will rule here and the Barns will rise again. Those that exist here will exist under a different leader—perhaps one who is even stricter, more cruel than he who reigns here now. I would not put that burden on any of you."

"You don't trust us?" asked Blackjack, amazed.

"I trust you. But what is at stake here is more than the future of my breed. It is the future of the Appaloosa, and the future of us all. This is a task for a stallion. Who knows what torture may lie ahead? Who knows what the Black Lord knows—and what he will do to those of us here who bear knowledge to destroy him? If I give you the Name, I give you certain death. Without it, you may escape, somehow, if we are captured. With it, you will certainly die."

"Tell us," said Shaker. "Blackjack is right."

"I'd just as soon not know," said Hank, "but I see Blackjack's point. I think you should tell us all, Piper."

The stallion shook his head.

"Pride," said Blackjack, troubled.

"That's as may be."

"No trust in the herd."

"I trust you with my life," said Piper simply. "And I am responsible for yours. I cannot add to your burdens more than I have already."

"You can," said Blackjack.

"You must," said Shaker. He crept near Piper and looked up at him.

Piper shook his head. His eyes were gentle. "I cannot." He turned to the Road before them. "Follow me. Quietly."

They followed in the order they had established in the tunnel, Piper leading, Blackjack at the rear. They pushed their way through the infertile side of the mountain to the hot dry sands below.

Ahead, the Black Barns beckoned, a weeping sore on the horizon's flank.

They walked, and the still dead day wore on. The

heat rose to a fever. They walked, and as they picked their way between the rocks and holes cleverly concealed to trap unwary feet, the Black Barns drew no nearer.

"We should stop a while and rest," said Hank finally. "Shaker's having a tough time of it."

Piper glanced around. Shaker plodded forward, head down, sides heaving. The stallion stepped close to the bay and lipped at his sides.

"He's stopped sweating," said Hank, his own coat discolored with sweat. "That's not good, is it?"

"He needs water," Piper agreed. "We all will, soon." He looked off in the distance. "There was a pool ahead. I saw it from the ridge." He frowned. "We've been travelling at a good pace. We should be nearer to the Black Barns than this. Yet there they are—and it seems as though they've come no nearer."

"It's a desert, a phantom place, and your eyes will deceive you," said Hank. He stepped carefully around a low-lying shrub, avoiding the sharp spikes that seemed to grab at his ankles. "When I was younger, I lived near a desert, where hay had to be trucked in for much of the year, and the water holes dried to nothing at the end of the summer."

"Well, there aren't any trucks here," said Blackjack, gazing at the desolation around them. "No trees, no grass, and no water, as far as I can tell. Just these thorn bushes." He eyed the brush carefully. "I wouldn't care to take a bite of one either."

"Night will come. Perhaps there will be dew," said Hank.

"We'll keep on," said Piper. "Even demons cannot exist without water."

They walked on. The heat grew, even as the black night came on. They walked through the heat and the dryness and no dew fell. Their tongues grew thick and their muzzles began to split and peel.

They walked through the night. No creatures stirred in the thorns, or in the sand under their feet. There was no moon, nor any suggestion of it. They dozed as they walked, and even their dreams were of silence and thirst.

A dirty yellow light was all that came with dawn. They seemed no nearer to the Black Barns, although the thick stand of trees which Piper had said concealed water were now visible to them all.

They walked. One foot ahead of the other. Piper kept his head high, but the others slogged forward, watching their own hooves stumble through the sand.

Late in the afternoon, Shaker fell to his side in the sand. A sudden cloud of small, stinging insects attacked his eyes and ears. Hank blew them away.

"Shaker," said Piper, "get to your feet."

The bay shut his eyes, and moved his legs in the sand, as if he were walking.

"Come, Shaker," said Piper. "A horse down is a horse beaten."

"Leave me," said Shaker. "Go on. I hear my herdmates calling me and I must answer."

"I don't hear a thing," said Hank practically, "except the sound of my own heart. Your herdmates aren't calling you, Shaker."

"And if they are, you'll not find them here." Piper bent and bit Shaker firmly on the ear. "Rise! You cannot lie there."

Shaker grunted and rolled to his chest. Painfully, he extended his forelegs and heaved himself to his feet. He hung his head and breathed out with a harsh sound. "I'm thirsty, Piper," he whispered. I'm sorry. I don't believe I can go on without water."

"We're all thirsty," said Blackjack. "Hank's tongue

is hanging out like the edge of a saddle pad under a saddle. Come on, one foot in front of the other." He nodded his head and gave Shaker a weary nudge.

"We'll wait for a while, until Shaker catches his breath," said Piper.

"How sure are you that there's water ahead?" asked Hank. He spoke thickly through his protruding tongue, as though he wore a rubber bit jammed between his teeth.

"I'm not sure," said Piper. "If there is water on this desert, I will find it for you all. I promise you." There was pain in his tone, and Blackjack flicked his tail impatiently.

"We're all in this together, Piper. It's not your fault we're here. We wanted to come."

"We can't let our mission die from thirst," said Hank. "You're taking this better than any of us, Piper. Your time in the mountains means that you are stronger, more able to handle this kind of thing. You go on. Leave us here, and when you find water, come back for us."

"I'll wait," said Piper. "I won't abandon you. Shaker will be able to move out soon, and we'll find water together." He sighed. "Then we'll be able to go on."

The night wore on, hotter and dryer than the day before. The earth pulsed with heat under Piper's hooves, and he lifted his muzzle again and again to scent the air for the taste of water.

Hank and Shaker slept on their feet, heads down. Blackjack dozed off and on, jerking himself awake when deep sleep crept up.

Piper himself shoved aside the thought of thirst, ignored the wool blanket taste in his mouth and tested the air again. His nostrils stung with dryness, and when he rubbed his nose against his forelegs to ease the itch, the sensitive skin split, and he inhaled the scent of his own blood.

He snorted in disgust.

"What is it?" asked Blackjack. He looked at the blood clotting Piper's muzzle. "Oh."

"I'm not going to be able to scout water with a noseful of this. I'll walk on. There has to be water somewhere in this god-forsaken country. You keep them right here. If anything comes, hide in the thorn brush. I'll be back before dawn, no matter what I find. Don't let Shaker go down again—he'll never get up."

"Piper . . ."

Piper, impatient, looked at Blackjack.

"What if something happens to you?"

"It will not."

Blackjack blew out in a single explosive sound which expressed his anger. "The heart of the Black Lands themselves, surrounded by evil, the Pack of Harrier Hounds undoubtedly hunting us, and you believe that you're invulnerable. It's just too dangerous for you alone to know the . . ."

Piper's chest swelled. His eyes gleamed in the dark. The scent of his rage permeated the air. Blackjack stood still, head slightly lowered in the submissive stance. "We are protected," said Piper evenly, after a moment. "The Courts themselves approve this journey."

"Approve you, you mean."

"I am Lead Stallion, Blackjack," he snapped. "Are you disputing this?"

"I do not, Piper."

"Do you, a gelding, challenge me for leadership of this herd?"

"I do not, Piper."

"Very well then." The scent of rage died and Piper

blew out. He sighed heavily, and Blackjack, head still down, glanced at him from under lowered brows. "But I—a gelding—believe that when a stallion walks alone, he invites destruction. And there is more at risk than your body or mine, Piper. It's our souls, and the souls of all our herdmates. Foals, mares, weanlings, yearlings—all our kind."

"I've assumed that risk." Piper stood tall, pride in his neck and head. "But I'll tell you this, Blackjack; there's no one I would trust more to leave in charge of the herd. Guard well, Blackjack. I'll be back before this excuse for a sun rises."

"Fare well, Piper, in your search."

Piper stepped through the night, his every sense alert. The bank of thorns which held the water he had seen from the mountainside lay ahead, a darker shadow against the stifling night. Freed from constraint of responsibility for the herd, he moved out at a swift trot, breaking occasionally into a canter, pushing his weariness aside.

He hated this land, its dead air and its unresponsive earth, and he used that hate to drive himself forward. He moved quietly, despite his speed, testing the air, the earth, and thinking of his task all at once. The old collie popped unasked-for into his mind, and he could see the grave, tawny face as though Cory himself were at his side.

Piper's gait faltered. Was he wrong? The knowledge he held, the Name of the Dark Horse himself, would destroy the bearer. He had no hope for himself at all. If he gained the Black Barns—and he *would* gain the Black Barns—the destruction which would follow would consume them both.

Could he doom the others to certain death?

Piper shook his head as he ran. He couldn't. He could not allow that sacrifice. The others had a chance—for escape, for life. He did need them, that he admitted, to divert the enemy and allow him to reach the Dark Horse. But at least they would have a fighting chance to free themselves.

Confronting the Dark Lord himself, none of them would have any chance at all.

The air grew cooler, and he saw, wondering at the deceptive way light and distance could bewilder in these deserted wastes, the trees where the water must be. He slowed to a walk, the cooler air moving more easily in and out of his chest. The blood dried in his nostrils and he breathed deeply.

That was it. A sweet scent. Faint, but unmistakable. Water.

Tension drained from him. He could hear the water, a faint slap-slap against the sides of a gravel bank, and thirst rose up and shook him by the throat. He coughed, stopped, and inhaled again. It was a small pond, more than enough for the four of them.

Should he drink himself, right now, and return for the others after he had slaked his thirst?

He shook his head to rid himself of the betraying thought; this was not like him at all, he knew. He turned in a wide circle and went back at a gallop, the desert dust rising in a cloud beneath his heels.

"What's he doing now? Where's he going now?" A skull-headed hound rose from his resting place beneath a thick thorn tree. "Let me bring him back." His reddish eyes glowed sickly in the black night.

"He'll return." The sleek black mare beside Scant scraped contemptuously at the ground. "He's gone to get the others."

"Before he drinks? What a fool!" said Scant. "What of your plans, o sweet brood mare? What if they drink before he does?"

"I've considered the possibility. It's been taken care of."

"Just in case, I'll call the Pack," said Scant, his rat thin tail curling with eagerness. "It has been a while since they've had a good hunt and they grow restless." He grinned, his jaws gaping in a hungry yawn. "And they love to feed, to drive the prey. And Anor, too, is hungry."

"You'll do no such thing." El Arat flattened her ears against her skull and her teeth gleamed. "They are destined for the pit. You shut your filthy mouth and wait, as I've told you to."

"What if he doesn't come back, sweet one? What if he suspects a trap?"

"He will." She lowered her head and murmured, "He is afraid for them and for their thirst. He is very like his sire—his pride drives him, as I thought it would."

They waited, concealed.

The sound of four horses moving near came first to El Arat. She pressed her hooves into the sand. One horse, moving well and strong: Piper. Another two walking firmly, but with less strength. The geldings. The fourth: she curled her lip over her teeth and hissed in satisfaction.

"Out of the way, hound. They are here." She turned and glided swiftly through the trees to the edge of the Watching Pool. She panted a little with eagerness. She stared deliberately into the waters for a long moment; the sound of horses came nearer.

El Arat leaned forward, her silky mane swinging over the water. She breathed out, a long harsh, flame-laden breath. The waters bubbled. She called, softly, "El Mordant, Dreadlock. Rise. It is time, my darlings."

The oily waters of the Pool boiled high. A yellow-green light burst from the center and thrust a column of light to the sky.

Two fillies stepped from the column of light and stood beside the Pool: one red, one black.

They were young and slender, and in the light from the column, eerily beautiful, with a wild grace which spoke more of inexperience than innocence.

"Mother," said the red filly. Her eyes were clear, and shone with a light which held no color at all.

"Mother," said her black sister. Her eyes were amber, as though strong sun shone through the shed skin of a snake.

"Stand here beside me," said El Arat. "Do not move forward until I tell you to."

"Horses come here!" said Dreadlock, the red. She trembled with eagerness.

"Stand concealed, and be silent!"

The fillies walked from the banks of the Pool and waited.

"He will let the others drink first," Scant hissed, "you have guessed wrong, Soultaker. You are a bigger fool than I thought. All his kind allow the weaker members of the herd to drink. It is a way you cannot know. You've failed."

Piper broke through the trees at a trot, head up, eyes large.

"Water!" shouted Hank behind him. The gelding stumbled forward. Piper moved back to let him drink.

"Stop!" cried Shaker. "Stop! Stop! Stop! Piper, have you drunk from this water? Do you know that it is safe?"

"It *smells* safe," said Hank doubtfully.

"How can we know, in a land as deceitful as this?" Shaker crept forward eagerly. His eyes darted from side to side. Blackjack, a furrow between his eyes, looked at him with a worried expression.

"It's safe," said Hank, running forward. "We can smell it. It smells wonderful."

"It may be poison, Piper!" said Shaker. He shrank lower, and in the dark, looked more dog than horse. "Of course, if you wish us to try, and perhaps be killed . . . You are stronger than we, as stallion. You're right. Hank can test it for you."

"Yes!" said Hank, pushing forward.

Piper shoved him out of the way with a single push of his shoulder.

Hank stood obediently back, his eyes fixed on his stallion. "May we drink the water, Piper?" he asked humbly.

"Wait." Piper nosed the water. It smelled sweet and fresh to him. His throat choked him.

"Just one sip," whispered Shaker, "your honor will be satisfied if you take one sip to see that it is not tainted. And then you can step aside and let us drink. Why, it is *more* of a test of your honor that you take one drink and stop."

"Piper," said Blackjack, uneasily. "Piper, I . . ."

Piper drank.

Shaker grinned.

Blackjack screamed. "NO!"

The water slid down Piper's throat like a sweet, sweet snake and he drank long and deep.

There was a roaring in his ears.

The dark that surrounded the Black Lands rolled back, blown by a soft summer breeze. The scent of green and growing grass filled the air. Piper turned, and saw that he was in a meadow, thick with summer hay, hock-high with clover and timothy. The sun sailed yellow-bright overhead, and the sky was a clear-washed blue. He took a step forward, and from beneath his hooves, corn sprang high and thickly green. A yellow ear, heavy and ripe, swayed heavily on the stalk. The leaves unfurled in anticipation, moved aside by the late summer wind.

Piper bent forward and ate.

He was at peace, his thirst and hunger slaked.

"He is eating thorns!" cried Hank. "Blackjack, stop him!"

"Well done, Shaker," said El Arat, stepping out from behind the trees. "El Mordant. Dreadlock. You may come forward now."

Piper raised his head, the corn a miracle in his mouth. His herd was safe behind him; the soft rustlings and grazing of the mares reached his ears. He whistled for them, and they came forward through a grove of beech trees. Two mares, maidens still, one red as the flowers which nodded in the grass at her feet, the other as black as a bird's wing. They moved gracefully through the field, with small, finely carved ears, and shimmering falls of mane and tail.

Piper stepped forward to meet them.

• 10 •

A Mission of Mercy

For most of the day after they left Piper near the Old Mare's Mountain, Duke and Alvin jogged along in companionable silence. At seventeen hands, Alvin towered over Duke, and the difference in the lengths of their legs made progress slow. In addition, the Connemara was fussy about where he put his feet. When he came to a puddle of melting snow, he would halt, deliberate, and then make a long detour around the puddle, his ears pinned back against his head. Sometimes the only dry path would be through a patch of last year's teazel and he carefully pulled the dried husks from his feathers before he would go on.

"Don't you think we should go faster?" Alvin asked him mildly. The big Standardbred waited patiently for Duke to rub his muzzle free of a spider web.

"Why?" Duke shook himself thoroughly, then moved out. "We have a lot of time. The moon won't be full for twenty-four turns of the sun's wheel, and we won't be able to Walk the Path to the Moon before then. And I really don't like mud, or damp, or sticks in my hair."

"You moved along pretty quick when we were with Piper," Alvin observed.

"Herd stallion," said Duke briefly. "Had to."

Alvin stopped to grace a clump of spring grass. Duke took a few bites, looked up at the sky, then said, "There'll be quite a fuss when we get there, I expect."

Alvin swallowed, nodded, and broke into a slow, ground-eating trot. Duke pumped along beside him. "I mean to say, the *mares* will be quite upset. Shouldn't wonder if they didn't fuss for days about having to Walk the Path to the Moon."

Alvin thought about this.

"Chattering away night and day, day and night," Duke said.

In unspoken agreement, they slowed their trot to a walk.

"Duke," said Alvin after a moment, "what if it's possible to Walk the Path to the Moon when it's not at the full?"

"Clover said it wasn't."

"Clover's a range mare. And you know what Frosty's like. Maybe they don't know all they need to know."

Duke drew his lips back over his teeth, then clapped them together.

"I'll tell you what, Alvin. Did *you* see the dream in the Pool?"

Alvin shook his head, regretfully. "I've always wanted to see Her," he said. "She's beautiful, Piper said, gold like the sun."

"Well, I don't know that I believe any of it!"

"You don't?" said Alvin in denial. "You can't not believe, Duke, not after all we've been through."

"After all what we've been through? A three day

trek to the mountains. *Easy* trek," said Duke, throwing out his chest a little, "and a pair of gabby foxes. That's all I've seen."

"Huh." Alvin looked at the sky. The sun was leaving the mountain and the cool presence of evening was in the air. "The moon will be the size of a hoof clipping, now. And on these spring nights, it sometimes shines quite brightly. Brightly enough to make a bit of a bridge between the sky to the water and back again. I think we should go to Sweetwater as fast as we can and make Frosty try every night until its eye is wide open."

Duke grunted, then said reluctantly, "I don't believe it, mind, but perhaps we owe it to Piper to speed up a little." He groaned, and walked faster.

"Either that," said Alvin, "either that or we try it ourselves."

The two geldings stopped and looked at each other.

"To save the Breedmistress," said Alvin, "and," under his breath, "to see Her."

Duke flicked one ear. "If it worked, and I say if, mind, we'd certainly be remembered. We'd even have a Tale of our own. If it's true. If it worked."

"Duke, the Brave," said Alvin.

"Alvin, the Wise," said Duke.

"We probably could get back to Sweetwater stream in two days, if we didn't stop to sleep," said Duke.

"All *right.*"

The geldings moved out at a steady jog, passing familiar landmarks from their journey up the mountain the day before. When night fell, the sky dark except for the sliver-moon, they ate and drank and pressed on.

By mid-morning, they moved at a steady pace through the meadow where they'd picked up Shaker. The faint scent of burned timber and horseflesh lingered in the air and Duke wrinkled his nose in distaste.

"Poor Shaker," said Alvin, "do you suppose he hears the voices of his herdmates all the time? That they follow him like flies in summer?"

"Perhaps," said Duke. He was breathing heavily. They had made several stops for grass and water during the night; after the last, Duke's trot had been slow and heavy. The sweat never seemed to leave his withers.

"Sometimes I think I can hear them, too," said Alvin dreamily. " 'Come on!' they're crying, 'Come on!' "

Duke stopped, a frown between his eyes. He pricked his ears forward and looked steadily at a long stand of oak and maple to the west. "You're not hearing dead herdmates, Alvin. You're hearing a search party. And it's very much alive."

Alvin snapped out of his reverie, startled. The sound of many horses moving came from among the trees. He heard the eerie call of men: 'Come on!' 'Come on!'

"Do you suppose David's sent a search party for us?" Alvin said. He inhaled. "It's odd—they don't really have any scent to mention."

Duke hadn't moved from his intent inspection of the grove. "This doesn't feel right," he muttered. "Strange men on strange horses."

A party of men on horseback broke into the meadow where they stood. Duke and Alvin, used to the sight of riders, watched them curiously, without alarm.

"It looks as though they want us," said Duke, as the riders moved slowly toward them.

At a voiceless signal, the group heading toward them broke into two sets of riders, each directed to the geldings' offsides.

"RUN!" said Duke with sudden intensity. "RUN!"

"Why?" asked Alvin. "It's just men. We've seen them before."

The cowhand nearest Duke rose in the saddle, a lariat whirling around his head. The horse he rode looked straight into the Connemara's eye; there was no flicker of welcome, or of recognition there. The cowhand swept on; the horse swerved and Duke saw a crescent-shaped brand, almost the shape of a giant hoof on the horse's flank.

Duke charged straight at the horse and rider. "Go, Alvin! Get away to Sweetwater. Tell Frosty . . ."

Alvin snorted, bucked, and whirled on his hindlegs. He sprang into a gallop as though the start gun had gone off in his ear. He covered an astonishing amount of ground with his racer's stride.

Four of the riders gave chase.

Duke swerved as the lariat was let fly; the loop flew past his ear and slipped harmlessly off his shoulders. Two riders closed in on him. One shouted, "WHOA!" and in Duke, old habits died hard. Almost involuntarily, he slackened his stride. A cowhand snatched the rope free of the saddle tie, swung it once, and the loop settled over Duke's head.

He ran. The loop tightened around his poll and under his chin. Duke shook his head furiously, gasping, and the rope slipped down with his sweat.

The rider wound the end of the lasso around the saddle horn with three fast movements, and Duke sprang forward in a last, desperate lunge. The rope held. He choked. The world swam red, then dark, and Duke rose to his hind legs, pawing the air desperately. He fell into the side of a strange gelding, and wondered briefly at the unnatural feel of the horse's hide. He felt the tough scrape of leather chaps along his cheek. He bit down and a human scream split the air. "The Lion!" thought Duke.

The rider hit him hard between the ears with the heavy handle of his quirt. White light shot through the dark before Duke's eyes. He came to a shuddering halt.

The riders milled about him, their horses' bodies jostling Duke off his feet. He went down, hindquarters first.

The rope slackened. He could breathe again. The horses backed off, and Duke struggled to his feet and stood still.

"Alvin!" he gasped hoarsely. "Run!" His voice came out no more than a whisper. He tried to draw in air to his tortured lungs; he thought he would never take in enough. His legs trembled, and his heartbeat filled his ears.

It would be all right.

It would be all right still, if Alvin got away. Only one of them had to reach Sweetwater with news of the treachery.

His vision cleared, and he caught his breath. The noose around his neck tightened imperatively, and he turned obediently at the command.

"Duke," Alvin said, "I'm sorry, Duke. I ran as fast as I could."

Two ropes circled the Standardbred's splendid neck, the ends coiled tightly around the saddlehorns of two riders.

They were trapped.

The cowhands pulled them through the brush at a hasty scrambling jog. They headed south down the mountain, away from Sweetwater. Duke jogged along reluctantly, head extended against the rope, ears flattened with resentment.

"What Herd are you from?" he demanded of the gelding on his near side.

No answer. Duke bared his teeth and took an ineffectual swipe at the gelding's flank. The mare on his offside grunted and cowkicked, unsettling her rider. The kick caught Duke in the stomach and he stumbled. The rope jerked him upright. "Where are you taking us?" he gasped.

Anther kick, aimed with precision at his ribs. Duke pulled himself together after a moment. The rope bit into his neck, against raw flesh. He stopped resisting, and the noose eased.

They scrambled down an incline, and followed a newly broken trail through a stand of brush. Duke inhaled. There was a road ahead, the smell of oil and gasoline polluting the air. They broke through the brush and onto a man-made road that stretched as far as Duke could see in both directions. A large cattle truck was parked on the shoulder, the loading ramp down.

The hands dismounted and led Alvin, then Duke, up the ramp into the truck. Old straw littered the truck bed, smelling of urine and manure long dried. Duke peered out between the slatted sides. The hands shoved the cowponies one by one into the truck. After a moment, the engine rumbled to life, and the truck pulled out onto the highway. Duke and Alvin stood pressed close together. The land outside whipped by, headed south. Away from Sweetwater.

"Where *are* we going?" Alvin muttered. They twisted around and looked at the cowponies. Geldings and mares both, obviously a Working Herd from somewhere.

"I don't recognize any of them," Alvin whispered

to the Connemara. "I don't think we've seen any of them at the rodeos."

Duke shook his head. "There's something very strange about them. They're just standing there." He shifted a little, maintaining his balance in the swaying truck. "I'm Sir Duke, an unranked member of the Sweetwater Working Herd," he said loudly. "Who is your Herd Chief?"

A flea-bitten grey looked blankly at him. It was a mare, her sides gaunt.

"You? Is it you?" Duke rolled his lip back from his teeth. "We are members of Sweetwater Herd. You can't just take us away from our range like this. Look, my herdmate and I share the same brand." He turned a little so she could see the Sweetwater mark on his hindquarter. "Does this match your brand?" He looked scornfully at the crescent-shaped hoof mark on her buttock.

"Not even close," said Alvin loudly. "What's going on here?"

"Wild horses." It was a whisper, sounding as though it came from a long way beneath the earth. "Wiiiild."

"Who, you or us?" said Duke angrily. "You can tell just from our scent that we belong to men."

"Wild horsssessss . . ." The whisper trailed away. Alvin shuddered, and moved closer to the Connemara.

They stood with their heads down, feet splayed against the jouncing of the truck, for what seemed like a long time. The sun went down, and still the truck drove on, the endless length of road unwinding like a rope. By the time they stopped, night had settled deeply over the world, and a few stars were out, eclipsing the thin moon.

The ramp rattled down and the cowponies filed out, as silent as they had been all of the trip. Duke aimed another bite at the quarters of the flea-bitten grey as she turned to walk out of the truck. His teeth closed on hide that tasted dead and dusty.

Two hands drew Duke and Alvin roughly out of the truck and onto gravelled earth.

"What *is* this place?" asked Alvin quietly. "It's not a ranch."

"I don't know."

A series of interconnecting pens, looking like the cattle runs at the rodeo, only larger, sprawled over the landscape. A long, low shed ran the length of the yard; the ground around it was pocked with the imprint of many hooves.

Alvin sniffed the air. "A *lot* of horses have been through here. Many, many herds. More than I've ever seen in one place at a time."

Duke stopped and inhaled a lump of dried dung. The hand pulled him roughly forward to the shed. "That had the scent of wild horses," he said, puzzled, "range grass and all."

The cow ponies filed one by one into one of the open pens by the shed. A watering trough was built into one side of the fence and a few of them nosed the water.

"I'm thirsty," Alvin said.

"Looks like we're going in there, to that shed," said Duke. "There'll be water buckets, I should think."

But there were no buckets of any kind in the shed. The floor was buried knee-high in dried and decaying manure. Duke lifted his feet in fastidious disgust.

The door slid shut behind them.

The building had rows of cobwebby windows on either side, all but rusted shut with dirt. They were set high off the floor, close to the ceiling, and Alvin, craning his neck up, could just get his head to the panes of glass. American wire had been nailed to the window frame as protection against breakage. It was rusted, and the wire bent and sagging. Alvin thrust his head against the window and looked out.

"What do you see?" asked Duke, stretching his neck beside him.

"They've left the saddles on the cow ponies," said Alvin in disgust. "The men have gone into that little house." He waited a moment, then said, "There's hay in the pen where they are. Looks more like straw from here, lots of weeds and muck in it."

"I wouldn't mind weeds and muck at this point." Duke moved slowly through the muck, nibbling stray bits of straw interspersed with the dung. "There's something very *not-routine* about this place."

Alvin nosed a pile of ordure. "It's certainly the dirtiest barn I've ever been in. How could a horse stand this for a stable?"

"Use your nose. A lot of horses have passed through here, too. And most of them didn't stay very long."

"Perhaps this is sort of a rodeo," said Alvin doubtfully.

"Doesn't seem likely. Ho! One of the windows at the end there is broken. Put your head out and see if you can get one of those cow ponies to tell us where this is." He stamped restlessly. "I don't like this at all!"

Obediently, Alvin went down to the window and gave a loud whinny. There was a long pause. Alvin called out again. There was a brief, whispery reply.

"That grey mare," said Duke, "what did she say?"

Alvin backed carefully from the window. He turned to Duke, his eyes blind. A whicker started and died in his throat. He trembled a little. "A slaughterhouse."

"I see," said Duke. And they stood close together in the dark.

The night wheeled on, and no one came to bring

them water or hay. They ate what bits of straw they could find in the dung. They dozed, and once Alvin asked, "When will they come for us?" and Duke answered, "I don't know."

By morning, they were very thirsty. Alvin banged his forefoot against the metal side of the shed. They heard the murmuring voices of the men who had captured them coming out of the house. The scent of water drifted across the yard, and Duke raised his voice in loud appeal. Alvin looked out the broken window.

"They're filling the trough for the horses in the corral."

"Are they bringing hay?"

"Yes. For them."

"Did they take the saddle and bridles off during the night?"

"No."

Duke blew out in disgust.

The sun moved across the sky.

"My tongue feels funny," said Alvin, late in the afternoon. "Thick, like a blanket." He hit the side of the barn again, patiently. Thump. Thump. Thump.

They had nosed through the fetid piles and eaten all the straw they could find. The sun sank and twilight came on. The moon rose thin and pale through the broken window. A lethargy stole over them both, their bodies shutting down against starvation and thirst. Duke shook his head against the stealing fogginess. "Alvin," he said slowly, his mind as thick as his tongue, "ask those horses when. When will they come for us?"

Alvin moved heavily to the window and took a deep breath. "I can smell water," he said. "And grass."

"Ask them."

Alvin called out. The answer whispered through the night. The chestnut drew his head back in. "When the truck comes back, they said. Not the truck that brought us here, a different one." He looked puzzled. "A cold truck, they said."

"A cold truck."

"It's for the pieces, they said."

Duke's lower lip stuck out with a stubbornness Alvin had never seen before. "We can't just wait here," he said, "we have to try something."

"What? There's no way that I can see to get out of this barn. The sides and roof are metal. The door is locked shut. And . . ." He shrugged: this is our fate.

"That may or may not be true," said Duke to the shrug. "Our bargain with men is absolute. No one knows that better than I do. 'As man disposes, so must the fate of horse follow his desire.' I've known that ever since I was a foal. But this is more than mortal death that waits us here. It is, perhaps, the death of the Appaloosa. Perhaps of all our kind. We have to get back to Sweetwater. We have to do something."

"You do believe," said Alvin. "I knew that you believed."

Duke shrugged irritably. "Our herd stallion has set us a task which transcends our duty to man and our Bargain, that I do know. The rest is what Piper believes. And our first loyalty must be to our own kind, Alvin. Or there may be none of our kind."

Alvin waited patiently. Duke stood deep in thought. His thirst made it hard to think clearly, and the insidious desire for Twilight Sleep, which Equus gives to all horses who are hopelessly lost to starvation, tugged at his ability to focus.

"Dogs," he said clearly.

"What?" Alvin shook himself awake.

"When dogs bark, men come to see why they are barking. We must call out in the same way."

"Bark? We can't bark."

"No, we'll just—make noises. Until they come to see *why* we are making noises."

"Just noise? What kind of noise?"

"I don't know, anything," said Duke impatiently.

"Jehanna," said Alvin. "We'll call on Jehanna. Perhaps that will bring us luck."

"All right. Ready?"

They looked at each other and began a high-pitched, insistent whinny. They shouted, over and over again, at regular intervals. They whinnied until their ears rang with the reverberations of the noise against the metal-sided shed. Outside, the cow ponies in the pens called back in a ragged chorus, "Silent! Be silent!"

"Jehanna!" cried Alvin and Duke together. "JEHAN-NAAA!"

From the depths of the house on the other side of the pens a dog barked sharply.

"I'd do this a lot better if I had a drink," said Alvin. "JEHANNA!"

He stuck his head out the window and shouted once more, "Jehanna! Duke! There's a light on in the house! The door's opening! Someone's coming out."

They heard a man's voice, low and angry. The horses in the corral snorted and stamped. The two geldings heard the sharp crack of a whip. The dog barked again, "Quiet! Quiet! Quiet!"

"JEHANNA!" Shouted Duke. "JEHANNA! What's happening—JEHANNA—now?

"JEHANNA! He's coming this way."

"JEHANNA! JEHANNA!" they shouted.

There was a fumbling at the door and the bolt rolled back. A man carrying a rope loomed large in the darkness. He scraped at the wall and the light came on. Duke and Alvin stood blinking in the sudden brightness.

"JEHANNA!" shouted Duke and Alvin.

The man snapped the whip and came toward them.

Duke shook his head to clear it. The man walked up to Alvin and slid the rope over his neck. He raised the whip and cracked the gelding across the withers. Alvin, still shouting, began trotting forward, dragging the man with him.

"Whoa!" the man shouted.

It took three Sweetwater hands to stop Alvin from walking through the dipping trough; one slaughterhouse hand was no match for the determined Standardbred. He walked to the open door, dragging the man behind him. The whip whirled and cracked, raising bloody welts on Alvin's flanks. Alvin reached the door at a rapid trot, ducked his head and slammed through. The opening was only wide enough for one of them, and with a snarl, the man fell back.

He looped the rope over his arm and turned to Duke.

"Walk on!" shouted Alvin from the yard outside. "Ignore him!"

Duke walked, the whip cutting him on first one side and then the other. The man was strong and the little Connemara weak from thirst and hunger. He walked on, the whip slicing open his ears and muzzle. The lash narrowly missed his eye and he shied, pulling the man off his feet.

"Come ON!" Alvin shouted.

The man swung his right hand to the left, pulling Duke with him. Alvin charged back through the door and into the man's chest. The hand fell back, and the rope loosened around Duke's neck.

"Run!" Alvin ordered. "Run!"

They ran, unsteady on their feet, their hearts beating hard. They reached the yard outside, and drew in great breaths of sweet spring air. The pull of the watering trough was irresistible, and Alvin moved involuntarily toward the scent. Duke nipped him sharply, and he came to himself. They ran into the trees along the road that had brought them there. They ran stumbling and sliding through the woods, Duke panting heavily in his efforts to keep up. Behind them, the shrill cries of the men and whispered whinnies of the cow ponies in the pen died on the wind. The shouts of the man pursuing them were lost. They ran until the smell of the slaughterhouse was a memory. And then they stopped, sides heaving, sweat foaming down their sides.

"We've got to find water," said Duke, when he caught his breath, "soon."

Alvin nosed his friend gently. "We did it!" he said. "Duke the Clever!"

"Alvin the Strong!"

"There must be water somewhere," said Alvin practically. "These are mountain woods, and there's always water somewhere."

They walked through the trees, noses to the ground, and then to the air, searching. There should have been piles of snow left under the trees, relics of the winter behind them, but there was only grass, thick and obviously weeks growing. They ate. Spring grass is full of moisture, and this slaked their thirst. "This tastes like early summer," Duke mumbled a little worriedly. "We weren't in that shed for more than two turns of the sun, were we?"

Alvin shook his head, tearing great clumps of the grass between his teeth. They ate their fill, and as the sun came up, they locked their knees and slept, a healing sleep. Their strength returned quickly, and when they woke, the sun was high overhead. The dullness was gone from their minds, the Twilight Sleep forgotten.

Duke looked carefully at their surroundings. The stink of the slaughterhouse was gone; in its place was the fresh air of sky and land. He breathed in gratefully. His shoulders ached from the wrench the man had given him, and he was still very thirsty.

"We're free!" said Alvin, waking up beside him. "Isn't this air good? And this grass," he added, grabbing a huge mouthful.

Duke said nothing, a worried wrinkle between his eyes. Alvin nudged him. "Graze. It's great. I haven't tasted anything as good for months. It's thicker than the grass at home." He looked thoughtfully at the ground. "Why do you suppose that is?"

"Because we're not anywhere near home," said Duke. "Let's walk up that hill and see if we can get our bearings."

They climbed the slight grade and peered over the top. They were standing in a meadow which ended in a vast road, wider than any road of men they had seen before, overlooking a city of men. Trucks and other machines whipped by like huge hornets. The air curled up from the valley below them, heavy with the smell of men's homes and their bodies.

"I've seen places like this before," said Alvin, "when I was racing." Below them cars and trucks rumbled along the vast concrete path. "You've seen cities before, haven't you, Duke? This is a city."

"And it's not anywhere near Sweetwater," said Duke. He flattened his ears against his head. "Do you know where this city is? Do you know how to get back to Sweetwater?"

"We should follow the sun, shouldn't we?" said Alvin. "We've marked the sun on our own range.

And we'll know when we're getting close because of
where the sun goes down and where it comes up.
The air will tell us, too, and the feel of the earth
underneath our feet."

"And how long do you think it will take us?"
Duke's tones were grim.

"A turn of the moon," said Alvin. "We were in the
truck for a turn of the moon."

"Have you ever raced a truck against the pasture
fence? It eats up furlongs, faster than the fastest
horse. That truck took us many miles from Sweetwater,
Alvin."

"It can't be too many," said Alvin anxiously. "We
don't have that long before the moon opens its Eye
to the full. We can't be more days away than that."

"I hope not."

"Well, we'll get there," said Alvin. "It's just a
matter of one hoof in front of the other."

They turned their noses to the sun, and began the
long walk home.

• 11 •

In the Pit

A fierce, dry wind blew across the Black Barn's wastes. Thunderheads clung to the sides of the mountains surrounding the blasted valley, swollen purple and black, and shot with lightning.

A scattering of hollow bones marked the path to the Pit. The path lay open to the heavy yellow sky, and the sun pounded down with furnace heat.

Five Harrier Hounds sat on the lip of the Pit, looking down, guarding the mouth of hell.

The Pit had three levels. There was a vast arena in the center, ringed by pens that held the bodies of the animate Dead. In the center of the arena was the Pit itself, accessible through an abrupt slope marked by the well-worn tracks of cartwheels and horses' hooves. At the lowest point of the Pit was the mouth of a gaping hole, where nothing seemed to live but darkness.

Hank and Blackjack stood pressed together in one of the many rough pens which lined the first level. The floor outside the pen was covered with thick, ropy piles of what appeared to be stall leavings. It was stifling hot, despite the constant wind above their heads, and Hank coughed the dryness from his throat.

"It sure stinks," he said. He rested his muzzle on his friend's back and looked at their surroundings. The pens were backed by the high stone wall of the Pit itself; they had been hacked out of the rock, so that the walls at right angles to the back were also stone, and rose higher than Blackjack's ears. The door to the pen was just three hemlock poles, thick and heavy, set into U-shaped brackets protruding from the walls. When they put their head over the highest pole, they could see most of the activity which surrounded them. Staring, dull-eyed horses were jammed, like themselves, two and three to filthy stalls.

Hank worked his lips and sighed. "Some water'd be nice."

"No kidding." Blackjack flicked an ear. "They filled the trough over there this morning."

Hank inhaled. "Smells scummy."

"It always smells scummy." Blackjack bumped his nose against the topmost rail. It rattled loosely. "I know I can get this off," he murmured.

"You've said that at least once a day for . . . how many days have we been here?"

Blackjack blew out. "I've lost any sense of the sun or the moon. I don't know."

He rattled the pole again.

They were both thin, the ribs springing high beneath their dusty coats. A half-healed scar along Blackjack's barrel testified to a fight lost. They were both filthy, their manes and tails matted with burrs and tangled with sweat. Blackjack rattled the pole a third time, and Hank, irritated, rattled the other end. "Will you STOP? All that happens is that one of those Hounds shows up and tries to make a meal of our legs." He glared at the teeth marks on his foreleg and gave the pole another frustrated jerk.

"That's it, you know," said Blackjack, quiet excitement in his tones. "It's too heavy for me to bump off—but if we both do it . . ." He shoved at the end of the pole nearest him. It cleared the top of the U and fell back. "See?"

Hank bumped his end of the pole. A howl drifted down from the reaches over head. Blackjack whinnied back, contemptuously. "Damn Hound. Let's try it, quietly."

Hank, one eye on his herd mate, put his nose under the pole and waited expectantly.

"Go!" They pushed at the same time. The pole cleared the U, teetered, and Blackjack ducked forward and thrust his chest against it. The pole clattered onto the ground. They stopped, listening hard. Nothing moved in the pens but the bleak-eyed horses.

"Try the second one," whispered Blackjack excitedly. "It's like driving tandem, we have to work together."

"Like what?"

"Carriages—or like that damn cart we've been hauling up and down that bloody path to the rocks."

"Ah."

They shoved, and the second pole rolled free. Blackjack stepped over the lowest pole onto the arena floor. He looked over his withers at Hank, his eyes gleaming. "Come on! Scummy water's better than no water."

Hank lifted his forefeet carefully over the pole as Blackjack moved to the wooden trough. The Walker swerved sideways to avoid the ropy piles of manure. The pile heaved suddenly. Hank stiffened in shock. "Watch out!"

A snake the width of Hank's neck uncoiled. Its eyes glittered jet black and its mouth opened in a sibilant hiss, the split tongue darting out between its sharp fangs. It swayed upright, poised to strike.

"Stop," ordered Hank. "Back up, slowly."

Blackjack backed, his eyes locked on the snake's. His left leg struck one of the poles lying on the ground and the snake drew its head back in warning. Blackjack stepped over the pole in place with exaggerated care. The snake spiraled back into the dung, its mottled skin merging into the green brown mass as though it didn't exist at all.

"So now we know why the poles are easy to move," said Hank. "Something every where we look."

"Delightful," agreed Blackjack. Hank smelled the fear in his skin, and nuzzled him briefly. The Walker steadied himself. "Looked too easy. I suppose."

"Sure did."

"Well, this is a damn stupid way for us to end up," Blackjack said.

Hank grunted. Blackjack had tried a number of methods of escape: stealing past the guards in the opposite direction of the herd when they were all led to the scanty grass that made up the pasture topside; trying a direct assault on a Harrier Hound—which had earned him the half-healed scar on his side. Nothing had worked. They were reduced now to stealing water as a way to keep their spirits up. They knew that they'd eventually drink; the Hounds and their guards wanted them alive, and working, and they would quickly die without water.

Blackjack thoughtfully nibbled the lowest pole. "A horse down is a horse beaten, Hank. And we're not down yet."

Hank curled his upper lip over his teeth. "I'll tell

you what's going to go down, and that's Shaker. Look." The bay, an uneasy bravado in his step, was coming down the track that led to the wastes outside. There was a Legion Rider on his back, and the horse walked with mincing steps, his scrawny tail flagged. His eyes slid away from Hank's fierce stare. His rider dismounted, replaced the poles, and led Shaker back to the track outside.

"A true leader," Blackjack marvelled loudly, "a hero among horses."

"Indeed," Hank shouted, "and a reward we ourselves envy, don't we Blackjack? A mount for a soulless man. Praises, Shaker!" He spat at his feet.

"She is not ready for me, yet," Shaker called spitefully over his shoulder. "She came out of the fire with promises, and she keeps her promises. I will stand where Piper himself now stands—as soon as she is through with him! She promised—you three for me. And I did it! You three for me. That was the deal."

"We're going to get out of here," Hank said grimly, as Shaker passed from view. "And when we do, I'll track down that offspring of a mule and a donkey and I'll pound him into food for the Hounds." The gray gelding rumbled in a suppressed rage. "He betrayed his kind. His stallion's oath. He deserves worse than death."

"Can't get much worse than this," said Blackjack with a gleam of humor. "If we catch him, we can't do much more to him than's been done already. I wouldn't waste your breath on him. We've got to figure a way to get out of here—and how to rescue Piper."

"Rescue Piper." Hank stamped at the stall floor. To their immense disgust, the pens were left piled

high with manure for days on end. Both he and
Blackjack disliked standing in their own dung, and
made an effort to keep the waste piled in one corner
of the pen. At the end of four or five days, it didn't
matter how careful they had been: the manure was
up to their pasterns. "Shouldn't he be rescuing *us*?
He's not trapped in a crummy pen guarded by the
biggest damn snakes I've ever seen in my life, and
mucked out once every hunter's moon."

"He's trapped another way." Blackjack sighed heavily. "You saw him. He drank from that stinking
Pool . . ." Blackjack broke off, the memory of Piper's
frightening immobility as clear as though the stallion
himself stood before them.

"Right. Well, you have any more hot ideas?"

Blackjack looked long and carefully at the Pit where
the damned stood penned and helpless. Beneath this
level was the rock pit, where he and Hank were
harnessed to pull loads every day. And beneath that,
the mouth of the hole, diving to impenetrable depths.
He could hear the rumblings of the hole faintly beneath his hooves, as though a monstrous creature
turned in uneasy sleep below. Above, the deserts of
the trackless Lands. There could be only one way
out . . . and that was up.

"I've been thinking about the routine."

"Snakes are part of this routine," said Hank, "and
scummy water, and no grain, and the worst pasture
it's ever been my misfortune to graze on. Guarded
by those Hounds every moment we're up and out
and not harnessed to that damn cart. I'll welcome
whatever is *not-routine*—if it ever happens. Can't be
worse than this."

"Well, that's just it," said Blackjack, "the *not-routine*
is bound to happen. Always does."

There was a scrabbling sound above them, claws on rock, and the geldings came to watchful attention. "Now you see," said Blackjack, a little smugly, "the *non-routine*." He threw back his head and called out, "HO! Scant! You scum!"

A dog's head appeared on the upper rim, dark and scarcely discernible against the white-hot sky above it. A smell of decaying meat drifted in the air, and the sound of buzzing flies came clearly to both geldings. The creature disappeared briefly, then two yellow-green eyes gleamed in the dark of the entrance to the first tier. Scant, Pack Leader of the Harrier Hounds, slunk forward to meet them.

The muscles under Blackjack's dusky hindquarters clenched. Hank turned his face to the stony wall behind them, and lifted his tail in an insolent gesture.

"So, geldings. And how do you like our Pit?" Scant's tail trailed rat-like behind him, leaving an oily trail. Hank turned around and faced the Harrier Hound in disgust. "Easier than we thought, to catch that braggart leader of yours." The yellow-green eyes danced a little. "I came to tell you the news." His eyes widened in pretended disbelief, "You have not heard? It has taken some time—oh, you knew it would, you told me so yourselves, you said 'never' though, as I recall, and I said, 'soon'. Well, it has happened, my friends. Not much trouble at all to convince Piper to join our little herd. She had much to do with it, I won't deny that. But he's happy as a colt in clover, as they say. What kind of herd members were you, to make it such a relief to him to let you go so easily? Didn't you bow low enough to him? Didn't kiss the ground with sufficient gratitude when he led you into this?"

"I don't believe you," said Hank uncertainly.

"Such faith!" said Scant admiringly. "Such faith.

Did he have such faith in you, gelding?" The Hound came closer, his breath a miasma of rotting meat. "Did he trust you? Tell you things? Names of things perhaps?"

Hank looked blankly at the Hound.

Scant turned from the grey gelding to Blackjack. "No? He did not tell you? Well—all I have to ask you is this . . . if he knew this name—oh, say the name of anything, anything at all, wouldn't he tell it, if he were still a faithful leader to you and to your kind? How long have you been here? And has he set you free? When he could, with just one little Name?"

Blackjack's breath caught in his chest.

"Now, listen to me, gelding." Scant crawled closer. His eyes flickered from side to side, as though he were watching for those who would overhear. "If he mentioned any such name to you—wouldn't you want to tell me? Wouldn't you want to let me tell you how to use this power you might have?"

"He told us nothing," said Hank. "We don't know what you are talking about."

"Oh, I think you do." The Hound crouched close to the ground. "And I think you are wondering why he has not told us what he knows. So that you can go free." Scant's eyes narrowed to glowing slits and he said viciously, "But you see, he has not. And there is one reason, and one reason only. He has joined Her and Her Kind."

"Stuff it," said Blackjack. "Ignore him, Hank. He's a trickster."

"A trickster," said Scant, meditatively, "it takes a trickster to know a trickster." His eyes flicked back and forth from Hank to Blackjack. "It takes a trickster to know what is *not-routine*." He noted Hank's jump of surprise with satisfaction. "Oh yes, there's not much that goes on in the Pit without my knowing about it. Not much at all." He worked his claws into the filthy ground and wriggled with pleasure. "Souls, now. None of our guests here in the Pit have souls. If you won't exchange names with me—well—won't you offer yours to me and mine? You've been abandoned, left to your own devices. And you remember the First Law: A horse is a member of a company. A horse is one with his fellows. Why not *truly* become a member of our herd? Why not give up your souls? What use are they to you—really?"

"So that's what you're after, Scant. Our souls?" said Blackjack.

"Offered freely, yes . . . and then, why I could get you out of the Pit. You could ride with the Legion itself. Two fine horses such as yourselves would have no trouble in moving right to the front of the ranks. You, Blackjack, would make a fine Herd Chief for the Soulless Legion," he crawled nearer, "and you would not have to work in here, with the damned." He peered eagerly into Blackjack's face. "You do not need your soul. You will not miss your soul." Scant's eyes closed to gleaming slits. He grinned, then said with soft emphasis, "Your stallion certainly doesn't. He gave up his today, to She Who Watches By The Pool. A long wait, you may say, but a worthwhile one."

"He wouldn't," said Hank uncertainly. Then, with a positive nod of his head, "He wouldn't break his herd oath."

"And we won't," said Blackjack. "We have not yet set hoof on the Green Road, Scant, and until we are judged at Summer's Gate, you have no right to call our souls from us. You cannot call them here. You can only hold our bodies."

"Brave talk. From a gelding. But I do have your

bodies now, don't I?" Spittle ran from the Hound's mouth and he licked it away with a rotting tongue. "Tasty bodies. And I can hasten your departure for the Green Road, if I so choose, so that you may leave your bodies here for me and mine." He turned. "The Guards are behind in their quotas. I do believe that you will have to work twice the time you worked for us before—it's a matter of productivity, you understand. So you will work a double shift. One shift for your bodies, and one for your souls. Unless, of course, you decided to join your stallion."

They were hitched to the carts with a leather harness that was cracked and dry. The girths wore the hair from their bellies, and the breast bands bit hungrily into their chests. The carts were piled high with gravel and stone, and when the drivers cracked their whips and shouted "GEE!" their hooves skidded on the stony earth and split. They strained to pull loads that were just short of immovable. Their rations were cut to almost nothing, and Hank rolled an eye of longing at the scum-filled trough as they labored up the trail to the open.

They pulled the carts up and down all day, as the sun rose and the heat increased to an intolerable, fiery hammer. The others quit, and were unharnessed and let loose to graze the scanty range. Hank and Blackjack had a new driver, and they hauled on. The trips were all the same, up hill, straining against the vicious breast collar, the unloading, the reloading, then down again, slipping and sliding on the rocky path, fearful of the overburdened cart losing the rusty brake and crashing into their legs to fracture a bone.

Scant crawled up to them at the change in shift, whining with an eerie laughing cry. "You'll miss the evening feed, geldings. Sooo sorry. Too bad. You'll

get water and food in the morning—that is, if you're
unhitched in time to feed with the others."

And for what seemed like a numberless time at
the top, they waited while the driver dumped the
loading back. They each staled a little, passing a
scant foul-colored urine that dried as soon as it hit
the ground.

"I just might give up my soul for water," Hank
joked grimly in the earlier hours. But as time wore
and the weight of the loads increased, they became
too tired to communicate at all, until bleeding and
weary, the harness was removed, and they were put
into the pens, for what remained of the night.

Hank raised his head, and looked at Blackjack. "I
don't believe that Piper sold us out."

"Of course he didn't."

Hank scraped wearily at the floor. He began to
shake. "This place reminds me of . . ."

"Of what?" Blackjack spoke in a sharp, urgent
whisper. "There's no roof. Don't think of it. Don't
say anything. If they find you can't stand to be penned
in, that's the first thing . . ." Hank rolled his eyes.
Blackjack, despairing, said harshly, "I'll just bet that
Piper sold us out."

"What?"

"One swallow of that water from the Pool—you
remember, don't you? And phhht. Just like that.
Frozen as stiff as that calf we found in the blizzard at
Sweetwater."

"Not Piper," said Hank, his eyes clearing.

Blackjack pressed on, "Magic. It must have been
magic. We've got to find him, Hank, and get him out
of here. It's the only thing that can save us—*all* of
us. Once he sees us, hears us, I'll bet he'll remember his oath to the herd. It's a binding oath. He'll

remember, and the magic will disappear. We won't be here forever . . ."

"Why not? Who escapes from here? Who . . ." Hank stopped himself with a shake of his head. "No. You know, you were right. They hold our bodies, but they can't call our souls until we're judged in Summer." He flattened his ears against his skull. "We aren't anywhere forever, are we, Blackjack. We'll just be here until," he swallowed hard, "until we die. Our bodies."

"That goes for barns with roofs, too," said Blackjack. "All that can happen is that you'll lose your body."

Hank nudged him. "That's enough." He hung his head, closed his eyes, then muttered, "Thanks."

"We're going to get out anyway. I've thought of a plan."

"Yeah?"

"I watched the routine. All the harnesses hang on that wall over there. It's just like the barn at home; we each have our own tack, adjusted just for us."

Hank moved his withers wearily, "Isn't such a good adjustment."

"It doesn't matter. It's the same harness, don't you see? Now, when the driver gets off the cart, he goes behind us to unload, right?"

"Yes."

"The harness is old and crummy. You chew mine, I'll chew yours. The men can't see us. They're as blind as new kittens; they can only see in front of themselves. It might take us a couple of days, but we can chew through the harness eventually, and then— paah! We make a break for it."

"Ha!"

"We go back to the Pool where Piper's at the

thorn tree. We make him see us. And we go to the
Barns and finish what we came here to do."

"Pound Shaker into dog food."

"Maybe, after we have Piper call the Name."

Hank nodded, then muttered, "Equus, we need
more food and water. Soon."

Just before dawn, they both woke from an uneasy
doze to the sounds of the first shift beginning the
day's work. Their shoulders and chests were sore
with the extra pulling they had done the day before.
Hank's hindquarters were stiff, and he stretched in
the cramped space, trying to ease the frozen muscle.

"You're not tying up, are you?" asked Blackjack
anxiously.

"I don't think so." The grey gelding carefully flexed
his hocks. "Much more of this and I might."

They watched hungrily as the skeletal men brought
bales of dusty hay and scattered them near the watering trough. One by one, the riders opened the
pens, and the Soulless Horses jostled each other to
the feed, in an unnatural silence. Their first shift
driver lifted the poles to their pen, and Hank and
Blackjack stumbled quickly to the feed. "Either Scant
hasn't told him we're to starve, or the Hound plans
to draw the punishment out by giving us just enough
to survive," said Blackjack.

"Who cares?" Hank shoved his way through the
eerily quiet herd.

"Watch the edge," Blackjack warned. Hank's
hooves, split and cracked with the rough work, slipped
on the rocks. The trough was near the rock slide, and
below it yawned the mouth of the Hole. The Walker
rolled his eye at the depth of the Hole; the ground
below heaved and shuddered as they passed.

The Soulless Herd was tightly bunched at the

feeding station. Blackjack, hesitating, drew breath
and shoved his way among their bodies. He hadn't
met the Herd Chief and didn't intend to—he doubted
that herd protocol applied here, and shoved his way
through without caring what rank was in his way.
Hank followed closely, his nose at Blackjack's hindquarters.

"Move!" said Blackjack to the dank-coated horse in
his way. He took a sharp nip and the horse moved
lethargically on. Blackjack spit out the taste of a
corpse long buried. The scent of water overrode all
else, and in some part of his mind as he pressed
through the Soulless ones, he thought, "I'd be terrified if I weren't so thirsty." And then he and Hank
reached the tank and drank as though it was not
scum-filled and stagnant. They ignored the foulness.
After a few long swallows, the trough went dry.

"No more?" said Hank. He turned to the horse
next to him with outstretched neck and the quick
exhalations which is a sign of greeting a strange
horse to a herd. "Is there more water?"

"More water?" The horse responded slowly, the
tones as deep as a tunnel in the earth. "Water?"
echoed the others. "Water?" They moved together, a
wave, their hollow eyes fixed on Hank. "Water-water-
water." They pressed close.

Dead weight.

Hank breathed hard. His head swam. The night
sky pressed in on him like a falling roof. The Soulless
moved this way and that like a school of blind fish in
a dying river. He backed up. He cried, "Do you feel
the building move? Does the floor shift beneath your
feet?" He backed up, confused, and he heard the
barn collapsing again and again as it had in his dreams,
over and over again. "Do you feel the walls move?"
he shouted.

"Hank!" cried Blackjack. "Hank!"

The Soulless pressed closer, long-dead eyes mocking him, the weight of their bodies stifling him.

"Watch out!" Blackjack shouted. "Watch out!"

Hank leaped backward into the air, past the rock pile and into the Hole. He whinnied long and high, like a bird calling.

Blackjack gazed frantically into the Hole, as Hank's body spun down into the dark. "Hank!" he screamed. "HANK!"

The whinny stopped, cut off.

Hank fell for a long, long time. He spiralled like a bird, head over heels, spinning faster and faster as the earth pulled him into her grasp. He fell through dark that pressed on his eyes and ears like a pair of giant hands. He landed hard, in water. The breath left his body in a massive expulsion of air.

He swallowed and went under. He thrashed to the surface choking, thinking "no water for days, and now this!" Paddling and plunging, Hank felt the depth of the water through his skin, heard the depth of the water in the hollow smack when the water struck itself in great gouts as his legs churned the surface. Instinctively, he turned and swam, four legs pumping, for shallower depths. His feet scraped pebbled shore, and he urged himself up and out, pushing against the weight, abrading his flesh on the rocks.

He was half in, half out, and his mind went dark.

He came to consciousness slowly. His chest hurt. His first impulse was to get up and run. Hank knuckled his forelegs under his chest and pulled himself halfway up. Pain shot through his barrel and he fell back with a grunt. He lay there, blinking and the dark resolved itself to half light. He gathered his forelegs underneath himself once more, and heaved himself to a stand. His breathing was loud in his ears, and as it slowed, Hank realized that there was nothing to hear *but* his own breathing, and that he was absolutely alone. He heard his breath, his heart, and the slow groaning of the water as it moved through the underground cavern.

Blackjack's monster, he thought. And all this water under their feet, and they hadn't known it. He bent his head and drank until his belly protested. The water was cool and sweet, like the water from his ranch at home.

Like water from the world of men.

Hank looked up. Far above him was the Hole of the Black Barns. Scant and his Harrier Hounds. The Soulless Legion, and He Who Should Not Be Named in the Dark.

And Blackjack and Piper—trapped in the regions above him.

His thirst sated, he and looked around, trying to make sense of where he was. The river snaked away in the half-light. Mushrooms grew in patches by the water, and a green fungus on the rocky walls. He hesitated and then ate, the taste woody and unfamiliar. He scraped the lichen off the walls with his teeth, licking and biting as though it were a salt block.

Except for the slap of the water, it was dead quiet. Hank shivered. The cavern was high, and the roof sailed away to unimaginable heights. Should he go back—to see if he could rescue Piper or Blackjack? His strongest instinct was to join the herd. Should he call out, tell Blackjack to jump? He raised his head. Too far; he was lucky he hadn't broken a foreleg—if he'd been fighting the air instead of letting it take him, he would have fallen harder, perhaps drowned.

And the Hounds could follow, if Blackjack jumped.

He breathed in deeply. There was a faint something in the air, a sweetness. Like spring. And the water was good, not filled with green and stagnant. The river flowed downhill; if he followed up, would he find its source? Would he be back in the world of men?

Maybe. He walked against the water's flow for a long time. When the bank narrowed, he waded chest-deep in the water, then scrambled back when the shore widened. The mushrooms and the lichen were plentiful, but unsatisfying. He longed for good green grass.

He stopped every now and then to doze, his knees locked. He searched the silence even as he slept, waking quickly at imagined sound. Once, a rising fish splashed near him as he trudged up the gravel banks, and he called out hopefully.

He woke, and walked, woke, and walked, and eventually, the cavern began to narrow.

He ignored it at first, refusing to believe that the walls were pressing down on him, that the roof was getting closer and closer.

"Only my body can die," he told himself and snorted, because he valued his coat, his legs, the way he moved and the feel of his mane on his neck. He didn't want this body to die—he wanted to reach the open.

The river narrowed abruptly. It flowed faster here, winding away behind him.

The air was clearer, and much cooler. Somewhere up there was a spring in full flood. A spring in the world of men. He could taste it: clover, timothy, the bitter taste of buttercups.

He thought of Alvin and Duke, safely at Sweetwater. If he could just get home! If they all could just get home!

He walked on. The roof closed in, brushing the tips of his ears. The dam of stone walls pressed close to his side. The stream narrowed to a rivulet.

He stopped. To get through, he'd have to hunker down, crawling forward like some dog in a rabbit's tunnel.

He took one step, and then another. His heart began to pound. He lifted his tail and staled nervously. He stood still and awake, let the memories come . . .

He had been asleep in his stall, piled thick and high with straw against the winter, and outside the snow had begun to fall. Flier had been restless in the stall next to him; the Quarterhorse was older, and Hank's first herdmate after his gelding. The Quarterhorse had always seemed tall and strong to him, and he woke now to see his herdmate circling his stall in fear. "There's something wrong," Flier had cried. "Do you feel the walls swaying? Do you feel the floor move under our feet?" And then, with a tremendous, rolling crash, the roof had caved in, the snow tumbling down in an avalanche, the rotted timbers that held the roof falling. All along the barn, horses screamed and pounded at their stall doors.

Hank, struggling through a blindness of fallen timber and whirling snow, kicked out futilely again and again to free himself. His hindfeet landed on something yielding and soft and when he had fought his way to his feet, he turned and looked and saw that he had been pounding helplessly at Flier, who stared sightlessly back.

Flier's eyes were wide open, staring, and the snow fell on them as the dark brown color turned to green . . .

* * *

Hank shook himself. His sides hit the tunnel walls. He backed up. The scent of spring drifted through the air.

"I am getting out," said Hank aloud. "I am getting out, and I will find Jehanna if I have to Walk the Path to the Moon myself, and I will get Blackjack out of there." His whinny bounced against the walls, and he added loudly, "And Piper too!"

. . . And Piper too, came the echo. He inhaled, then stopped in astonishment. Piper's mark, and Blackjack's and his own spoor were mingled in the breeze from the outside.

He considered. They had come to a fork in the tunnel the day they had challenged the First Gate. Was he coming up to the fork? On the path they had not taken? The smell brought the memory, sharp, insistent. The path they did not take *was* here. And out there—a way to help his herdmates. Fear rode him like a jockey, clinging to his withers, whispering in his ear. You could stay here, the fear told him, and eat the mushrooms in the river. You'd be safe. He remembered Piper, and the night he had taught them to fight in the mountains. He remembered Blackjack, comforting him in the dark of the Pit.

He shut his eyes and walked.

The tunnel pressed closer and he scrabbled like a rabbit in a snare, his legs working frantically to get through the narrow passage to the world outside. The stone walls scraped his sides, breaking open the wounds from the harness, pressing on the bruises from his fall, squeezing his chest. He shut his eyes and crawled doggedly on, not noticing when the walls fell away, only dimly aware of the incline up, automatically moving into the sunshine with his eyes shut until . . .

"Will you watch where you're going, you silly horse! That's my tail you just stomped on."

Hank opened his eyes to blue sky, green grass, and a familiar pair of foxes.

"Well," said Dill, "we haven't heard a thing. You're marked up like you've been in a fight with a mountain lion. Where's Blackjack? And what in the name of the One has happened to Piper?" She closed her eyes in a double wink. "We thought you all might need some help—so we stuck around. Now this is what we're going to do . . ."

Wild Summer

Piper looked up at the ridge overlooking the valley and waited for Clover and the brood mares to come to him over the ridge. He had dreamed last night that they were in danger, and that he had somehow failed to save them. He couldn't remember that he had slept, only that he had dreamed. It wasn't unusual for his Lead Mare to stay out of his sight. But he couldn't scent them—and that was disturbing. His Dreamspeakers had told him all was well. He shook his head and blew out, clearing the fog from his mind. He was, Dreadlock had told him, overanxious about his herd and his duties as the stallion. This was why, she explained, her breath sweet in his ear, neither she nor El Mordant had borne his foals this summer.

There had been a brief rain this morning and the grass in the meadow surrounding him sparkled in the light from the rising sun. Under the trees, jonquils crowded in thick bursts of orange-yellow in the hock high grass. Piper took a mouthful: it was purple-green alfalfa mixed with flowering clover, the best

241

forage possible for a herd of brood mares and their weanling foals. It was curiously tasteless going down.

A stream trickled into a rock-lined pool off to his left, and he walked through the meadow to reach it. The water there always smelled sweet, but like the grass, it had little or no taste, and failed to slake his thirst. He drank deep and raised his head, unsatisfied.

Perhaps he should have listened to Cory's desperate plea, and left Sweetwater to find his dam and sire. Dreadlock and El Mordant had both pled with him; Clover had too, hadn't she? He had listened. A stallion must listen to the herd Dreamspeaker and the Lead Mare if the herd is to thrive—this Piper knew and knew well. What exactly was it that Cory had asked him to do—to abandon his appointed role as Lead Stallion to chase after a pair of renegades? Had Cory told him that? Or had it been El Mordant? He shook his head as if to get rid of flies, but that was ridiculous, since there were no flies here in the meadow, and never had been. Curious . . .

"Piper."

A soft, musical whisper destroyed his concentration. Dreadlock, her chestnut hide a deep red flame in the sunlight, breathed lightly on his muzzle, as a mare will when she meets a favored stallion. Her mane flowed like falling water over her neck and to her knees.

"You're thinking again," she said. "What is wrong?"

"Nothing," said Piper, "except . . ."

"What?" She nibbled at his chest, her breath a sweet mixture of lavender and wild grasses.

"I dreamed of dark, of terror, of an enemy who hides from me. I dreamed that I ran down a mountain far from here, and that I couldn't reach the bottom of the mountain."

"Hush. Rest."

Piper moved restlessly away from her soft muzzle. He looked up at the sky. "Another day of sunshine, and no flies. Another day where it has rained—lightly—in the morning before the sun is up, so that the Queen Anne's lace grows well by the pond."

"This is good," said Dreadlock.

"There is no balance to this summer. It is all too—quiet." Piper moved restlessly in the grass.

His Dreamspeaker's transparent eyes fixed on him. "When you stand there, Piper, I smell the crushed grasses on your coat. The sunlight glances off your neck in rippling waves and I can see how your muscles move." She snorted gently and whispered, "Walk with me, Piper, and I will tell you what these dreams mean. They are nothing."

"Tell me now," Piper said.

Dreadlock tossed her head, her mane drifting around her ears and muzzle in a cloud as light as dandelion seeds. "They mean that you are great among stallions. That you are envied, that others wish to take your place. That you must stay here to guard us from these enemies, or we will be stolen away by those who wish us harm." She moved close to him. "These dreams are a warning to you to stay here, to keep your oath and guard us from those who would do us harm."

Piper stamped the ground. He reared halfheartedly and stood on his hindlegs. He dropped to all fours with a heavy thump and said listlessly, "Walk the Path to the Moon tonight, Dreadlock. Speak to Jehanna. Ask her about my dreams."

"I cannot, you know that. The moon is not yet at the full. And even if it were, Piper, would she answer me? I am your Dreamspeaker; she would tell you to listen to me."

"You are young," said Piper uncertainly. "Perhaps . . ."

"Perhaps nothing." She turned her hindquarters to him and ran up the hill, glancing over her withers at him with her clear crystal eyes. She squealed, a flirtatious, lighthearted sound. Piper gazed lethargically after her. There was a whisper-whisper-whisper in the summer grass, and El Mordant stepped out from around a small hummock where she had been grazing. Her black coat shone purple dark as a crow's wing, and she moved gracefully through the meadow, light as air.

"Piper is not happy with us," Dreadlock said. She let her lower lip hang loose in an attractive pout, and flattened her ears against her fiery head. "He dreams, he says, and will not listen when I tell him what his dreams may mean."

"You are honored with two Dreamspeakers, Piper," said El Mordant. She danced close to her sister mare, and they peered at him from beneath their forelocks. "Two Dreamspeakers, which has never happened in any herd that I've ever heard of, and still you will not believe? Do you wish *me* to speak your dreams for you, Piper, and not my sister mare?"

"I wish to see Clover," said Piper, "I must ask her what she believes."

"You spoke to her yesterday," El Mordant said.

"You spoke to her this morning, before the dawn graze," said Dreadlock.

"You spoke to her last night, when the moon was high and full," said El Mordant.

"I thought you told me the moon was dark," said Piper sharply. "And I do not recall Clover yesterday, or this morning, or the day before."

The mares moved closer, and he inhaled their sweet female scent. Their voices rose together, so that he couldn't distinguish one from the other.

"Race with us in the meadow."

"Walk with us to the Pool and watch how a rainbow forms in the waterfall."

"You're confusing me," said Piper. "Go away. He shifted uncomfortably on his feet, feeling thick and heavy. "Leave me alone!"

"Drink," said El Mordant. "You are thirsty."

Piper, moving heavily, lowered his muzzle to the water. Behind him, his Dreamspeakers chattered, grazing the tasteless clover and alfalfa. Piper stared at his reflection in the water. The glossy black of his neck and chest looked grey in the bright sun. A mountain ash at the pond's edge moved, and he raised his head, his thirst forgotten. He eyed the tree with a glimmer of interest. He'd felt no breeze.

"Pssst!" Two rheumy eyes peered out at him from the branches of the ash.

Behind him, Dreadlock said, "El Mordant, Piper would have gone on that silly quest. He would have abandoned Clover and the foals—and us—to go chasing a dog's tale."

"A mare's nest."

"A false dream."

"A lie."

"He would have left his sacred duty . . . and this!"

"And this!" El Mordant sang. "For grass that never coarsens with the turn of summer's wheel. For rain that never brings thunder or lightning to threaten the herd . . ."

"For a place where predators never threaten the herd. Where all is safe and quiet," said Dreadlock.

"For death," said the voice behind the rheumy eyes in the ash tree. "Stupid stallion, you are. Can't you see that nothing ever changes here? Can't you see that life has just stopped? Fool!"

Piper stared at the ash tree, astonished. Something moved in his heart, and his eye sharpened.

From behind him, El Mordant sang, "He would believe that there is another place where we would be safer. He would take us to a place where the big cats wait in the branches of trees . . ."

A cougar perhaps? Here? In this safe meadow? Piper took a cautious step closer.

"Stand still, you damn fool," said the voice in the tree. "Just listen to me. And don't drink the water."

"Piper's thirsty," said El Mordant, coming to his side. She gazed into the ash, her eyes wide and angry. "Piper must drink. His throat is dry, and he longs for water, does he not, Dreadlock?"

"I cannot," said Dreadlock, in a loud tone, very different from her sister's silky whisperings. "I will not. Not anymore. He is beautiful and even as we watch him, his beauty is draining from him. He is greying out before my eyes. He is losing his color. He tastes of different lives, El Mordant, and of seasons where life goes forward and does not stand still. There could be a live foal in my belly, El Mordant, but there is not."

"Shut up!" hissed El Mordant. The black filly whirled and kicked ferociously out. "Shut up!"

"Listen to the red one, sonny," said the voice behind the old eyes in the mountain ash. "And wake up!"

Two things happened at once.

The sky darkened. The surface of the pool turned black and oily under his muzzle, the ash tree withered with a hot wind, and long thorns grew from the branches.

Piper felt a raking pain in his fetlock. He leaped away; he'd sensed no predator in the long grass at his feet. He caught a glimpse of a foxy face, and felt the brush of a white-tipped tail.

El Mordant dived for the ash tree, teeth bared and gleaming. An owl flew up and out of sight.

"Curse that devil fox!" came an angry shout. "Where is Scant when I need him!"

Piper shook his head, dazed. He stood beneath the thorn trees in the Black Barn's wastes. At his feet was El Arat's Watching Pool, and a rapidly disappearing image of Sweetwater mountains. He looked up. El Arat, the Soultaker, stood fire-eyed on the opposite bank. Two fillies, one black, one red, were at her side.

"It's Dreadlock's fault," said the black filly. "She wouldn't keep up her end of the song. She helped him, I swear it."

"I'll take care of both of you later," said El Arat grimly. Her tones sweetened, and she looked at Piper from between half-closed eyes. "You are thirsty, are you not, Piper? Drink again, strong one, and ease the dryness of your tongue and throat."

"Not if you value your ankles, pal," said a voice crossly from a nearby bush. Piper looked at his foreleg; blood oozed from a fox-sized bite. Piper lifted his head and looked. Blackjack, Hank, and the two foxes looked back at him from behind the bush. The stallion let out a great cry of triumph and despair.

"How long have I been like this?" he thundered. He rose in a mighty arc, forefeet cleaving the air. "How long!"

El Arat cocked her head, considering. Prudently, she backed away from the Pool's edge. "A long time," she said spitefully. "Long enough for me to call your precious dam's soul to the Barns, and your sire's as well. Both of them now live with him." She threw her muzzle contemptuously in the direction of the towering Barns in the distance. "Your dam services my master's needs. And your sire lies begging for mercy at his feet."

Beside her, at her flank, Dreadlock shook her

head slightly. Piper reared again, his scream a challenge that split the leaden air. "Blackjack! Hank! To me!" He spun, the black and cream colors of his coat a defiant banner against the thorn break. He swept down the path to the Third Gate, mane and tail streaming in the wind raised by his passing. From the brush surrounding the path came Hank and Blackjack. The Walker carried the remnants of a worn harness around his muscular neck. The grey gelding raced forward, ignoring the wounds on his chest which trickled bloody red.

Hank at his near side, Blackjack on the other, Piper raced along the path. Behind them, El Arat's screams followed in a futile barrage of rage.

Then in the distance came the faint yowling wail of a Pack in full cry.

"The Hounds!" snorted Blackjack. His lips curled in a grim challenge. Dill and Basil bounded along in the brush beside him. Dill cast a quick look at her mate. Her teeth appeared in a sharp white grin. "We'll take care of most of them," she called. "They won't give up the chance for a chase—and we've been idle far too long!" With a yip of excitement, the foxes dashed off toward the Pack.

Piper glanced sideways at his two friends as they galloped forward. "They'll manage to divert most of the Pack," he warned, "but not all; take care." Blackjack's harness flapped against the Walker's chest. Piper pulled his lip over his teeth in a mirthless grin. "Looks like you two have been in some fourth-rate rodeo. That's some breastplate."

"It looked better before Basil and Dill got it," Blackjack grinned back. "Hank led them to me. They chewed the harness off before the driver even knew they were there."

They rounded a curve in the path at a flat-out run.

And pulled to a plunging halt.

The Second Gate rose before them, closed.

Piper danced forward on the tips of his hooves. The crest of his neck swelled with power, and his spotted haunches rippled with muscle. He struck at the Gate with his forefoot. Once. Twice. A third time.

The third strike echoed. Silence fell. A hot breeze lifted Blackjack's heavy mane. Hank snorted and pawed the ground, looking fiercely around. Far behind them, El Arat and her two fillies stood at a safe distance.

"Call on the Executioner," she shrieked. "Anor waits for you beyond that Gate. You will not reach my master, spotted dung. Anor himself bars the way!"

The earth rolled beneath their feet, as if some great beast had stretched.

Slowly, the Gate swung open.

Anor came from nowhere, walking steadily down the path. His clawed hooves clicked against the rocky earth in a deadly rhythm. His jaws held the half-eaten carcass of a horse. Above the body his one yellow eye gleamed in dull rage. He caught and held Piper's gaze for a long moment. With a contemptuous toss of his head, Anor dropped the carcass and kicked it aside. It rolled, the gutted belly uppermost.

A familiar burn wound across the belly made Hank start. "Shaker!" he whispered. "Three for one. I guess El Arat wasn't too happy when we escaped." A grim whicker escaped his throat, and he challenged Anor with a look.

Scant crept out from behind the iron gate post.

"You come to see my master?" he asked, sly eyes darting back and forth. "You come to address He

Who Should Not Be Named in the Dark? You wish to speak to him?"

Piper nodded once.

Scant bellied low to the ground. Flies crawled in his ears and buzzed around his head. Those that swung upward in a lazy spiral toward the giant red stallion at the Gate dropped and died in the road at Anor's feet. Scant's tongue lolled and he grinned at the horses.

"My master will grant you an audience, spotted horse. If you can gain admittance from his chieftain here." The Hound cocked his head, as if listening to the monster beside him, then said, "Anor does not care to let you pass."

"He must step aside," said Piper, "or I will kill him."

Scant bent his head to his forepaws and giggled. "In that case, Anor will take you up on this challenge, Piper. And any of your pathetic herd that cares to follow you to the Final Death." He crept close to Piper, his voice low and eager. "Very clever, to send my Pack on a fox hunt. But you will not get past him, the Red for whom I speak. You know the penalty if you fight him and lose, do you not? There will be no Green Road for you. Anor is my master's executioner. He is a law unto himself. You will not be judged in Summer if you challenge him and lose. Oh, no. You will die, forever, your body left to rot before this Gate, like that sniveling traitor there." He glanced sidelong at Shaker's gutted body. "Can you imagine? His price for admission to El Arat's herd was these two geldings, delivered safe and sound to the Pit. And when they escaped . . ." Scant shrugged. "As you see. Your herdmates now, if they challenge Anor, they too can embrace death's sweet jaws."

Piper looked at Blackjack and Hank. "Leave now,"

he said. "This is my battle. The Legion Riders still roam the earth above us, and the Pack hunts our two quick friends. I cannot ask you to risk your souls. Any death would be better than this, this final one. You cannot risk your souls for me and for my breed."

Blackjack shook his head. "We can risk our souls for all breeds," he said. "We will not leave you, Piper, not now. But you must give me IT. I can slip by you while you fight and Call the Dark One myself. We are a herd. We are all in this together. Only you are strong enough to fight this thing. But I'm quick, and clever, and my task won't need strength."

"No way out," said Piper fiercely. "And I have been a fool. My pride's brought us to this, Blackjack. You were right." he turned to bring his muzzle to Blackjack's ear.

"So!" shouted Scant. "You whisper! You back off, stallion?"

Piper's temper rose. "I accept the challenge, Hound. One moment, only."

Anor charged. Head lowered, jaws gaping, he leaped into a gallop aimed straight at Piper's jugular.

Piper reared and danced sideways. He raked the red hide with his teeth as Anor lumbered past. Anor pivoted and charged again, leaping at Piper, clawed feet splayed wide. He raked his forelegs along Piper's flanks, and bright blood spouted from beneath his claws.

Piper kicked out with both hindfeet, catching Anor in the stifle. The Red buckled and fell to his knees. Black smoke rose from the wound in his side. Piper whirled once more, rearing high and coming down hard, burying both forehooves in the Red's belly. Anor rolled, knuckled both forefeet under his chest and heaved himself to his feet. Piper struck and struck again, hindlegs landing squarely on the Red's great

sides. Smoke welled from Anor's wounds, blackening
the air, filling Piper's nose with a choking stench.
With a snarl, Scant sprang at Piper's hindlegs, jaws
grabbing for the hamstring. Hank charged, grabbed
the Hound by the nape of the neck, and whirled him
in the air. The Hound squalled, and Hank dropped
him to the ground, then slammed down hard.

Unweakened by his wounds, Anor closed on Piper
with a sound like rocks crashing into a gorge. The
snarls and whinnies of the battle between Hank and
the Hound pulled Blackjack first to Hank, then to
Piper. Anor's clawed hoof raked Piper's forehead.
Blood dripped into the Appaloosa's eyes and muzzle.
The stallion backed up, snorting fiercely to clear his
nose of blood. Anor leaped on him, and Piper was
down.

Anor's jaws closed on Piper's throat. "Blackjack!"
he gasped. "The Name!"

Blackjack ran forward to them, dodging expertly as
the Red lifted his hindleg in a deadly kick. "Tell
me!" he shouted. "Tell me! The Red can never speak!"

Piper rolled his eyes desperately. His breath came
in great gasps. His muzzle moved.

Anor closed for the kill.

• 13 •

Hunter's Moon

"This doesn't feel right," said Duke. "The sun's turned around quite a few times now and the moon's nearly full. And I don't believe that we're anywhere near Sweetwater. We've gone in the wrong direction."

Alvin, head down, plodded alongside the Connemara without responding. They were both wet from rain, their forelocks plastered to their brows, manes and tails stuck damply to their skin. The two geldings were passing through a long, newly harrowed field that stretched horizon to horizon, from hill to hill. The spring rain had been steady and the field was thick with mud.

"It's too warm for this time of year," Alvin agreed. "The air at night doesn't have the bite it should have."

"Warm," said Duke, "warm doesn't mean anything. Remember the thaw this winter? We were hock-deep in mud for days."

"We're hock-deep in mud now." Alvin stamped

his feet into the ground, then pulled his hooves free with a sucking sound.

Duke turned and looked back the way they had come. The field was pocked with hoof-shaped holes in a more or less steady line.

"What's important," Duke continued firmly, "is the way the light from the sun falls. It's still wrong. And the air smells wrong, too much of men's cities in it."

"So what do you think we should do?"

Duke stopped and grabbed at a clump of grass that had escaped the harrow's blade. He chewed, swallowed, then looked up at the sky. "I don't know."

"Well, I do. I think we should try to Walk the Path to the Moon ourselves. I've thought that we should try to Walk the Path to the Moon for days now, and you've always said the same thing."

"No."

"That's it: No." In an unspoken understanding, they both broke into a slow trot up a rise in the field.

"Are you afraid?" asked Alvin when they reached the top. The field sloped down again to a line of trees. They moved out of their trot into a slow lope.

"I'm not afraid," said Duke sharply. "It's just that it's foolishness for us to try it. If all this is true, geldings can't do it anyway, and something awful might happen. If it isn't, well, then, we've made two donkeys out of ourselves by standing in a puddle howling at the sky. It's foolishness either way."

"You don't believe, after all, do you? After all we've been through, after all we've seen, you still don't believe."

"We haven't seen anything," Duke reminded him. "We've heard about what others have seen, that's all. We weren't at the stream with the brood mares. And we didn't walk into that cave with Blackjack and

Piper when they said the Old Mare showed them that stuff."

"Jehanna herself helped us escape from that slaughterhouse."

"We escaped from that slaughterhouse on our own."

"Then why did you come on this whole task?" Alvin's tone was curious, not aggressive, and Duke gave his question considered thought.

"I'm not sure," he said finally. "Piper was determined to do this. I've given Piper my oath, because he's herd stallion. And my loyalty's to him." They reached the trees and slowed down. "And Blackjack's right. Geldings never get a chance to do anything interesting."

"I think you want to believe," said Alvin simply. "That's why you've come. You want to believe and you can't. You should just do it, Duke. Just believe."

"Mmm."

They entered the stand of trees cautiously, and tested the breeze for predators. "Man's too close here for there to be anything dangerous," said Duke practically, after Alvin coughed with the effort of inhaling all the breeze he could catch. "We'll be all right."

The rain slackened as night approached, and they found shelter under a tall pine tree. They grazed, and gradually their coats dried. There was plenty of water, "too much," Duke grumbled, and they settled in for a rest before continuing on.

Duke was old, and he fell asleep at once in the grass, locking his knees and hanging his head. Alvin laid his muzzle carefully across his herdmate's back and dozed, then fell into a deeper sleep. The weight of the Standardbred's head woke Duke, and he moved out to lie down in the clearing beside the pines. He slept lightly after that, and woke once more, deep in the night, and looked straight at the Hunter's Moon.

It rode the shoulder of the sky, a grey-orange globe with a bite in the side as it was not yet completely full. The remnants of the rain clouds trailed across it. Water dripped quietly from the trees, and Duke heard the scrabble-slap of a family of rabbits feeding on the new grass nearby.

The moon shone orange. An owl hooted, and the rabbit family stopped their slight sounds. Duke imagined them cowering in the grass. A sudden sense of vastness filled him; himself a small mite in the middle of the endless sky, the incalculable reaches of the earth.

Duke had always been shorter than most of his herdmates in a herd of any size, and it had never bothered him particularly. It wasn't size that counted; it was wisdom.

"Can you touch wisdom? Can you taste it? Can you see it, smell it? Does wisdom exist as this fence exists?"

Piper believed it did, Duke remembered crossly. He rolled, seeking a comfortable spot in the grass. It was the moon that was keeping him awake. There wasn't even any proper moonshine from a Hunter's Moon, just the orange light of the moon itself, shining away like some fruit in the sky.

Memories came to Duke of a time when he was young, just weaned. He and a few other adventuresome colts had crept away from the mares at night to explore the pasture over the hill from their paddock. They had wriggled through a gap in the fence, and then gotten lost in the dark. And the wind had come up, taking away the familiar scents of their dams, whirling away the comforting smell of the herd stallion, and they had been truly lost, not knowing which way to go to get back to the safety of their mothers. The moon had come out from behind such clouds as these, and led them back. They'd gotten scolded, of course, but then the Caretaker, a nice young mare called Jonsey, had given them a song to sing. If they were ever lost again, she'd said, they could ask the moon to shine on and show them the way.

He had believed in his gods then, but he was young and foolish.

Duke carefully craned his neck. Alvin was asleep, breathing deeply under the trees. The Connemara got slowly to his feet. He looked up at the Hunter's Moon and sang under his breath:

"Jehanna who sows the sky with stars
Who breathes upon the night
Make the stars glow
Make the moon grow
That we may see its light."

The moon rode the sky, silent, and no light shone down from the yellow eye.

"Paah!" said Duke.

Alvin stirred under the trees, and Duke hastily folded himself into the grass. The rain started up again, a light fresh sweep of water, and in the forest Duke heard the "snick-snick" of an owl in flight. He closed his eyes to sleep. He thought, just before he dozed off for the last time that night, that he saw the owl itself, wings outstretched, lined against the rayless moon.

"I thought they hid from daylight," said Alvin, waking Duke.

Duke grunted and got to his feet. His knees were stiff and he stretched, forelegs extended. He yawned heartily, staled, and shook himself. The sun was up, the rain was gone.

"I said you'd think it'd hide from daylight."

"What would?"

"That owl there."

Duke blinked up at the pine tree. A horned owl sat on a low hanging branch, great wings closely folded. The owl blinked back at Duke. Its eyes were gold, startling in the black and white feathered face. Moon eyes, thought Duke. Hunter Moon eyes.

The owl looked steadily down at the Connemara. Its wings fluttered, extended, and the bird soared over the clearing where the geldings stood. It was very black against the bright sky. The owl landed at the top of a maple still in bud, and swiveled its head over its back to regard the horses with a wide warm gaze.

"Wish I could do that," said Alvin. "Swing my head around like that. The farrier couldn't sneak up on me like he does."

"Come on," said Duke, "let's move out."

"All right," said Alvin agreeably. "Where to this morning?"

"Follow the owl."

"The owl?"

Duke flattened his ears against his head. Alvin looked at the bird, then at the Connemara. His eyes crinkled at the corners, but he held his peace.

In the days that followed, the owl flew over land the horses would have avoided if they had been travelling alone. They crossed men's fields, and leaped fences. They skirted more than one cluster of villages. Many times, they crossed asphalt roads with trucks and other vehicles storming along the way like gigantic hornets from a split nest. They flung themselves across these roads in a panic, hooves striking sparks from the slippery surface, the hot, gassy air of the cars filling their noses with fear.

They kept up a steady ground-eating lope, halting

frequently to graze and drink. There was no time for Duke to pick burrs from his fetlocks, and not much time to sleep. Although Duke was sturdy, the furlongs began to take their toll.

They both lost weight. Hollows appeared between hip and barrel. Duke's eyes sank, rimmed with dark in his white face. Alvin noticed grey in his friend's muzzle for the first time. And the Standardbred developed scratches on his pasterns from the damp, the rash a tormenting itch. They kept on. The air and the position of the sun in the sky became more and more familiar. At night, the moon waxed brighter and rounder.

Stopping for a brief rest in a mountain pasture several days later, Alvin looked at the moon in wonder. The owl sat with folded wings on a neglected fence post nearby. "It's at the full," he said worriedly. "It is, and it won't last."

"Not quite," said Duke, peering up intently. "See, there's a bit of a dent in the side there, still."

"Maybe. How close are we to Sweetwater, do you think?"

"Close. We're coming around a different way, to be sure, and the mountains are ahead of us instead of behind us, but we're close."

"Duke the Leader," said Alvin.

"Alvin the Follower," said Duke. "Let's move out."

The Standardbred looked at his herdmate, and said gently, "Can we slow to a walk, do you think?"

"We're too close," said Duke, "trot on."

They trotted on, and toward the end of the day, the smells and sounds of Sweetwater were so close that they broke into a heavy canter. The owl, watching them cross the last hill that overlooked Sweetwater, blinked its great eyes once and sailed away. Duke, his breath short, his legs pumping with iron determination, had no voice to call farewell. Alvin raised a whinny, and the owl's wings dipped once, twice, before he disappeared into the sky, flying straight into the full silver moon.

"There it is!" Duke stopped, exulted, to catch his breath. Sweetwater lay below them, the ranch house dark, the brood mares dim shapes in the pasture on the bluffs. The geldings broke into a hard gallop and ran noisily to the barbed wire fence.

"Lead Mare!" Alvin's whinny was loud and rough. Duke pulled in great gasps of air behind him. "Clover!"

They heard the high-pitched squeals of foals wakened from sleep and the restless mutterings of the mares themselves. Half a mile away, the farm-house lights snapped on.

"It's us!" Alvin called. "We've come back!"

"Piper!" Clover's whinny, filled with hope and longing, momentarily silenced both geldings. They heard her eager gallop, and she emerged from the dark of the pasture, ears forward, body tense. A suckling foal ran awkwardly at her side.

"No, no," said Duke hastily. "It's Alvin and me. We've come back."

"And where is Piper? Why have you left him? What about the herd oath!" Clover jigged furiously. "WHERE IS HE?"

"We've come to tell you that," said Alvin quietly. "And it's no message for the little one to hear."

Clover took a deep breath and stood still. After a moment, she nosed the foal gently from her side, calling to Jessica to take it back to the brood mares.

"Well?" she demanded.

"We split up in the mountains," Duke said. "Clover, it'd take too long to explain it twice. Where's Frosty?"

"Back there. What do you mean, explain it twice?

Where's Piper? Why isn't he with you? Has he been hurt? Is he all right?"

"Stop pelting me with questions!" Duke ordered. He raised his voice, "Frosty! Come here, please."

"I am Lead Mare of this brood mare herd, Duke." Clover's tone was icy.

"You won't be for long if you don't keep quiet and listen to me. Frosty, there you are."

The Storyteller stamped to Clover's side and gazed nervously at the Connemara. She, too, had a colt with her.

"How dare you? What do you mean, I won't be for long? Who challenges me?"

"El Arat herself," said Duke.

Frosty's eyes rolled back, and she jumped, ready to bolt.

"Listen, Clover, and all you brood mares. We found the Namer of Names. She has agreed that we may call on Jehanna and that Duchess may be taken from the havens beside the Green Road to Summer."

"That's wonderful," said Clover sincerely. "BUT WHY ISN'T PIPER WITH YOU?"

"The Old Mare told us that El Arat has given birth to twin foals. That the Watching Pool has been grown over with scum, and that Equus and the stallions of the Army of One Hundred and Five have not been able to Watch for the whole turn of the moon. They do not know that there are now three Soultakers instead of one."

"Three!" said Clover. The mares moved back and forth in the darkness, and the scent of fear rose from them like a cloud.

"There will be no escape for any horse who tries to slip past the Soultaker now," said Alvin. "The Old Mare gave Piper the true Name of the Dark—you know—He Who Should Not Be Named in the Dark, and it's dark now, so I don't want to say it aloud. But Piper has gone with Blackjack and Hank and Shaker and Dill and Basil . . ."

"To the Barns," said Duke, cutting in. "To Call his Name, and destroy him and his land forever."

Clover shivered. "Oh, Equus," she whispered. "Piper! He'll be called! I know it. He will die. I will never see him again."

"There's something we can do about it if you'll just *hurry*," said Duke. "Whether Piper succeeds or fails may depend on whether Frosty can Walk the Path to the Moon. And it must be tonight, when the moon is full. *She* has called out the Soulless Legions, and they ride to the Green Road to bring Duchess and the Dancer to the Black Barns and imprison their souls . . . Equus and the Army of One Hundred and Five must be told. Now!"

Clover stood with her head down, then said, "Frosty."

"No!" said Frosty. "I done it once already," she added feebly.

"Then you can do it again." Clover nudged her sharply. "Come on."

"You have the message, right?" said Alvin. "We're going along, too, aren't we, Duke? We have to. We'll see Her."

Duke pricked his ears inquiringly at Frosty. She nodded. "Okay by me."

"Jump the fence," said Clover. "We'll move out of your way."

"You first, Duke," said Alvin.

Duke walked a few paces away from the fence, then ran and jumped, barely clearing the wire. Alvin, with a great, satisfied exhalation of breath, backed up and circled once at the trot.

Suddenly, they all heard the hurrying pad-pad-pad

of Meg's feet. "You, stop!" she barked. The slim collie, her coat glimmering snow and dark, dashed at the Standardbred and nipped at his ankles sharply. "Where have you all been? Where are the others? I can't believe that you abandoned the ranch the way you did. Back! Back!"

The horses heard David's running footsteps.

"Go on without me," said Alvin. "They may try and interfere. I'll lead them away from the pasture." The Standardbred galloped slowly toward the mountains, looking back to see Meg snapping crossly at his heels.

"Alvin a trickster and Duke a believer," murmured Jessica. "I never thought I'd see the day."

"Come on," said Duke, "to the stream."

Sweetwater's stream bubbled gently silver under the moon and stars. The sky was clear, the moon a glowing apple; its light shone straight down into the water to make a silver bridge, the light a part of the glimmering water.

Frosty dithered on the bank for a few moments, putting one hoof into the water and then drawing it back. "I don't remember the saying," she said, fretting, "I mean, I think I remember. Does it have to be exact?"

"Just try it," Jessica advised. "We'll help you."

Frosty stepped into the water. Her colt squealed and tried to follow her, and Jessica gently nosed it back up the bank. The Palomino grasped the foal gently by the curly mane at the nape of its neck and said indistinctly, "Hurry up."

Frosty sloshed to the middle of the stream and gazed up at the moon.

"Jehanna, Goddess Mare," Clover prompted.

Frosty stepped from one foot to the other. She

took a deep breath and shouted, "HEY YOU, OPEN UP, JEHANNA!"

"Oh, for Equus' sake!" breathed Clover, disgusted. "That's *not* . . ." She subsided with a mutter.

The cry seemed to knock against the moon itself. They heard a distant bark, and the sound of Meg chasing Alvin up the slope of the mountain.

"Hurry," Duke murmured to himself, squinting intently at the moon. "Oh, hurry!" And he pushed away the doubt that teased his mind.

The moonlight lightened to brilliance. Duke's heart lurched.

She stood there, a shining golden presence. The waters of the stream flowed around her radiant feet. Her eyes were the color of rubies and her voice was gentle. The chime of the stars mingled with the running voice of the water. Duke bent his nose to his foreleg and exhaled in a long, long sigh.

"Welcome, mistress," said Clover. She caught her breath. "We have need of your help. We have a terrible story to tell."

Duke was lost in wonder. The flower scent of the Goddess Mare made him dizzy. The light she carried with her stopped his ears and filled his eyes.

"Tell me, Lead Mare, what is it that troubles you? The Pool is even now beginning to clear, and soon we will be able to Watch how Piper fares in his task."

"May the one who knows of the Tale tell you, mistress?"

The incandescent ruby eyes turned to Duke. The delicate head nodded, and Jehanna's silky mane swung over her withers. "You, gelding. I remember you. You called on me some days ago, I think, but the Pool was dark from the scum left by El Arat's mane, and I was unable to help you."

Duke's knees trembled. He bowed his head, and his voice tangled in his throat. He had a feeling that she knew of his doubts, his disbelief and that she didn't care.

"I and my herdmate, Alvin, travelled with Piper and the others to find the Old Mare, the Namer of Names."

"Then you are twice blessed, gelding, for a brave horse and a believer."

Duke's skin prickled with embarrassment. He coughed, and although he tried, he could not get the message out.

Jehanna walked forward, and the warmth of her light fell on the little Connemara. He squared up, then said, his tones surprisingly firm, "El Arat has borne twin foals. There are now three Soultakers instead of one. Piper has gone to the Barns to call the Dark Horse to his death."

The light from Jehanna grew cold, and Duke began to shiver.

"The Old Mare has said that you may call Duchess from the Havens. But El Arat has let the Legion Riders loose. Even now they ride the Green Road to look for her."

The light surrounding Jehanna dimmed to a faint glow, and for a moment, the Sweetwater horses saw her as she appeared to those in the Courts, a finely boned mare with an elegant head and ageless dark ruby eyes. She raised her head slowly and looked directly into the Eye of the Moon. She breathed out, and suddenly the light flooded her again with the suddenness of a spring storm. It grew so bright that they could barely stand to see her. Jehanna lifted her voice in a great cry like a bronze bell. The sound of it rose and sailed among the stars.

The Path from the water to the moon sprang high

and wide. Jehanna placed her forelegs upon it, and turned to look back at Duke, her gaze tender and wise. "Well done, Connemara."

She moved with stately elegance up the Path to the Moon. At the very top the Path dissolved into the Eye of the Moon itself, and Duke, his gaze intent, jumped and gasped in wonder.

Stallions were marching down the Path to meet the Goddess Mare. They were led by a flood of silver light, and Duke saw the face of his god. Behind the silver glow of Equus marched the stallions of the Army of One Hundred and Five. A rainbow arched over a space behind Equus' silver cloud, and then Hakimir, the Arabian, his bearing noble, came slowly forward, followed by a serried rank of stallions, each perfect of its kind. Somewhere in the orderly brilliant mass, Duke caught a glimpse of the Connemara stallion, and despite himself, a call of welcome escaped his throat.

The stallions marched, and Duke and the mares stood in awestruck wonder.

The light died away.

The night was quiet.

"Well!" said Meg, bounding out of the dark to stand at Duke's side. "There you are. Back to the barn for you."

There was a lot of fuss, as Duke had expected there would be. He was poked and pried at. His hooves were cleaned, and his coat brushed, followed by a very satisfying feed of warm bran. He was put into a stall next to Alvin.

"You saw her," said Alvin sadly. "What was she like?"

"Gold, like the sun," said Duke.

"And you told her what we knew?"

"I did," said Duke steadily. "She knows that both of us came back, too. I mentioned your name."

He bent his head to his herdmate and said, "The Army marched. I saw Himself. And behind him— the Connemara."

"And Gold Acre? Did you see him?"

"Big fellow, looks a lot like you?"

"Yes," said Alvin eagerly. "My Breedmaster."

Duke nodded, "I believe I did, Alvin. I believe I did."

"Well. Perhaps things will come out right after all."

Duke swallowed a last bit of bran mush that had stuck in his teeth.

"Perhaps," he said.

BLACKJACK

· 14 ·

The Final Gate

The eerie ululations of the Pack followed Blackjack as he raced from Piper's battle with the Executioner, and he ran with the dogs of hell at his heels. The larger part of the Pack bayed in the distance, chasing Basil and Dill. He sent up a brief prayer for the foxes, which stopped abruptly as he rounded the last curve in the gritty path.

The Black Barns rose before him.

He stopped, his flesh cold. It was very quiet. The Great Door was open. Beyond it, a dim red glow flickered in the silence. Terror overtook him, and he backed away wildly, his eyes rolled almost white. He felt the hot breath of the Pack on his hindquarters. They dived for his legs to hamstring him. He reared and whirled to meet them.

They flowed like an oily current along the road, rattails leaving a slimy wake. Their eyes glowed yellow-green in their nightmare skulls. They leaped at his face to tear at his muzzle, their breath hot and fetid. They whined and yipped, flakes of rotting flesh dripping from their tongues.

Blackjack spun, kicked and spun again. A Hound's yellow eye glared straight into his own, and he jerked away, off balance at the mindless evil in the soulless stare.

"Kill him!" they hissed. "Kill him. Kill him. Kill him."

Blackjack struck out again and again, his hooves slicing open a skull, crushing a rib cage, breaking legs. He put his head between his forelegs to protect his ears and muzzle and kicked out wildly, a fierce satisfaction in his chest when his hooves connected with solid flesh. He plunged both forelegs in a Hound's belly, and the creature rolled over and over, screaming its agony as it crawled away. He grabbed a third in his powerful jaws, whirling it over his withers, where it crashed headfirst into the roadway, neck snapped.

A Hound leaped at his near side, teeth raking a long wound on his shoulder. The frayed harness around his neck broke and dropped to the dirt. Another sank its fangs deep into his vulnerable belly. One leaped for his underthroat, and bit deep. Blackjack fought free, driven by a grim determination to get into the Barn, no matter what the cost. But the Hounds came at him like wolves in the mountains, in relays, with four or five taking over when their fellows fell back in exhaustion.

And Blackjack bucked violently. A snarling Hound on his neck whined and fell, chunks of flesh torn free as he catapulted beneath Blackjack's feet. The aisle was behind him, its darkness ominously still. Blackjack gathered in his powerful haunches and leaped the last few paces, twisting in mid-air so that he landed sideways, one eye on the darkness within, the other on the Pack.

They would not approach the door.

The Pack milled, climbing over one another, eerie whines and yips rolling away to silence. One by one they crouched, tongues lolling. A one-eyed bitch grinned evilly at him. Blackjack shifted his weight to his hindquarters, chest heaving. Blood trickled from wounds on his neck, flanks, quarters and belly. But his legs were whole, and he could see. He was wounded, but not mortally, and he curled his upper lip over his teeth in defiance.

"Game's a little different when you have to come at me one at a time, eh?" He blew out in contempt.

"So, my friends, my dearest ones. You will not take him? You will not approach the home of our master?" Scant crept out from behind the bodies of his Pack. He whined, nosing the one-eyed female, and eagerly licked the blood from her eye. She growled and snapped at him, and he backed off, giggling, and crept his way to Blackjack. "My master waits inside, my Pack without. You have your choice, gelding. Out here with us—or in there, with him. What will you do, gelding? Where will you go?"

Blackjack turned and looked down the great aisle. The oak stall doors were barred shut with iron. He heard faint scuttlings in the stalls, and shuddering, he edged out into the sullen sunlight. A crab-like creature, dried and black, scrambled beneath his hooves. He stamped in disgust, and the creature scuttled to a stall and slipped beneath its door. A shriek from a horse in agony split the air, then cut off, dying as swiftly as it had come. A sucking sound came from behind the door, then silence.

"My master waits," hissed Scant, creeping forward on his belly. "His time is precious to him, sweet gelding, and so your meeting will be brief. Go, go on. You are welcome there." And he opened his jaws and grinned. "You have something to say to him, gelding, do you not? Or do you simply wish to worship?"

"A word with him," said Blackjack grimly, "just one."

A look of unease flashed in Scant's eyes. Blackjack stamped, turned, and walked arrogantly down the center aisle. At first, he stepped out boldly in the rack, his legs working high, his tail flagged, his hooves beating against the silence. But the aisle seemed endless, the silence complete, and his confidence ebbed. He quickly lost any sense of the world that lay beyond this length of concrete.

Then the silence was broken with a long, in-drawn breath, as of a giant creature, waiting.

Blackjack flexed his poll against the dark. He faltered and forced himself forward.

He was sharply aware of his heart beating in his chest, the sweat drying on his flanks. He had never felt so alone.

The fear stole up on him, almost unnoticed at first. He was cold in the heat that pulsed softly from the end of the aisle.

He stopped finally, in front of a simple barred gate.

The Last Gate. And it was closed.

"Ho!" said Blackjack to the empty air.

Something moved in the black beyond. Blackjack worked his muzzle. Just say it, he thought, just call the name and then run like hell itself. He snorted. He was in the middle of hell itself. He worked his muzzle again. Just say it, and we can all go home.

Home . . . Grief swept over Blackjack like the

wings of a black bird. He thought of Sweetwater and its green pastures, of the mountains on a clear spring morning.

The movement came again, a flutter, and a black crow with red eyes flew out of the darkness and settled on the Gate post, wings folded.

Blackjack almost burst with relief. He drew breath and said, "Is your master here? I need a word, just one, with him."

"Bold gelding," said the crow. It hopped nearer, one sly eye fixed on Blackjack's wounds. "Brave gelding. My master is not here. You may leave your word with me."

"It's the Dark Horse himself I need to see," said Blackjack, some part of him amazed at his own courage.

"It *is* a bold gelding who heralds this Gate," said the crow admiringly. The bird fluttered its wings, then carefully groomed a pinion. "A horse who perhaps was born to rule rather than to be led. One who was born to cover mares as a stallion does, to lead the herd as a stallion does."

Blackjack opened his eyes, fear forgotten. "I am a gelding," he said simply. "I swore an oath to my stallion. I have no need to lead." As he said it, he knew that it was true and he exhaled in satisfaction. A weight seemed to lift from his withers.

The crow regarded him thoughtfully. "My master could fix that. You tell me what is your deepest desire, gelding, and I will carry your message to him, under my wing, like so," and the crow lifted his wing. Blackness swept beneath, and Blackjack felt the terror the bird carried with it.

"Message taker. Fear carrier," he said aloud. "I have not heard of you before, crow."

"Oh—all do, eventually." The crow clicked its beak. "Few get this far, I must admit, so perhaps that is why you and your kind have not heard of Crow."

"Well, after I see your master, I will return and tell them of you," said Blackjack. "Call him, if you would. I haven't much time myself."

"You really wish to see him? He will consume you, gelding. He will take your blood and bone from you as if he sipped water."

"Then why are you bargaining for him?" said Blackjack boldly. "How stupid do you think I am?" He shifted on his feet, his courage growing. Piper should see this, he thought. The Dark Horse himself hiding behind a carrion bird. "Why doesn't he just appear and suck me up like you say he can?"

"The Hounds wait for you outside. My master waits beyond," said the crow. "*I* have no need to trick you, gelding. You are trapped. My master admires your bravery, that is all, and as is his way, he always offers the touch of peace to those who come to him. He is always looking for new—talent. Some of our best recruits come from your side, you know. Our lady mare El Arat herself, for example."

"No thanks," said Blackjack. He stepped forward, and nosed at the sisal rope that closed the Gate. "Out of my way, crow. I would speak with your master."

"Bravery, honor, quick wits," the crow murmured. "That such a gelding could be here, in front of me. You are sure you could not teach us your ways, Blackjack? It is Blackjack, isn't it? Perhaps *we* could be taught these things. If we had an inspiration." The crow ducked its head and picked at the sisal. "Let me help you. And perhaps you will help us."

"Paah," Blackjack blew out in contempt.

The crow picked up the end of the rope in his beak, and regarded Blackjack with a sparkling eye. "So, do you wish to see my master?"

"I certainly do." Blackjack stepped forward confidently toward the Gate, his neck outstretched to step inside.

With a motion swifter than flight, the crow picked the rope free. It swung and formed a loop. The loop settled over Blackjack's neck. Holding one end of the rope in its beak, the crow flew up. As it flew, it grew in size to a vast, amorphous shape, an unendurable stench spreading from beneath its wings.

The rope tightened around Blackjack's neck, cutting off his wind. It pulled his forelegs off the ground and he swung by his neck, choking. The crow squealed, "Eeehai! Eeehai!" and the bird call changed, grew and transformed into the bellow of a gigantic stallion. Red fire sprang high. Blackjack twisted by his neck. Endless night stretched over Blackjack's head.

Two pinpoint red eyes glowed in the middle of the vast dark. Demon's eyes. *His* eyes.

Choking, desperate, Blackjack tried to draw in air. The lasso tightened, and the eyes—calm, dreadful, red—swam mockingly in front of him. The rope slackened. Blackjack dropped to all four feet. The noose remained tight, too tight for breath, and his sides shuddered with the effort to draw in air.

The floor heaved beneath Blackjack's hooves, and "Click!" the Black Horse walked forward and "Click!" the fire flared around him in a torrent, and "Click!" the gigantic shape of the stallion sprang out against the flames.

And he said, "Welcome, Blackjack."

The gelding struggled with silent ferocity.

What goes around comes around, Blackjack thought. If I die here, strangled on this rope, I'll walk the Green Road, I will live in the Courts, and another horse will live to take my place.

With this thought, the terror ebbed.

"Oh, there will be no Courts for you," said the Dark God. "Do not reassure yourself with that. You have, after all, challenged Me. I will be owed your soul at the very least."

A high-pitched wheezing came from Blackjack's throat. The red eyes filled his world. Blackjack bowed his head and stopped struggling.

"Good." The Dark God bent his great neck in satisfaction. "It will be easier this way." And ONE! he advanced one step and TWO! his eyes loomed larger and Blackjack knew he would fall into those red depths forever and THREE! the great mouth opened and there was no end to that spiralling emptiness and FOUR!

Blackjack breathed in. Ducked. Spun and was free.

He shouted the Name. And the voice that came from his throat was not his own, but the voice of all his kind. He shouted, and the Name ripped its way through his swollen, bleeding throat, and the Name took shape and exploded into a great, blinding light, and in that light stood a stallion, rusty black, dwindling even as Blackjack took his next breath.

He shouted, and the stallion dwindled to the crab-shaped, dried up thing that he had seen as he first stopped on the great aisle, and the thing dried away to a fine powder and spiralled away into . . . Nothing.

Blackjack, emptied, felt nothing, saw nothing. Time waited for him.

The earth heaved beneath Blackjack's hooves. A great rumbling shook the Barns. The iron-bound stall doors which lined the great aisle burst open and the airy souls of the horses damned to this black land soared free.

The aisle cracked wide open. Timbers, slate, bricks and concrete tumbled into the caverns gaping there. Blackjack whirled. Somber daylight beckoned at the distant entrance. Blackjack leaped for freedom, his hooves striking sparks from the concrete floor. A narrow bridge was all that remained of the great aisle, and racing swiftly, Blackjack singlefooted his way across, the Barns crashing into rubble all around him.

While Hank and the foxes stood helplessly by, Piper battled Anor back to the Second Gate, where El Arat stood guard at her Pool. The two stallions, one red, one stippled black and cream, were covered with dried and drying blood. Piper gathered himself for one last mighty effort. The Red, legs splayed, head swinging in exhaustion, stood dully in front of him, fanged teeth dripping gobbets of Piper's flesh.

Piper screamed a final, furious battle cry, and lunged at Anor's throat. He hit the jugular, and dark red blood burst into his mouth. He pushed his chest against the Red's and they struggled in a grotesque embrace.

Suddenly, the ground buckled and Anor's hindfeet slipped. He fell back. Piper lunged, forcing Anor to the waters of the Pool.

"No!" screamed El Arat.

Piper sank his teeth into Anor's neck and pulled with the last of his great strength. Inch by straining inch, he pulled the massive bulk to the roiling waters of the Pool. His breath was raw, the world around him dark.

Anor tumbled back into the pool with a scream.

El Arat sprang back from its edge as the waters foamed high. Anor thrashed helplessly and roared in naked rage. The water cascaded into his throat and he choked, legs churning up the oily liquid. He struggled to the bank.

Piper watched him, spent. His head was down, his lips drawn fiercely over his teeth. Trembling seized him.

The sky rattled with the sound of thunder. A wind came blasting across the plains. There was an immense noise, of mountains falling, of an avalanche of rock and stone. The wind smelled of death.

"Mother!" shouted El Mordant. "The Barns!"

Lightning shot across the sky over the Barns. The buildings erupted, sending wood and stone spinning in tornado gusts of wind.

The wind blew to hurricane strength, carrying the sands of the soulless desert away in great billowing clouds.

Hank struggled to Piper's side and the two stood close together.

The wind struck the Watching Pool with a solid fist. The waters fountained, faster and faster, and Anor, with no purchase for his legs, whirled wildly in its center. His bellows were lost in the thundering wind.

The waters sucked him down.

The wind died.

The air cleared.

Far away, at the very edges of the sky, Hank and Piper heard the cry of the Pack in full retreat.

The waters of the Pool calmed and went still. The thunderclouds rolled on, an occasional rumble shaking the earth and sky. It began to rain, a soft, drenching torrent. Piper raised his muzzle and let the drops soak his torn mouth and tongue.

El Mordant and Dreadlock plunged and squealed in the downpour. "What is it, Mother?" cried Dreadlock. "There's water falling from the sky!"

"It's rain," said El Arat, her voice brusque and ugly. "Where there should be no rain."

The torrent lessened to a downpour and in the grey curtain, the horses saw a dark shape moving toward them from the direction of the Black Barns. El Arat raised her voice in a triumphant whinny. "Yes!" she screamed, "Yes!"

The rain slackened, then stopped altogether, and the dark horse stood revealed.

"Ha!" said Blackjack, picking his way carefully through the thorn trees. "So much for your 'Yes!', mare. Did you think I was your master? Blown to bits, I'm afraid, in the general upheaval around here."

"Blackjack," said Piper, simply. "Thanks Equus."

"You did all this!" Hank exclaimed, looking at the devastation surrounding them. "The wrecked Barns, the Pool, puddles of rain in a land where no rain ever falls."

"Nah," said Blackjack. His neck was scarred with a fearsome wound which entirely circled his throat and neck. He twitched his ears ironically, and he greeted Piper with the three brief exhalations which mean a gelding acknowledges a leader of the herd. "We *all* did this."

He cocked his head inquiringly at Piper, indicating the great gouges of flesh on the stallion's chest and withers. "Just standing around waiting for me to show up? What happened to the big red guy?"

"In the Pool," said Piper. "I tried the Bear just as the world exploded. Lucky shove." He sniffed curiously at the raw ring around Blackjack's neck. "And you?"

"Lucky duck," said Blackjack. Hank began to lick

the blood from the Walker's neck, and Blackjack slumped, his knees shaking.

"Well, your luck's run out," El Arat hissed. "Look! The Legion Riders!" She shrilled a loud command. In the distance, along the path that led to the First Gate, the Soulless Legion rode. Hundreds of horses and their riders, moving forward with the automatic movements of the damned.

Hank stepped to Piper's near side, his neck arched, ready for battle. Blackjack ambled thoughtfully to the other.

El Arat walked forward on the tips of her hooves, her yellow eyes alight. "They come to me," she said, her voice guttural. She slid her eyes sidelong. "They come to me. I must thank you, stallion, you and what passes for your herd, because it is you who have made all this possible for me." She grinned, her satisfaction deep. "You see what has happened. You see what you have accomplished for me. This is my land now, mine. A Dark Mare rules here now."

The Legion came toward them at a steady, purposeful gait. The Lead Rider appeared over the slight rise that led down to the Watching Pool, eyes blank in its stony face. A whip in its right hand rose and fell, scarring the sides of the horse it rode.

"Brothers," said Piper, stepping forward, "we have no quarrel with you. Your Dark Lord is gone, and you are free."

"Ridiculous," spat El Arat. "Capture them, take them to the Pit!"

Something flickered in the Lead Rider's eyes.

"The Souls were freed in the Barns," said Blackjack to Piper. "Do you suppose that . . ."

"Yes," said Piper. "I do."

The Lead Rider pulled to a halt. The others filed behind him and pulled up.

"Welcome, brothers," said the stallion, stepping forward. The creamy spots on his hindquarters glowed in the weak sun. Despite the wounds, his head was high and confident. "Free yourselves. Ride on."

"You will do no such thing!" El Arat screamed. "You are mine! These are mortals! They are nothing to you. Take them, and all will be as it has been before."

The Lead Rider gazed blindly past them to the Pool. He turned in his saddle and looked at the devastation of the Barns.

"We will rebuild," said El Arat. "I swear to you. A finer Barn than the Black Land has ever seen before." She squared up, her silky mane floating in the wind. "I am your mistress now. You will obey me."

There was a spell of quiet, broken only by the shifting of Hank's feet. Then the air moved softly near Piper's cheek, and involuntarily he glanced up. There was a slow flailing of wings.

"No!" El Arat screamed. "I will not have this!" Her teeth gleamed and she leaped into the air, snapping at the bird flying overhead. "This is mine now! I have the right!"

The Great White Owl, one wing black, one wing white, floated effortlessly overhead. He hung motionless, buoyed by a current of air.

"A sign!" shouted Blackjack. "A sign!"

Slowly, the white wing dipped.

El Arat tore up great gouges of earth with her hooves, her muzzle distorted in a rictus of rage. "I have worked too long for this!" she shrieked. "It is mine by right!" She spun and raced down the path to where the ruins of the Black Barns smoked under a clearing sky. She paused, looked back, and gazed directly at Piper, a terrible look in her eyes. She trembled with hatred.

Her challenge reached them all:

"I curse you for this. You and all your get! No mortal will defeat me, Piper. Watch where you go in the future!" She reared, and screamed, "You will see me once again!" She ran then to the Barns, her body swallowed by the ruins.

El Mordant and Dreadlock melted into the thorn break after her.

Piper looked up. The Owl had flown. He walked forward and faced the Legion Riders. "Brothers," he said, and there was an undercurrent of desperation in his voice. "My dam, my sire, do they travel with you? Have you brought them back, or does my dam still wait in the Havens?"

The Riders sat motionless, impassive. All at once, the Lead Rider dismounted, and all his Riders with him. They gathered into a column, horses at their sides, and began to walk forward in synchronized rhythm. The horses, heads up, moved automatically at first, but as they progressed farther and farther away from the Watching Pool, they began to move on their own, tossing their heads, rolling their bits in their mouths.

Piper ran with them, his eyes pleading. He looked into their faces, and cried, "Duchess! Where is Duchess? Stop, please."

Blackjack ran after Piper, shouldering him gently back to the devastated Pool. "You see where they are headed, Piper? They do not go to Her—to the Barns, but to the desert. Only it's no longer a desert—it's growing grass out there."

They all turned and looked. The ground which had been sand-struck and barren beneath an iron sky had been touched by the steady rain, and now swelled with a creeping tide of green. The sky shone more blue than yellow-grey, and the weak sun spread warming light on the burgeoning fields.

"They go to graze," said Hank. "Isn't that something?"

Piper, desolate, watched the Legion reach the newly growing pasture, disperse, and disappear into the new meadow.

Hank touched Blackjack lightly on the withers. "It's time," he said. "We should go home."

Blackjack nodded. "Come on, Piper. We can be home in three turns of the sun. Think of it! Oats again, and well-cured hay. Sweet meadow grass and water that doesn't taste of dead fish or worse. Walk on!"

"I cannot leave," said Piper, "not until I know what's happened to my dam. Not until I know if my sire is safe."

"Well, that's why we're getting back there, isn't it?" said Hank practically. "To find out how successful Alvin and Duke were in getting Frosty to Walk the Path to the Moon."

He looked at his two herdmates with keen attention. Blackjack and Piper both would have to move slowly, eating and resting along the way. The gouge around Blackjack's neck would heal into a frightful scar, a grisly reminder of what they all had faced. And Piper, his spotted coat flecked with blood and his own chewed flesh, would never stand with a purple ribbon in any conformation class in this world or the next.

"What has happened here?" Piper asked bitterly. "The Barn's destroyed, but El Arat and the Soultaker's daughters run free. The Pack is scattered, but not gone, and we see no signs of Basil or Dill. There is meadow in the Dark Lands, where desert was before, but the Soulless Legions graze there. Blackjack has a scar that will never leave him—and who knows where Anor has gone? Where are my dam and sire? What have we done? What have we gained?" He pawed at the ground. "Where are our gods when we need them?"

"Come on," said Hank gruffly. "Follow me."

So it was Hank who finally led them back, down from the Dancer's mountain to Sweetwater Valley, four days past the full of the moon.

• 15 •

El Arat's Revenge

Back at Sweetwater, Piper and Blackjack healed slowly. The scar of the noose around Blackjack's chest and withers filled in with proud flesh, thick and grainy. At a distance, Piper's savage gouges looked like ordinary Appaloosa mottling; it was only close up that they looked like what they were: the mark of a cannibal.

David turned Blackjack, Hank, Alvin and Duke out with the brood mares for the summer to recover completely; three of the barren mares from the Sweetwater herd composed the new members of the Working Herd, and Blackjack would watch them ride out mornings with a wistful eye.

"They think you tangled with a mountain cat," Meg told them after the exuberance of their return died down. "And that Blackjack ran into rustlers. Hank they figure just fell into a ravine or something. He healed up, and you two didn't. You sure you don't want to tell me exactly what happened?"

"Someday," Piper said. "When we know ourselves."

He didn't know what had happened to his sire and

285

dam, and the thought tormented him. He had obeyed his Laws, the demands of the Balance—was he never to know the ending? The ways of his gods—of the One himself—remained a mystery still, and he picked restlessly at the questions in his mind. Why? Why am I not to know?

The brood mares were having a good year; as summer rolled slowly on, the foals they'd dropped grew tall and strong. All but a few were brightly colored. This, Piper took as a good sign; if his dam were still lost in the Havens, Appaloosa get at least were still alive and whole in the world of men.

As the full moon waxed in June, Piper persuaded Frosty to Walk the Path to the Moon once more. But her efforts failed. The Path was closed, and Piper, uncertain, doubting the justice of his gods, was restless, plagued with dreams and worry.

It had been a dry spring at Sweetwater, and the summer was even drier. The pasture grass developed the thin, crackly feel of hay. Days passed when the sky was the clear blue that meant no rain would come for days. Sweetwater Stream slowed to a trickle, and the weanlings splashed fearlessly from bank to bank, the water barely covering their hocks.

The four geldings were closer now than they ever had been before; the brood mares treated them with a nervous respect, and they walked tall and proud. It was Piper who suffered, Piper who stayed thin and gaunt while his herdmates put on weight, Piper who doubted that what he had done had brought anything but battle scars to his herd mates, who was haunted by terrible dreams.

Alvin, Duke, Hank and Blackjack at the far end of the pasture overlooking the bluffs one hot afternoon when the weather finally broke.

"If we had a Dreamspeaker, you wouldn't have to

wonder what happened to Duchess," Alvin said to Piper. "And she could tell you what your dreams mean."

"I doubt that a Dreamspeaker could help," said Piper. "It isn't dreams that I have precisely, more an uneasiness when I'm sleeping. I feel that I'm being chased, toward what, I don't know."

"Perhaps you are being chased to your destiny," said Duke gravely. "Perhaps you are after all to be a Breedmaster."

Piper shook his head. "No. They still live. I have to believe they still live."

"We may never know," said Duke softly. "We have played our part, Piper. The Dark Horse himself is destroyed, and El Arat chased to some far corner of the Black Lands. Scant and his Pack are scattered, and the Soulless Legion grazes in pastures where no grass grew before. Perhaps this is all we are meant to know. The story's over. The Balance has been served."

Piper sighed. "You can't be right."

"Take it easy," said Alvin comfortingly. "Next year, things will be back to routine; you'll be back on the rodeo circuit, and the Working Herd will ride again. And we'll forget all of this—the Black Barns, the Pit, El Arat and her creepy fillies."

"El Arat," said Piper, remembering.

They grazed lightly in the sultry heat. Lightning flickered through banked storm clouds to the west, and Piper's wounds began to itch fiercely, as though he were plagued by flies. Hank and Duke engaged in mutual grooming, then stopped, and stood nose-to-tail, switching the pasture gnats out of each other's faces. Alvin grazed the clumps of grass near the bluffs of Sweetwater canyon. Blackjack, an anxious eye on Piper, stayed close to the stallion's side.

Piper roamed the wire fence surrounding the brood

mare's pasture, his ears twitching, his muzzle raised to the air. Blackjack followed him, and finally Clover loped over, her ears flattened crossly against her head.

"What's the matter with you two?" she asked irritably. "You're upsetting the weanlings. And look at Rocket, will you? He thinks something's up. He keeps rounding up the fillies and taking them to the gate and I have to go scatter them again. It's too hot to pace around like this."

"Storm's coming," said Piper. "And there's something foul in the air. Keep the herd together." He pawed restlessly at the dry grass, then looked abruptly at his son.

"Rocket did well while I was gone?" asked Piper.

"You've asked me that once too often, Piper. Yes, he did. He's going to be a great stallion in another year or so. I can tell. And the men can, too. He works every day in the corral with David."

Piper nuzzled her neck affectionately. "Good."

"I wish you'd tell me what's wrong," she said wistfully. "Everything's all right now, isn't it? You did what you set out to do. What could happen now?"

Thunder rolled, an ominous series of beats. The wind rose in a sudden burst.

"Quiet!" Piper, stiff-legged, raised his head and strained his eyes to the mountains. He blew out with a hollow, breathy snort like the bellows the blacksmith used. He trembled, then pawed the ground.

"Get Rocket. Gather the mares together, foals in the middle of the herd."

"What?"

"Do it. Now!" He ran forward a few paces, his eyes fixed on the horizon. An intense black mass was forming in the center of the oncoming storm. Underneath the long slow wave of thunder, a hissing came, as of hornets swarming from a gigantic nest in the sky.

Clover inhaled; the stallion smelled of rage and fear. "You're scaring me, Piper. It's just a thunderstorm. What is it?"

"Black flies! Headed this way! Blackjack! Round up the mares!"

Clover froze. She wheeled and reared, shrilling a warning to the herd.

Black flies drove animals to suicide, descending on their helpless victims in a devil's fury. Once fastened on an animal's ears and eyes, the cloud moved as a being of one mind, closing to kill, stinging again and again. They crawled into the body's most sensitive spots: eyes, ears, sheath, mouth.

The pain drove animals mad.

They bred in the long grasses beneath the trees, reaching maturity when the days were long and the weather hot and dry. They rose in a body to strike from cool shade, to kill ferociously and without mercy.

Clover screamed again, racing in a wide circle to bring the herd together. The brood mares huddled, weanlings pressed close in the center of their ranks.

Piper raced to the pasture gate, bellowing to Meg for help from the Sweetwater hands. Blackjack raced to Alvin's side by the bluffs, and the Standardbred raised his head in astonishment.

"Black flies? Here? There aren't any trees within furlongs."

"I know," said Blackjack grimly, "but they're headed this way." They watched the cloud with intense concentration.

At first, it looked like a thunder cloud, a welcome harbinger of rain, rising from the horizon. But it moved with the speed of a tornado, a roiling furious mass.

And beneath it ran a familiar shape.

Blackjack jumped in appalled recognition. It was a horse, and even at that distance, he could see the yellow-green glow of its eyes.

"El Arat," he whispered. "She's back."

A half mile away at the pasture gate, Piper saw her, too. El Arat's curse came back to him, and he watched in horror as she raced toward them, leading the deadly cloud straight to the mares he was sworn to protect. He whistled an imperative command to Blackjack. Blackjack sprang into a gallop, calling to Alvin as he raced, "Guard the bluffs. Turn the herd back. The flies will drive them this way. The mares will be killed if they fall into the canyon beyond the bluffs."

Alvin nodded curtly. Blackjack galloped after Piper, who had a good quarter mile advantage. The brilliant black and white of his stallion closed on the Soultaker and her demon followers. The cloud swept past El Arat. She stopped. Reared in triumph. Lightning flashed behind her—and her body shone yellow/green/black. She shrieked, once, in terrible triumph, then leaped into the storm's embrace and disappeared.

Piper reared up to the cloud, beating desperately at the mass. Blackjack crashed to a halt, his heart constricted.

The black flies, armed with a deadlier purpose, flew high over the stallion's head and on to the mass of huddled brood mares.

"No!" shouted Piper. "NO!" He screamed a long challenge.

The cloud flew directly over Blackjack's head. For a long moment, the Walker's world grew dark, and he was back at the Final Gate, staring straight into the jaws of hell. Demonic red eyes glared down at him from the formless thousands. Blackjack shook with fear, then struck out at the cloud with both forelegs.

The cloud flew on.

"The mares!" Blackjack shouted. "Save the mares!" Piper's sons and daughters, he thought. El Arat's curse. Damn her. Damn her!

The cloud descended on the herd, and the mares lost their heads. They jostled together and shut their eyes, the foals squealing in terror. The buzzing squall drove them to the bluffs where Alvin stood guard.

Alvin watched them come. Jessica was in the lead, her creamy mane whipping wildly in the wind, her golden coat damp with sweat. Her eyes rolled completely white. Blind terror filled the air. Alvin, shaking, fought the impulse to run as mindlessly as the mares.

The mares drew closer, terrified screams mingling with the hornet sound.

Alvin called on the strength he'd had when he raced for men. He shot into a flat out gallop as if from a starting gate. He ran as he had never run before, long legs covering the ground at an improbable speed. The vanguard of the cloud reached him. The flies descended in a vicious shower. They attacked his back, hindquarters and flanks. Flies buzzed angrily in his ears and mouth. "The Snake!" he thought, and ducking his head low, he cannoned into Jessica at the crumbling edge of the bluffs. She turned aside, running blind. Men shouted from somewhere far away, calling the mares to the safety of the pasture gate. Jessica thrashed her way to the cowhands, and the herd followed her, turned from the treacherous bluffs.

At the tail end of the herd, Frosty lumbered on, deaf to all but fear. Eyes shut, ears back, she galloped straight to the canyon's edge. Alvin stopped, and stood his ground, his big body a barrier. He swerved hard, knocking her off her feet. She fell heavily, and Alvin reared to keep his hooves from plunging into her vulnerable body.

His forefeet came down—met nothing—and he plunged over the bluffs to the canyon below.

Frosty scrambled to her feet and ran on to the safety of the gate.

The deadly cloud flew over Sweetwater canyon to the pine trees beyond.

Piper ran to the edge of the bluffs, great sides heaving. Alvin lay still on the gully floor, a bright mass of chestnut against the dried earth. His long neck was stretched against a boulder. His eyes were half open.

Blackjack thundered up, Meg at his heels. Duke, puffing hard, sweat-soaked, stumbled up with Hank.

The horses looked down at their herd mate.

"He's just stunned," said Duke after a moment. "Like that time at the rodeo when the steer got him. I'll go down and get him to his feet."

Hank exchanged a look with Blackjack.

"Let Piper go down," Blackjack said gently.

"Alvin the Reckless," sighed Duke. "Who'd have thought it? We'll go down together, Piper. He'll need both of us to get him up."

"Duke," said Meg gently, "you come back to the gate with me. I'll get some of the men to come and help."

Duke, his breath a little faster, challenged them all with a steady look. "Let men help him up? We're his herdmates. He'll want us to help him up."

"He's not going to get up," said Hank roughly. "Can't you see that, Duke? He's—come on, Duke. I'll go with you back to the gate."

"He'll be fine, once he hears me," said Duke, stubbornly. He leaned over the edge and called out in a long whinny, "Alvin! Alvin! Up!" Duke backed up and shook his head. "He's always been a little lazy, like we all are. But he'll get up for me."

"Come," said Hank. "We'll let Piper and Blackjack take care of it. Come, Duke."

"Jehanna," said Duke loudly, as the collie nudged him away from his friend. "I'll call on Jehanna! She can help."

Piper and Blackjack picked their way cautiously down the gully slope. The breeze picked up, then died away. The sun beat down from the cloudless sky.

"He's breathing!" said Blackjack. "I thought—"

"So did I," said Piper.

The area behind Alvin's stifle moved up and down in faint jerks. Piper moved forward and blew on Alvin's face.

"Alvin."

The Standardbred's eyes flicked open. The corners wrinkled with an unspoken question.

"Yes," said Piper. "The mares are safe. And the flies are gone."

A small sound escaped Alvin's chest. His eyes closed, then opened again. They were very cloudy.

"Alvin," said Piper simply, "we love you. Please don't leave the herd."

"I. Will. See. Her." His breath was a hopeful whisper.

"Damn," said Blackjack. He scraped at the ground with his foreleg.

"Jehanna?" said Piper. "The Gold One. You, of all of us, Alvin, will see Her. But not now. Not now." He nosed Alvin's cheek, and moved his muzzle softly against the gelding's neck.

Alvin trembled. A rictus shook him. His eyes darkened.

Piper stamped in fury. His tail flagged, his neck rigid, he raised his voice to the sky. "Equus!" he shouted. "Equus! Save this member of my herd. He has given all to save the mares. Don't take him now! I will stop questioning the fate of my sire and dam. I will go forward as herd stallion. I will not question your ways again. Only save his life. Do not call him now."

A green mist rose from Alvin's body, and took shape into a path.

"You cannot take him! Not yet! Let him stay! He died because of a filthy trick, a curse I brought upon him. It is my fault." He paused, and lowered his head, staring sightlessly at the ground. He murmured, "If you must take someone, Equus, take me." He raised his head once more, the anger gone from his eyes, his face gentle. "Take me."

The scent of spring flowers drifted through the summer afternoon. The odor of hyacinth grew strong.

Jehanna's ruby gaze gleamed through the green mist around Alvin's body. Behind her stretched the long Green Road, a steady upward path to the sky. The end lay lost in the mist.

"Take me, Mistress," said Piper, "I am ready now."

"It is Alvin's time," she said.

"Where have you been until now?" Piper said. "Why have you abandoned us until now? Why come to me now, only to take my herd mate?"

"So you would turn your back on the Courts,

because you cannot bend the will of Equus to your way?" said Jehanna. "Would you undo what you did—even if Alvin's life is at stake?"

Piper looked deeply into the gold mare's eyes. Alvin, breathing heavily now, answered for them all, his voice a mere whisper.

"We. Would. Not. Mistress."

Piper trembled with grief. "He's right. I would not undo what I did. But must this be part of the price?"

"We do not set the price, Piper. I grieve for you. I am sorry. But the Balance rules over us all." She bent her head and the air around her was fresh and sweet. "We are animals, only, under the rule of the One, El Arat and Equus alike."

"Then I challenge HIM!" Piper shouted to the sky. "I call on the Owl, his messenger. I call on the Balance, to judge whether the life of our herd mate is owed."

Jehanna stood motionless, ruby eyes calm.

The silence around her stretched on like a living thing.

The sounds of the earth stopped.

The sun hung suspended in its journey across the sky.

Then, from the very center of the sun itself, a small speck fell toward them. The sound of beating wings filled the air.

The Owl swept overhead.

He circled the horses once, twice, and then again. As the Owl's wings raised for the third time, the sky, sun and earth vanished.

Piper was alone, in a vast space that had nothing in it, but was somehow full. Blackjack and Alvin were near, although Piper could not see them, and Jehanna, too, a warm gold presence. Piper looked. Slowly, the peace of this place filled him, eyes, ears, skin and heart. Although there was no light—he was not in shadow. Although he stood alone—he was not separate. The horse, all animals, and man himself—all were creatures of the One. Each being had a place in the presence of the One—and the One was present everywhere. Although he could not see, he understood. He, Alvin, the mares, all were part of one mighty whole. The moving of one part to another meant little.

A sweet noise filled his ears, like the cascading of a waterfall, a music that melted his heart with the promise of a fresh and joyful spring. The One who played the pipes played on. Peace enveloped Piper in a celestial light.

"I understand," said Piper. The grief lifted from his heart.

The tender sounds of the pipes faded into the vastness of creation.

The sun grew bright.

The earth was rough beneath Piper's feet.

"Praise be the One," Jehanna sang.

Jehanna knelt on her forelegs by Alvin's head. She rose and breathed lightly on Alvin's neck, then turned and walked up the Green Road.

She reached the top and turned to nod farewell. Ahead, the Green Road opened to a vast and flowered meadow. A silver shining, Equus, moved to greet Jehanna, and beside him, a rainbow arc of light.

"The Dancer," Blackjack said. "And behind him, Piper, look!"

Duchess, her mane and tail as black as a crow's wing, her coat the color of dried grasses in autumn, nodded to her son. Her eyes were bright, and a radiance came from her. "Piper!" she sang. "Well done!"

The Dancer's colors glowed more brightly still, and a familiar call split the air.

"Piper!" His sire's shout was like a great bronze bell. "Well done!"

"Father!" shouted Piper. "Until we meet once more."

Their colors died, as a rainbow will when the light is lost.

The Road dissolved and faded into ordinary sunshine. Sweetwater came to life beneath Piper's feet.

Alvin struggled to his haunches.

"I think," he said clearly, "that this foreleg's broken. Are the men coming to get us out of here?"

• 16 •

Sweetwater Sunrise

"Now *that*," said Newton the farm cat, "was the part I wanted to see the most of all, the part where they had all three of you slung up on that big rig and picked you up with it and put you in the truck and I didn't get to see any blood at all, hardly any." She looked hopefully at Piper. "Do you think any of you will bleed today?"

They were all together in the barn several days later. Alvin hung from a giant sling suspended from the cross beams above his stall. His left foreleg was encased in a hard bandage from shoulder to coronet band. A hand came twice a day to flex his other legs and rub him down.

Piper and the geldings had been brought into the barn that morning, and Piper was trying to discover why from the barn cat.

"I'm NOT a barn cat," said Newton firmly, "I got promoted, I told you. And I get to go into the house to eat where I have my own dish and when I got promoted I got wormed, which is why I missed everything, and it's also why I have a normal-size stomach instead of that big barn cat belly I had when I was a barn cat, which I'm not now." She rolled over and put a paw on each side of her face. "Worms," she said reflectively, "are pretty disgusting. Would you like to know what happens when you get wormed? Meg explained it because her puppies got wormed too, same as me." She gazed unwinkingly at Piper, her eyes huge. "Did I tell you I got promoted?"

"You've told me everything except what I want to know," said Piper. "Let's start again. We were all brought into the barn because . . ."

"Because it's great to visit the barn and not to live here."

"Give it up," advised Blackjack. "Here's Meg. We can make more sense out of what she tells us. Ho, Meg."

"Ho," the collie replied absently. "Newton, go back to the house. You'll get stepped on if you hang around here today."

"Who would dare step on a house cat?" Newton puffed her copper-black fur to gigantic, indignant size. "I say, who would step on a house cat? Now a barn cat, there's a cat that has to keep out of the way. That's a cat to step on. Fat, wormy barn cats."

"The new geldings might step on you, that's who," said Meg. "Now go on back to the house." She barked once, and clicked her teeth at the little cat. Newton stalked stiff-legged out the overhead doors. Meg, distracted, turned back to the horses. "Too much to do, and not enough time to do it," she muttered. "That cat!"

"Do you know what's going on?" asked Blackjack.

"Of course I do. Rocket went to auction yesterday. He fetched the largest price ever for an Appaloosa colt. You should be proud, Piper." Busily, Meg trotted up and down the aisles, inspecting the empty stalls. "David's bought more heifers, and more geld-ings to work the cattle, and some new mares, I think." She paused to sniff carefully at a loose board in the wall. "I guess things will be even busier from now on.

"Blast, so that's how she got in." She pawed at the wall, then turned and faced Piper, a worried wrinkle between her eyes. "Piper, I was out on my rounds this morning and I found a fox." She scratched her white ruff furiously. "This fox wanted to give you a message and it dropped *this* on my fur." A sprig of dill fell on to the concrete, and Meg turned it dis-dainfully over with her nose. "That's from the gar-den." She looked significantly at Piper. "The garden next to the hen house, and the rabbit hutches."

"Many a caged rabbit in my time," snorted Alvin in amusement. "It's Dill!"

"Did any of the rabbits—ah—disappear?" asked Piper.

"No," admitted Meg. "But, by Canis, Piper, if any of them do, it'll be your fault. What do you mean by bringing a fox to this ranch?"

"I doubt that she'll stick around," said Piper. "Did she have any message for me, Meg?"

"She did, said she'd leave the ranch in peace if I gave it to you, but I don't trust foxes, Piper, and you shouldn't either. They are wild, uncontrolled meat eaters, and they don't know enough to stay away from chickens!" She flattened her ears and showed her teeth. "A horse who's friends with foxes is not a friend of mine, and she better not set up a den around here, or she'll regret it."

"She'll keep her word," said Duke. "If you just tell us what she wanted Piper to know."

"The Dark Lords in the Havens. The Old Mare's safely asleep. Now what does all that mean?"

Blackjack, memories of the red-eyed crow alive once more, stared unseeingly into his hay rack. Hank snorted. Duke and Alvin put their heads together against the wire mesh that separated them.

"And what does it *mean*?" demanded Meg. "Blast! Hear that?" The collie's ears tuliped forward, and she dashed down the aisle, barking. "Truck's here! Already! Blast!"

"Are you all right, Blackjack?" asked Duke.

Piper blew out comfortingly in the Walker's direction. "So what you did has had some effect, Blackjack."

The Walker rolled his withers. "The scar hurts," he said softly. "The place where . . ."

"The rope," said Alvin. "We know."

"I remember, sometimes," said Blackjack. "In the dark, when the moon is down."

"It'll pass," said Hank. "It's all over."

"Is it?" Blackjack's eyes were tragic. "We've all been retired to pasture. Will the herd ever work again? I think not. Men don't trust me, now. This scar's a permanent reminder that I left my duty as Herd Chief. That we all abandoned our duty. They're bringing a new Working Herd in now. This wouldn't have happened if we hadn't left."

"It's over," said Piper, "and we never expected to win everything."

"I saw Her," said Alvin softly, "we destroyed the Black Horse, and El Arat's disappeared. What more can we ask, Blackjack?"

"A worthy life," said Duke. "That's what we can ask."

The sounds and scents of new arrivals came to them, and they moved restlessly in their stalls. Piper called out, a loud challenge, and subdued whickers answered him.

"Quite a few geldings," Hank said, his nose lifted to the air.

They heard the rattle of the gate let down on the stock trailer. The ramp was rolled into place, and the clatter of several horses descending made them all look inquiringly at the open doors. Piper rumbled deep in his chest. A ranch hand led the first gelding into the barn. A tough, well-formed Grade, with an intelligent eye, he had a springy, elastic gait. Meg darted through the door after him, and indicated Blackjack with her outthrust nose. "That's your Herd Chief," she said, "The big Walker right there. And of course—your stallion. But you've heard of him already." She disappeared again, then shepherded in a liver chestnut, a Quarterhorse with the well-defined interior muscling that mean the best of his type. At the Quarterhorse's rear was a compact, chesty Half-Bred, and a young Morgan with an alert eye.

They looked at Piper sidelong, and bowed their heads in respect. They acknowledged Piper's presence with the proper sequence of breaths—one sharp expulsion which announced their name and breeding, two long whistles which requested permission to join the herd.

Piper nodded, flexing his poll. "Welcome." He turned to his Herd Chief. "Blackjack," he said, "they're all yours."

The Walker squared up. His head arched, and his thick mane parted to show the scar around his throat. "I am Blackjack," he said briskly, "Herd Chief, by . . ."

"No need to introduce yourself to us, sir," said the Grade, gruffly. "We've heard of you. All of you. Sir, we're proud to join you, if you'll have us."

The Morgan pranced a little as the ranch hand let him into his new stall. "We can't believe it," he blurted out. "To be part of Blackjack's working herd! Blackjack the Magnificent!"

Alvin and Duke exchanged a significant look.

"Blackjack the Magnificent Blowhard?" murmured Duke.

They blew out in delight.

"Here we go again," said Hank. He settled his haunches comfortably against the side of his stall and watched his friends in amusement.

"All in and settled?" Meg said in front of Piper's stall.

"Yes. That's quite a Working Herd, Meg."

She glanced quickly, counting. "Hank, Blackjack, Duke, Alvin, Red, Eagle, Old Glory and Brewster. And the barren mares, Piper. They're out in the corral, but they're going to be a permanent part of the Working Herd, too."

"Blackjack will be busy," said Piper. "Good."

"So will you," said Meg. "You ready?"

Piper pricked his ears. David came into the barn, a hackamore in his hand. He slid open the door to Piper's stall. For a long moment, Piper looked into the man's strange, small eyes, then he bent his head and shoved his muzzle into his master's chest. "Saa, saa, Piper," said David. He ran his hands down the stallion's neck, probing at the healed scars. A faint signal came from his hands, and Piper rubbed his face in his master's shirt in affection.

David slipped the hackamore on and led Piper down the aisle. The geldings fell silent out of respect as the stallion walked, and he exchanged a quick wink with Blackjack. "Fought the Executioner, he did," the dunn whispered to the Morgan. "See those scars? We're part of Piper's Ranch now."

"All right," Piper heard Blackjack say briskly. "Where have you all worked before? We're top cutters here, and we work hard."

"It's long hours we're used to, sir, and hard work," the dun replied.

His voice faded as Piper stepped out into the drive. The sun was shining. Sweetwater hummed with activity. Ranch hands—several new ones among them—were adding a large addition to the corral. In the Cow Barn, he heard the blowing and rustlings of at least fifty new head of cattle.

And in the drive, a new rig gleamed silver and green.

David handed the reins of the hackamore off to a young hand, and hurried to the rig's back door. He let down the ramp and stepped inside. There was a soft murmuring whinny.

David backed a mare out of the truck and stood with her.

She was an Arabian, fine boned, milk-white, with a silky mane and tail. Her eyes were large and dark, and she greeted Piper with a sweet call.

"Sweetwater's Sunrise," said Meg, appearing at Piper's hocks. "Your new Dreamspeaker, Piper, at least that's what she tells me."

Piper plunged both forefeet striking sparks from gravelled ground. He greeted his Sunrise with a shout of delight.

EPILOGUE

In the Courts of the Outermost West, Jehanna blew into the clear waters of the Watching Pool and an image formed in its center.

The stallions of the Army of One Hundred and Five stood shoulder to shoulder, their expressions grave.

Like a banked and glowing moon, Equus moved among them and they parted ranks, a slow easing before his flood of silver light. Jehanna greeted him with a whicker as the Horse God stepped to the pond's edge.

"The Balance is restored," she said sadly, "praised be to the One."

"There can be no good without evil to balance it," Equus said.

"There can be no evil without good to challenge it," she responded. She looked away, and Equus bent his head.

Reflected in the Waters were the ruins of the Black Barns. They were half-buried in a thriving green meadow. The Pit was empty to the blue sky, and the Watching Pool glimmered clean in the pale sunlight. Anor's gate lay in shattered pieces, strewn beneath the thorn trees. The thorn themselves were covered in white blossoms, the petals stirring in the light breeze.

But in the concrete canyons of the Great Aisle, three shadows moved: El Arat and her daughters, starting to rebuild.

APPENDIX

The Laws of the Herd

I.   A horse is one with the herd
II.   A horse is one with the Balance
III.   The least shall be best
IV.   Fences shall not be broken
V.   The stallion will be obeyed
VI.   The Lead Mare shall govern the mares
VII.   The Herd Chief shall value his work
VIII.   The horse shall keep the Bargain with men
IX.   The whole is greater than its part
X.   The young shall survive at all costs

The Laws of the Herd are passed on orally, from Storyteller to Storyteller. Some, like Frosty, forget. All horses know the First Law. Most remember all ten, if you catch them on a sunny day when the grass is green, but they may not remember in the order listed here.

The Laws for Men, of course, are quite different.

Order exciting 11'' x 17'' sepia prints of your favorite characters from PIPER AT THE GATE - signed by the artist.

Mail order to: Bob Clarke Prints, 55 Brook Road, Pittsford, NY 14534

Please send me the following:

		Quantity
Piper	$7.95	_____
Blackjack	$7.95	_____
Cory	$7.95	_____
Basil & Dill	$7.95	_____
El Arat	$7.95	_____
Complete Set	$35.00	_____

I enclose $_____ (please add $2.00 to cover postage and handling). Send check or money order - no cash or C.O.D.'s please.

Mr/Ms _____

Address _____

City/State _____ Zip _____

(Note: Make checks payable to ''Bob Clarke Prints'')

Please allow 4-8 weeks for delivery. NYS residents - please add 7% sales tax.

A CHOICE OF DESTINIES: "Melissa Scott [is] one of science fiction's most talented newcomers. . . . The greatest delight of all is finding out how she managed to write a historical novel that could legitimately have spaceships on the cover . . . a marvelous gift for any fan."—*Baltimore Sun*   65563-9 • 320 pp. • $2.95

THE GAME BEYOND: "An exciting interstellar empire novel with a great deal of political intrigue and colorful interplanetary travel."—*Locus*
55918-4 • 352 pp. • $2.95